CW01336776

MISTLETOE, MALICE AND MURDER

A Smiley and McBlythe Mystery

Mistletoe, Malice And Murder
Text copyright © 2022 Bruce Hammack
All rights reserved.

Published by Jubilee Publishing, LLC
ISBN 9781958252055

Cover design: Streetlight Graphics
Editor: Teresa Lynn, Tranquility Press

This novel is a work of fiction. Names, characters, organizations, places, events and incidents are either products of the author's imagination or are used fictitiously. All characters are fictional, and any similarity to people living or dead is purely coincidental.

All rights reserved. No part of this book may be reproduced, or stored in a retrieval system, or transmitted in any form or by any means, electronic, mechanical, photocopying, recording, or otherwise, without express written permission of the publisher.

MISTLETOE, MALICE AND MURDER

A Smiley and McBlythe Mystery

BRUCE HAMMACK

Also By Bruce Hammack

The Smiley and McBlythe Mystery Series
Jingle Bells, Rifle Shells
Pistols And Poinsettias
Five Card Murder
Murder In The Dunes
The Name Game Murder
Murder Down The Line
Vision Of Murder
Mistletoe, Malice And Murder
A Beach To Die For

The Star of Justice Series
Long Road to Justice
A Murder Redeemed
A Grave Secret
Justice On A Midnight Clear

The Fen Maguire Mystery Series
Murder On The Brazos
Murder On The Angelina
Murder On The Guadalupe
Murder On The Wichita

See the latest catalog of books at brucehammack.com/books/

1

Christmas music filtered softly from the speakers of Heather's SUV as she wove her way through Houston's snarled traffic. She stole a glance to her right. "Are you telling me we're supposed to solve a murder that hasn't happened yet?"

Steve adjusted sunglasses over his sightless eyes. "I didn't say we're to investigate, only to listen to an old man's story. You've done nothing but work since our last case. Every now and then you need to get away from spread sheets, meetings, emails and the incessant phone calls. Sometimes I think your phone is glued to your ear."

Heather couldn't contradict him and right on cue, the speakers in the Mercedes SUV erupted with shrill rings. She huffed a breath of displeasure, glanced at the caller ID and pressed a button on the steering wheel. She spoke to herself as much as to Steve. "They can leave a message."

"That may have been the smartest decision you've made today."

Heather saw movement to her right and shifted her gaze to Steve. His right foot tapped quietly in time to *Frosty the Snowman*. "It's nice to see you enjoying a little Christmas this year. I was beginning to despair it would ever happen."

"It still hurts to go through Christmas without Maggie. It's been nice the last couple of years to have the distraction of a case to solve during the holidays. I may go somewhere warm and quiet this year."

"The day isn't over. Maybe some sort of case will come out of this appointment."

The onboard voice from the navigation system told her to turn right at the next intersection, which took them off a four-lane street and into Houston's posh River Oaks residential community. Steve raised his chin and sniffed. "I smell money."

Heather couldn't help but grin. It was his off-the-cuff statements that made Steve Smiley a joy to work with—most of the time. The impromptu statement about wealth rang true as a silver bell. Heather gave a nod of appreciation as she took in the stately mansions set far back from metal entry gates. Individually, the homes and manicured grounds would look better on the rolling hills of an English, French, Tuscan, or Spanish estate.

Curiosity drove Heather to say, "I give up. How did you smell money?"

"No pot holes. They're strictly forbidden in River Oaks."

"Did you ever work a homicide in this patch?"

He shifted in his seat. "Yes and no. A trust fund college student staged her death by drowning. Leo and I tracked her to Madrid, where she and her Spanish tutor, Raul, pretended to be married. Working with her father was fine, but her mother was another story. She blamed everyone but herself for her daughter's antics. I'm pretty sure the self-administered martinis she used to ease the pain of being so wealthy didn't help the situation either."

"Did you charge the girl with anything?"

"By the time she made it back to Texas, her parents had greased the right palms with either money, promises of election support, or both. The newspapers killed the story."

The voice coming out of the car's speakers told Heather they had arrived at their destination. She wheeled into a long driveway blocked by a metal gate and pulled up to a security box mounted on a pole. She punched the silver button on the box and a voice came back after only a few seconds. The man sounded cordial, yet firm. "Please state your name and purpose."

"Heather McBlythe and Steve Smiley. We have an appointment with Mr. Green."

"Which Mr. Green?"

Heather looked at Steve, who was already leaning her way. "Mr. Sid Green."

"Thank you," came the voice. "Proceed to the front door, where someone will meet you. Please have your keys ready and he'll park your car."

The gate opened like a sideways yawn. Steve's next words made her realize she'd momentarily slipped back into a lifestyle where the chauffeur's job was driving and her responsibility was to add to the family fortune. "In case you don't remember, the pedal on the right is the one that makes this jalopy speed up."

She came out of the memory fog and sped up to a sedate, but reasonable, speed. Before her lay a Tudor-style home, testament to a style popular in the 1920s with people who had enough money to match earlier generations of British lords who built manors. This stunning example had a massive center section with asymmetrical wings jutting out toward the driveway. The roof pitch, multiple gables, exposed timbers, and rock walls all spoke of a home meant to last for centuries, not mere years.

As promised, a bright-eyed young man of college age met Heather and Steve on the front porch with hand extended to take her keys. She handed them over and cast her gaze past the young man to a stern-faced older man wearing hospital scrubs. Despite his thick arms, barrel chest, and military haircut, his voice was soft as a cat's purr. "Follow me. Mr. Sid is expecting you."

Heather slowed to get a protracted look at the great room. The modern furniture collided with what could have been a room built for one of Shakespeare's tragedies with exposed beams in the ceiling and a massive rock fireplace. She also noticed there wasn't a Christmas tree or bit of tinsel in sight.

The man in royal blue scrubs slowed and cleared his throat, a sign she'd tarried too long. With Steve's hand on her arm and him tapping his way down slate hallways, they eventually wove their way to a large bedroom at the back of one of the home's two wings. The room was spotless, except for medicine bottles dotting the top of one nightstand.

"Come in," commanded the man sitting in a motorized wheelchair. He possessed a fringe of white hair on an otherwise bald head. Instead of waiting for them to draw near, he pushed a joystick and came toward them at an alarming clip. Luckily, there was nothing wrong with his depth perception, as he stopped in plenty of time.

"Butch, you can go. Shut the door behind you."

"Negative," said the man with a soft tone, like thin padding over steel.

Steve turned to face the man who defied the command of an employer who was at least fifty years his elder.

"Navy Seal?" asked Steve.

Butch shook his head. "Fleet Marine Force."

"What's that?" asked Heather.

Steve answered for Butch. "He started out as a Navy corpsman, but served with the Marines. Fleet Marine Force means he passed a grueling test and earned the FMF pin. I bet he has it tattooed on his forearm."

Butch thrust forth his arm for Heather to see.

Steve continued. "The Navy taught him how to save lives, and he learned how to kill with the Marines." Steve lifted his chin. "Isn't that right, Butch?"

"Affirmative, Sir."

"All right. I'm not going to argue with you." Sid Green pushed the joy stick on his wheelchair to the side and maneuvered it to a seating area in the room that contained a leather couch with a matching chair. "You two might as well make yourselves comfortable. This could be a long meeting, or a short one. I've made deals all my life and I'm used to getting my way." He looked at Heather. "What do you think of that, Ms. McBlythe?"

Heather waited to speak until she settled Steve on the left side of the couch and she sat on the right. "I'd say you're not the only person in this room who makes deals. Steve and I must agree or we don't take the job. I'm reserving judgment until I hear more, but right now I'm not inclined to take the case because there is no case." She paused. "It's obvious you researched us before we came, so I'm not saying anything you don't already know."

"You're a plain talker. I like that."

Steve leaned back. "We drove an hour through horrible traffic to get here, and I say that deserves a good story. Why do you believe someone is going to die?"

"Don't you want to talk money?" asked Sid.

Steve's voice lowered. "This will go faster if we dispense with the Texas two-step. You already know you can't buy us at any price. You have a body guard that watches you closer than a drill sergeant watches new recruits. He's also a first-class medical man who can treat everything from colds to gaping gunshot wounds." He turned to Heather. "Tell me about the security."

"Multiple cameras around the perimeter of the property as far as I could see. The dog tracks on the front steps looked to be from a Doberman."

"Two Dobermans," said Sid. "They're trained not to molest any family members. Anyone else is fair game."

Heather continued her report. "All windows and doors are wired, and multiple cameras monitor the hallways. There are even a couple of cameras in this room." She took a breath. "Of course, I haven't checked the entire house, but that's a preliminary report."

Steve took over again. "Your wheezing tells me those old lungs won't hold out much longer. I can hear the flow of oxygen. I'm betting you have a canula in your nose. You're nearing the end of your time, and you genuinely believe someone is going to die." He paused. "Is it you or someone in your family?"

"You two really are as good as I've been told," said Sid. "As to who will die, it could be any of us. I also wouldn't put it past someone in this family doing away with someone next door."

Heather looked at Steve and then faced Sid Green. "Perhaps you'd better start at the beginning and give us the complete story."

The ringing of a telephone caused Butch to reach into his pocket. With long, quick, cat-like steps, he retreated to the bathroom. The only word he got out before he shut the door behind him was, "Yeah?"

The door stayed shut only a few seconds. When it opened again, Butch returned to Sid's side with quick strides. He bent over and whispered into his employer's ear.

Sid put his hand over his heart and nodded. "Go! And take Ms. McBlythe with you."

Butch produced a pistol from the small of his back as he cast his gaze at Heather. "Follow me."

Heather reached for her purse and withdrew a .9mm from a holster designed for quick access. "What's wrong?" she asked as she stood and slipped the seven-shot semi-automatic into the pocket of her jacket.

The body guard was already at the door with weapon in one hand and keys in the other. The voice of Sid Green came from behind Heather as she covered the distance from couch to door. "Lucy's dead. Go to her room before the police arrive. I want a report as soon as possible."

Butch locked the door as soon as Heather stepped into the hall and said, "I wondered who'd be first."

2

Powerful strides carried Butch to the nearest stairwell. He took the stairs two at a time, causing Heather to run after him. They wasted no time traversing the second-story halls across the front of the home, then turned down the north wing hall. A crying woman dressed in the monochromatic attire of a domestic maid stood outside a closed door.

Heather caught Butch by the arm as he reached for the doorknob. "Don't touch it."

He spun with a look that could freeze boiling water, but Heather didn't drop her gaze. She reached into the inside pocket of her lightweight blazer and pulled out latex gloves. "The police will dust it for fingerprints. If you don't want to be a suspect, stay here while I go in."

He turned to the crying woman. "Pull yourself together, Sylvia."

Heather concluded Butch might be a capable bodyguard and a first-rate medic, but tact wasn't his strong suit. She took the distraught woman by the hands, spoke soothing words, and eased her against the wall. Then, gently, she directed the woman to have a seat on the floor, facing away from the room. The woman's brown eyes twitched with fear and apprehension.

Still holding her hands, Heather said, "I'm going in the room. When I come out, I'm going to ask you a lot of questions about what you saw and heard when you discovered the body. You can practice with Butch. Tell him everything you remember."

Butch glared down at her. "I'm going in with you to clear the room."

It took less than a second for Heather to decide that a full-frontal assault on Butch would yield the best results. "Are you an attorney?"

"Negative."

"What about a former detective with ten years' experience as a cop?"

He shook his head.

"Do you want to hang on to that Model 19 Colt or have the cops take it from you?"

He shook his head again, not wasting his breath on responding.

"If you go in, you'll leave trace material and the police will question you at length. You're not trained in what to look for or how to process a crime scene. I am." She pulled her pistol out of her pocket. "I'll clear the room, take photos, and film the room. I'm very detailed. You'll get an email with all photos and the video. I don't have time to argue about this. You're to stay here and record Sylvia's first statement on your phone. I expect you to do a thorough job." She squared her shoulders. "Questions?"

She halfway expected a salute, but he answered by stepping away from the door.

Heather entered the room and allowed Butch to view it from the hall. He scanned the room, nodded his approval, and backed away. She closed the door, more to keep death away from Sylvia than to block Butch from watching her.

The first thing that struck her was, unlike the rest of the house, this room bristled with Christmas decorations, including a tree with presents ringing the base.

She moved to the bed where a woman lay facing upward with

closed eyes. The pallor of the skin and a check of the artery in the neck confirmed death.

Heather completed a quick sweep of the bedroom, closet and bathroom, then returned to the body. A movement came from under the covers. Heather stepped away from the bed, almost tripping over her feet as her right hand found her pistol again. She assumed a shooter's crouch position with her weapon pointed at the lifeless body of Lucy Green. Keeping her pistol trained on the movement, she jerked back the covers.

A bleary-eyed, long-haired cat of the Persian variety looked up at her as if to challenge the interloper who'd entered her domain. It let out a hiss.

"I apologize, kitty. I'm afraid I have bad news for you."

The cat moved to Lucy's face, sniffed, and backed away. It looked again at Heather and let out a low growl.

"Don't blame me. I didn't kill her."

The cat went to the door, turned around, and stared at Heather as if to say, "Don't just stand there. I need a litter box and my brunch."

Patience wasn't a virtue the cat possessed in much quantity. She let out a screech of discontent. The door flew open, and the cat learned a lesson about standing away from it. Butch stood with his pistol at the ready as the kitty shook her dented head and shot past him. With his weapon lowered, Butch mumbled a few choice words about cats and shut the door.

A visual exam of the body revealed little. No sign of a struggle, no blood or bruising, nothing visible embedded under the manicured nails. Then, she looked at the headboard. A single sprig of mistletoe was taped to the headboard, exactly halfway between where a man and woman would rest their heads.

She moved away from the body to examine the room in more detail. A check of the windows found them firmly locked, unmolested by any sort of tool to make entry.

The room did yield one potentially significant finding. A mostly-full bottle of wine sat on the nightstand beside Lucy's bed with only the dregs remaining in a stemmed glass. She examined the label on the bottle. She'd seen the name before but wasn't familiar with it.

Heather stepped into the bathroom. Prescription medications abounded in a tall, narrow cabinet. The top row comprised partial bottles for physical ailments consistent with a post-menopausal woman. The next row held a smorgasbord of orange bottles whose contents fell under the purview of an overly helpful psychiatrist. Heather examined the dates on all the bottles and concluded Lucy Green had tried almost everything, but had not found the magic pill. A mixture of prescription drugs and a glass of wine might explain the death. Perhaps this wasn't a homicide after all.

Her last stop was a massive walk-in closet. Racks and rods held enough clothes to supply a small village with mostly name-brand garments. Price tags dangled from some. Shoes and hats lived on rows of vertical shelves while designer purses hung like tree ornaments on special poles down the center of the closet.

The search wasn't exhaustive, but she did take the time to snap numerous photos and even captured a video of all the rooms and the victim. She closed the door behind her once she entered the hall. Butch looked at her with eyebrows raised in question.

Instead of answering Butch's unasked questions, she said, "I heard Sid call the woman in the room Lucy. Who is she?"

"Lucy Green, Sid's daughter-in-law. Howard's wife."

Heather nodded. "Has anyone called it in?"

"Negative."

"Make the call. Is there someone else who can open the gate for the police and let them in the home?"

"Chad's on the property. He's Sid's great-grandson."

"How old is he?"

"Twenty-one."

"Give him enough information to direct the cops upstairs to me. You make a quick survey of the downstairs rooms and check for a break-in. After that, go to Sid's room and stay there. I'll be here with Sylvia when the cops come."

Butch punched 911 into his cell phone as he walked to the nearest stairway.

Heather turned her attention to Sylvia. She looked recovered enough from the initial shock, so Heather began her interview with what she hoped would be a comforting smile. "Tell me your movements from the time you came up the stairs until you left Lucy Green's room."

Sylvia swallowed hard, looked to the stairway, and then back to the closed door. "Miss Lucy never sleeps past nine thirty, so I was concerned when it was almost ten and she hadn't come down for her morning coffee. She always starts her day with a double espresso. I thought about bringing her one, but she likes to have her coffee on the back patio."

Heather nodded to encourage her to continue the narrative.

"I came to check on her, knocked on the door, and found it unlocked."

"Is that unusual?"

"Not really. She usually left it unlocked unless she and Mr. Howard had a fight."

"Her husband?"

Sylvia nodded. "You probably noticed they no longer share a bedroom." She was quick to add, "It's not that they fight very often, it's that he's a large man and uses a CPAP machine at night. They both sleep better apart from each other."

"Go on," said Heather, cognizant of time ticking away.

"I knocked, opened the door enough to announce myself, and peeked in. I watched Miss Lucy for what seemed like forever, but it was probably only thirty seconds. There was no movement, and she's prone to loud snoring if she's on her back, which she was."

The words flowed, so Heather did nothing to slow them. She nodded frequently and gave positive groans and grunts.

"I went to her bedside and watched her. The hand sticking

out from under the duvet felt cold, like she'd come in from outside. That's when I ran from the room, called Butch, and waited until you showed up."

"Did you notice anything unusual when you entered the room? A smell or something out of place?"

She closed her eyes for several seconds. "Everything seemed normal—except she wasn't breathing."

"Was it normal for her to drink wine at night?"

"She didn't make a regular practice of it, but last night was their anniversary, and I guess she celebrated."

"Alone?"

"They had dinner with the family, but I don't think Mr. Howard stayed here last night."

The sound of footfalls and keys jangling brought the conversation to an abrupt end. A Houston police officer took quick steps toward her. He withdrew a notepad from his shirt pocket as he approached. His gaze rested on Heather first. "Your name, ma'am?"

"Heather McBlythe."

"Are you a member of the family?"

"Attorney. Here on another matter."

He looked past Heather. "And your name?"

"Sylvia Lopez. Maid."

"Who found the body?"

"I did," said Sylvia. Her voice was now much stronger. She matched Heather's answers in brevity.

"Did you touch anything?" asked the officer.

"Only Miss Lucy's hand. It was cold."

His gaze shifted back to Heather. "What about you, Ms. McBlythe? Did you go in the room?"

She reached for the gloves in the pocket that didn't hold her small pistol and showed them to the officer. "I was a cop for ten years. It made sense for me to clear the room and check for signs of life."

"Any sign of life?"

"Not human."

He turned his head and raised his eyebrows. "Can you explain?"

"There was a cat under the covers that didn't move until I'd cleared the room."

"Are you armed?"

She nodded. "Front right pocket of my blazer."

He smiled. "Mind if I borrow your gloves? I left mine in the car."

Heather handed them over.

"Both of you wait here while I take a quick look. Is the door unlocked?"

Both women said yes at the same time. Once inside the room, the officer took only enough steps to draw near the body. He checked the neck for a pulse and keyed the microphone attached to his epaulet. A series of numbers and cryptic words followed. Heather understood the language, but didn't explain to Sylvia. Soon the house and grounds would be swarming with people, each with tasks to perform.

The man backed out of the room, and faced Heather. "Where were you a cop?"

"Boston."

"And you're an attorney now?"

"Among other things."

"Oh? Like what?"

"I own an investment company, and I'm a private investigator. You might know my partner, Steve Smiley?"

He'd been looking down until she mentioned Steve's name. His head snapped up like a Jack-in-the-box.

"Do you know Steve?" she asked.

"More by reputation than anything. I've heard stories about him that can't possibly be true."

"He's here. Maybe you'll have a chance to meet him," said Heather. "Tell the detectives to come to Mr. Sid Green's room when they get through with the crime scene."

The officer ran a hand down his cheek. "Do you think this is a homicide or natural causes?"

Heather shrugged. "Better safe than sorry. Treat it as a homicide for the time being. The autopsy should tell us for sure."

What Heather didn't say was that Steve had a way of knowing if the death was a homicide long before the medical examiner received the body.

3

Heather gave three sharp knocks on Sid Green's door and waited for Butch to release the lock and allow entry. She directed her first words to the nurse/bodyguard. "Any sign of entry on the bottom floor?"

Butch shook his head. "All doors and windows are secure, and the security system is, and was, fully functional."

Sid's voice rose in volume and intensity. "Don't stand over there whispering. Tell me what you found in Lucy's room."

Heather bristled at the tone, but the patriarch had a right to demand answers. After all, his daughter-in-law had died in his home.

Butch melted into the background while Heather took her previous position on the couch. She began what proved to be a ten-minute report, beginning with her and Butch leaving the room and concluding when she knocked on Sid's door.

No one asked questions during the narrative, but Sid cut to the chase as soon as she finished. "Well? Is it a murder or not?"

"Too soon to tell," said Steve.

Sid shifted rheumy eyes to look at Steve, who took in a deep breath. "From what I heard, there are several potential causes of Lucy's death. Some involve homicide, while others don't. First, it's possible Lucy Green died of natural causes. Second, a combination of prescription pills and wine might have been enough to kill her. The question becomes, if pills and alcohol are involved, was it accidental or intentional? There's no crime if it's accidental. If intentional, then did she commit suicide, or did someone force her to ingest pills? Finally, the wine might contain poison."

Sid considered the options. "Lucy thought too much of herself to engage in any sort of self-harm." His gaze shifted back to Steve. "Cut to the punchline, Mr. Smiley. Was she murdered or not?"

"The police will know after the medical examiner completes toxicology tests."

The old man rubbed a hand across the stubble on his chin. "I told you someone would die, and now they have. I wasn't sure who it would be, but I didn't suspect they'd go after Lucy."

"Why not her?" asked Steve.

"She's a Green by marriage only. She was the peacemaker in the family. Thought the feud that's been going on between us and the Webbers was stupid."

He rubbed his face again. "I'm not long for this world. I think someone in the Webber family wanted to hurt the next patriarch of the Greens. They poisoned Lucy's wine to get back at me and Howard."

Heather joined the conversation again. "We're getting way ahead of ourselves by speculating with no proof. Until we know the cause of death, talking about murder is a waste of time."

Sid's eyes narrowed as he challenged her statement with words of absolute surety. "I know without an autopsy."

"How?" asked Steve.

"The same way I know if a well is going to come in rich with crude or if it's natural gas. I feel things in my bones, and I'm telling you, this is murder."

The air in the room took on the feel of cold fog. Several seconds passed before Steve spoke again. "I understand what you mean by knowing things, and I'm not one to minimize something just because I don't understand it. However, it always helps to have proof."

Heather added, "We won't have a lot of time before detectives knock on the door, so tell us how the feud started between the two families."

Sid spoke over his shoulder to Butch. "Get me a bottle of water. I'm not used to this much talking."

A small kitchenette stood in the corner, which included a refrigerator. Instead of returning with one bottle of water, Butch brought three. Steve and Heather accepted the hospitality and issued words of thanks.

"My father was best friends with Peter Webber," began Sid. "Both men were self-taught geologists. They worked the oil fields in Pennsylvania in the late 1800s and knew they'd never get rich if they didn't do something big. In 1901, someone poked a hole in the ground near Beaumont and oil shot a hundred and fifty feet in the air. Dad and Mr. Webber watched from a distance for six months and realized everyone was concentrating on finding more oil around the big find at Spindletop."

"Not the rest of the state?" asked Heather.

"The rest of Texas, Oklahoma, and Louisiana were wide open. The two men found enough financial backing to support themselves for two years; then they hit the road, buying up mineral rights for next to nothing. Enough wells came in to keep them on the road for the rest of their working lives. By the time they educated me enough to go with them, they'd been on the road so long my dad was ready to turn over our half of the business to me. That's when the big split began."

Heather nodded in agreement to keep the old man going. His faltering voice needed regular sips of water to keep the words flowing. As further encouragement, she asked, "What triggered the severing of the partnership?"

"Mother was ill with TB. They called it consumption back then, and Dad must have caught it from her. That old buzzard, Peter Webber, didn't think I deserved a half cut of the leases because I was new to the game. He was used to dealing with Dad, and didn't like the idea of someone my age having as much authority as him. Things dragged on, Mom died, Dad got sicker, and Peter Webber wouldn't agree to a reasonable division of assets.

"By that time, I'd hit my stride and concentrated on the big ranches in West Texas and Oklahoma. Mr. Webber was a hard worker, but I worked hard and smart. He may have signed more leases, but I locked up a lot more land that produced a better quality, and quantity, of oil."

Sid required another sip to continue. "The strain of losing Mom, and Peter Webber's insistence that he be in charge, was more than Dad could take." He lifted his chin. "I'll admit I was mad enough to kill Peter Webber for the way he treated my father. He had no sympathy for all the years Dad spent with him. When my father couldn't perform any longer, Mr. Webber threw him aside like a used rag."

Steve asked, "Did he do the same to you?"

"Worse. At least he respected Dad until he couldn't go any longer. He never trusted me to do anything, and he sure didn't value my opinions."

Steve nodded and asked, "Who started the big split?"

"I did," said Sid, pride peppering his words. "Peter Webber had stopped talking to me altogether and I needed to protect what my father and I had worked for. I hired the best lawyer I could find while Peter went cheap. That old German squeezed a nickel until it screamed."

It was Heather's turn again. "I'm reading between the lines, but it sounds like the Webber family may think the division of assets wasn't fair."

Sid shrugged. "You of all people should appreciate the need for good legal counsel in business deals. Old man Webber thought he'd made a good deal when he received fifty-five percent of the leases to my forty-five. He didn't realize until later what a mistake he'd made."

"How much more production are you talking about?" asked Heather.

He grinned. "It's varied over the years. Overall, the Green wells have produced about seventy-two times more oil and gas than the Webber leases."

Heather realized the Webbers had seventy-two reasons to hate the Greens.

As if he could read her mind, Sid looked at Heather. "Peter Webber swore he'd kill me, and tried to, once. The shot only nicked my leg, but it was enough to send that old man to prison for three years. He came home in a pine box. His son, Peter Jr., came close to running me down with his car, but I was still quick enough to dodge him. Now, he's dead and buried, too."

Steve leaned toward the wily old man. "Any other attempts to kill you or any members of your family?"

"Not until today." He waved a dismissive hand in the air. "There's been a running battle in the courts, with each family finding something to squabble about, and the occasional throwing of a drink in the face at some social gathering, but nothing serious enough to hurt anyone.

"My son Howard is smart enough to let attorneys do his fighting."

"And he married Lucy?" asked Heather.

Sid nodded.

"Any ex-wives lurking about?"

"None," said Sid emphatically, before he issued a coy smile. "I take some credit for the absence of divorce in this family. I have people do extensive background checks on any women who get too close to the Green men. If something surfaces that keeps me from sleeping, I present them with what amounts to a prenuptial agreement. The main stipulation being they'll have to live in this house and they'll get none of the Green family assets if they divorce."

Heather had a mental checklist of the Green family men, but wanted to make sure she cemented the genealogy in her mind.

"I'm missing a generation. Your son is Howard, whose wife Lucy is now dead?"

"That's right."

"Howard and Lucy must have a son?"

"Tim, whose wife is Tammy. Howard and Lucy also have a daughter, Carol, who's a handful. She's the only Green in ten generations who divorced, and her ex didn't get a penny."

Heather nodded. "If you're a great-grandfather, there should be one more."

He issued a deep sigh. "That's Chad, Tim's son. Smart as Einstein, and marches to the beat of his own drum. Doesn't believe in the feud and is engaged to be married."

"Can't you scare her off the way you did the other women?"

"It's not that simple this time around."

"Oh?"

"Her name is Anna. Anna Webber. Lives next door."

Heather didn't mean to groan, but it escaped her all the same. She tried to cover it with quick words. "By any chance, is she of the line and lineage of Peter Webber?"

"She's got the blood, but not the personality. I don't know how or why, but I like her. It's her family I can't stand."

"Will her parents allow her to marry someone named Green?"

Sid threw up his hands. "Neither family can stop it. They're both twenty-one, finished college two years early, and have decent jobs. They own one little car, but mainly ride electric bicycles. I think they're both vegan."

Steve then asked a question that crossed Heather's mind. "When's the wedding?"

"Three weeks from now."

"On Christmas day?" asked Steve.

"Yep. I'm not sure if that's going to change now that Lucy's dead, but I doubt it. It's a destination wedding. I don't fly and neither do some of the others, so I booked all the close family on a cruise."

"What about the Webber family?" asked Steve.

Heather followed with her own question before Sid could answer. "Let me guess. Both families on the same ship?"

Sid chuckled, "That's the plan." He issued a mischievous smile. "Do you know if they have morgues on those overgrown barges with beds?"

"Deaths at sea aren't uncommon," said Heather after she swallowed hard. "They have ways of keeping bodies cold until they get to the nearest port, or the home port. They also have a brig for anyone who rushes the dying process."

The knock on the door brought the macabre discussion to an end.

"That will be the police," said Steve. "The knock sounds familiar."

4

Heather watched as Butch opened the door enough to allow a woman's hand to stick through the opening. She held a badge case with ID and shield. "Detectives Keita and Vega," she said with an accent that sounded like it came from a different continent. "We need to speak with Mr. Green."

Butch opened the door and allowed them to enter.

"Leo," said Steve. "You're the only cop I know that knocks five times instead of three."

Heather's smile parted her lips. Prior to the night when drug-addled thieves took the life of Steve's wife and he lost his sight, Leo had been his partner. Since forming their private investigator firm, Heather and Steve had helped Leo solve a couple of murders and he'd been a benefit to them in terms of inside information and bending some rules when the occasion required. Steve labeled the indiscretions as necessary "work-arounds" instead of violations of departmental policy. The results spoke for themselves. The duo never violated a law. Policies were another story. It was good to know a level-headed detective would be working this case.

Steve and Heather rose at the same time. Leo gave a smile

and nod to Heather, and treated Steve's hand like a handle on a water pump.

Sid Green's head lolled, which caused Butch to spring into action. "I can't let you interview Mr. Green."

Detective Keita took a step toward Butch and tented her hands on narrow hips. "Who are you to tell us what we can and can't do?"

Butch had the unique ability to speak in a way that didn't allow a challenge to his authority while remaining unflinchingly calm. He held up his index finger, and in a monotone, said, "One: Mr. Green's attorney says you don't have permission to interview any family members without him being present." He held up a second finger. "Two: As Mr. Green's caregiver, I'm telling you he needs to rest. You'll endanger his health if you persist."

Butch lifted the sleeping patriarch from his wheelchair and gently laid him on the bed. He checked Sid's pulse and covered him with a fleece throw before returning to the living room section of the suite.

Leo looked at Heather. She nodded. "Mr. Green has been through a lot today. He's already started his nap, so I suggest we do as Butch says. Steve and I can fill you in on what we know."

"Are you the one who interfered with our crime scene?" demanded Detective Keita.

Heather chose the tone of a parent correcting a child. "No, Detective. I'm the one who put on gloves and preserved your crime scene."

"You sound like a lawyer."

"I am, and at the time I entered the room I was representing Mr. Green."

Steve cleared his throat. "Butch, is there a place where Heather and I could meet with Leo and..." He paused. "I'm sorry, I didn't catch your first name, Detective Keita."

"That's because I don't give it to strangers."

Leo bristled. "They're not strangers and if you want to stay on this case, you'll drop the tough-cop attitude." He turned to face Steve. "Her first name is Ayana."

Jaw muscles flexed but the junior detective kept quiet as Steve moved on as if she'd said nothing but kind words. "I take a little getting used to, Ayana, but I think you'll find me to be a harmless, lovable, teddy bear."

Leo chuckled. "With big teeth that can rip chunks out of your backside."

Butch spoke next. "With cops swarming all over the house, I recommend you go to the back patio. I'll call the kitchen and have them send out coffee."

"Almost perfect," said Steve. "The only thing that would make it better would be some little something for a late morning snack."

For the first time, Butch's top lip quirked into his rendition of a fleeting smile. "There's always something good at this time of day. The easiest way to get to the patio is to go through the great room at the center of the house and through the sunroom."

It wasn't long before the foursome sat at a round table with Steve's back to the pool. The other three completed the circle. From his prior comments, Heather concluded Steve wanted to get on Ayana's good side by getting her to talk about herself, so she asked, "How long have you been stuck working with Leo?"

Her response came back stiff and guarded. "Not long."

"Three weeks," said Leo.

"Four," Ayana corrected him. "The first week they kept me in the office doing menial tasks."

Steve chuckled. "Don't feel bad. Everyone goes through hazing the first week in homicide. When did you catch on that you didn't have to empty everyone's trash?"

She looked at Leo. "Why didn't you tell me that was part of some silly initiation?"

Heather broke in to take the pressure off Leo. "If I'm not mistaken, you have a South African accent. Am I right?"

Ayana nodded. "I'm here for a year on an officer swap

program for detectives. I went through your academy and then they assigned me to homicide. Leo's my first supervisor."

Heather leaned toward her and spoke in a secret-sharing voice. "They gave you the best."

Sylvia, the maid who discovered Lucy Green, wheeled out a cart bearing two carafes of coffee, three kinds of baked goods, fruit, plates, forks, and napkins. Heather called the server by name and thanked her.

Steve lifted his head and sniffed. "Coffee and pastries. Perfect."

As Sylvia set the table, Heather directed her question to Leo. "Did you speak with Sylvia yet?"

"We were going to start with Sid Green. Ms. Lopez was next."

"No time like the present," said Steve. "Sylvia discovered the body. Why don't you let Ayana do the interview?"

Steve turned to face Ayana. "This way you'll get first-hand information from a witness and feedback from three experienced detectives."

The South African transplant squared her shoulders. "This isn't how we'd do it back home, but I'm here to learn."

Leo chuckled. "This isn't the way we do it here, either, but if there's one thing Steve taught me, it's to be creative. I must admit, drinking coffee and eating a cream cheese Danish while supervising an interview is a much more pleasant way to start an investigation."

Ayana pulled a notebook and pen from her purse. "Ms. Lopez, I need to ask you a few questions concerning your discovery of Lucy Green this morning. Bring that chair closer to the table. I'll expect your full cooperation."

Once settled, Heather made mental notes while sipping an excellent cup of coffee. Steve and Leo dove into the assortment of pastries that tempted her within an inch of her waistline. A glance at her newly-gained engagement ring reminded her there was someone besides her that would appreciate her discipline.

The interview progressed with Ayana asking pointed questions and demanding clarification in no-nonsense tones.

Sylvia's answers came back crisp. Heather had to admit she got little from Sylvia earlier, but concluded it was because of shock and grief, not because of a confrontational style of asking questions.

After Ayana told Sylvia she didn't believe some of her responses, Steve rose from his chair. "Leo, do you mind if I take over?"

"Please do," said Leo as he reached for another pastry.

Ayana returned her chair to its original place and wasted a defiant look on Steve. Heather helped him move his chair to sit at an angle to Sylvia. He settled in the chair, somewhat slumped, with arms crossed which matched her posture. His words came out soft. "Heather told us how shook up you were this morning. How are you feeling now?"

"Better."

"Good. We're here to talk. That's all. Pretend it's just me and you. I bet you're having trouble believing Lucy is gone. Am I right?"

She nodded as tears welled up in her eyes.

"Time will help you get to a new normal. Things will never be the same around here, but you'll get through this. You have my word on it."

Sylvia took in a breath and let it flow out. Her focus remained on Steve, the source of kind words.

"A few minutes ago, you said you began working here nine months ago. Is that right?"

She gave a nod of her head.

Heather said, "He can't see you, Sylvia. You'll need to answer him."

"Oh, I'm so sorry. Yes, nine months ago."

"How did you get this job?"

"There's a company that specializes in domestic help, gardeners, and general maintenance workers for the residents of River

Oaks. They promise their clients satisfaction or they'll have a replacement the next day."

Steve uncrossed his arms as he asked, "Is there much turnover?"

Sylvia mimicked Steve as she stopped hugging herself and relaxed her arms.

"It all depends on the family. Some workers last until they retire or die. Others don't make it a day." Her words picked up pace. "This is my third family, but I was never let go for not doing my job."

"Can you tell me about the other two families?"

Sylvia gave her head a nod. "The first family was the best. They were the Wilsons. I worked for them almost five years. They fell on hard times and had to sell their home. The next family was the Webbers."

Private finishing schools and law school taught Heather not to react to surprising information. She managed not to blurt out something that would interrupt Steve's interview, which allowed him to keep the pace of his interview going.

He leaned back, looking more and more relaxed. "Who did you report to in the Webber house?"

Sylvia's teeth came together as she gave a curt reply. "Mrs. Ingrid Schmidt-Webber."

Steve let out a simple. "Ah. I can tell by the way you said her name she was hard to please."

"I lasted longer than most. I later found out when she hired me, she really wanted someone who had worked for the Greens, but the agency didn't have anyone and she was desperate. When the agency finally found someone who had worked for the Greens, I was out the door."

Steve immediately asked, "Did Lucy hire you because you'd worked for the Webbers?"

Sylvia found humor in the question and allowed a smile to show off nice teeth. "I don't know that for sure, but the people who live in River Oaks want to know what's going on with other wealthy people. I know some workers who tell everything about their past employer."

"That sounds dangerous," said Steve.

"That's why I try to stay invisible. I have to admit, though, Miss Lucy was good at getting me to talk about my time with the Webbers. She liked it when I told her a fresh rumor, or remembered something that made the Webbers look bad."

Steve leaned forward. "You mentioned Ingrid Webber. Tell me more about her. What's she like?"

She didn't hesitate. "Very strict."

"Demanding?"

Sylvia nodded. "Very demanding."

"Was she that way the entire time you worked for her?"

"From the minute she interviewed me. Another maid said she got worse after her granddaughter Anna started seeing Chad Green." She paused. "Then again, the Webbers have money problems, too."

"I'm surprised the two families allowed Chad and Anna to see each other."

"Love will find a way," said Sylvia. "Especially when only a fence and hedges separate the two families."

Steve leaned back and rubbed his chin.

Sylvia shifted her gaze to Heather. "I meant to tell Ms. McBlythe that earlier, but I was so upset at seeing Miss Lucy dead."

Steve stood. "Thanks so much for speaking with us. I'm sure Detectives Vega and Keita will want to speak with you again. You've been most helpful."

Sylvia rose and scurried back inside. By this time, Leo had downed three pastries and two cups of coffee.

Steve moved his chair back to the table. Once seated, he leaned toward Leo who sat on his left. "That should give you plenty to start with."

"Thanks." He turned to Ayana. "What information did Steve get from Sylvia that you didn't?"

Mistletoe, Malice And Murder

"I asked the standard questions," said Ayana in a defensive tone.

"No. You demanded answers to standard questions. You used words as clubs to get information. Steve baited her with honey."

"Nice mixed metaphor," said Steve.

Heather poured Ayana a cup of coffee. "I thought you did a thorough job, but do you realize what Steve did for you?"

Ayana shook her head.

"He gave you several leads. Now you have things to follow up on."

"Do you mean with the employment agency?"

Leo took his turn. "Not just the agency, but the potential workers they send. If you want to know what goes on in the homes of the wealthy, talk to the people that work for them. Did you hear what Sylvia said about trying to stay invisible? That doesn't mean they don't hear and talk about things. Their employers forget that every person on staff has two ears and one mouth."

"Sometimes it's a big mouth," said Steve.

Ayana heaved a sigh. "What else?"

Heather corrected her. "You haven't had time to dig into the Greens' family history. After you've done your homework, you'll have a lot more leads."

Steve said, "You'll find Sid Green is a fountain of information as long as his voice holds out. If it turns out this is a homicide, I suspect you'll have your work cut out for you in getting answers from both families. Expect to be limited to asking questions through their attorneys."

Leo turned to Steve. "Any chance of us getting a copy of your interview with Sid Green?"

"Don't you want to know if it's a murder first?"

Leo rose and looked at Ayana. "You stay here with Heather. She'll tell you what she and Steve would do next if this turns out to be a murder."

Steve pushed up from the table and found Leo's arm. "I'm ready when you are."

Heather leaned into Ayana. "Steve likes to visit the crime scene. He has a nose like a bloodhound and can sometimes smell things that others can't." She didn't tell Ayana about Steve's other gift, the one that separated him from any other detective she'd ever met.

5

Steve and Leo left Heather to deal with Ayana's bruised ego. Once in the sunroom and out of earshot, Leo stopped. "We're where no one can hear us. What do you think of the partner they saddled me with?"

Sensing Leo needed encouragement, Steve decided to paint the assignment with as many bright colors as possible while not glossing over the truth of the situation. "Whose idea was it to swap detectives between Houston and South Africa?"

"The new chief, who's ninety-five percent politician and five percent cop."

Steve groaned. "I admit you drew the short straw, but someone must trust you to give you such a project."

"Either that, or they're trying to run me off." Leo let out a sigh. "She's not that bad, but you ruined me for any other partner by putting results over procedures."

"She seems smart," said Steve.

"Brilliant in some ways, but not much on creative thinking. She has two degrees in criminology and is halfway to her PhD. This year is research for her doctoral dissertation. I have her for two months and then she goes to another department."

Steve placed both hands on top of his cane. "At least it's a temporary assignment. You can put up with anything for a couple of months."

"It's not that simple," said Leo. "I'm to keep her next to me everywhere I go. Daily written reports are submitted to the captain, who passes them up the chain of command. It's like they have me under a microscope."

"Yikes!"

"Exactly," said Leo. "What would you do if you were in my place?"

Steve thought for a moment but nothing came to mind, except a little humor. "I'd find a doctor willing to take out my appendix."

Leo chuckled. "That's tempting, but I lost that body part when I was in college."

"Then pick another organ. What about a gall bladder?"

"I'm not that desperate yet, but I'll keep your suggestion in mind."

Steve tried again. "The best advice I can give you is to use her strengths and minimize her weaknesses."

"Can you put that in plain English—or Spanish? I'm fine with both languages."

"She's an academic. That means she spends long hours in front of a computer. Give her the tedious work that drives you crazy and assign her to write her own daily reports. I guarantee they'll be long and boring to people like you and me, but eye candy to those who like to read wordy documents. Review them, add a short addendum, and turn them in with both signatures. The higher-ups are more impressed with the number of words than content."

"That makes sense. I can spend my time doing the things that bring results, and tell her to document what we did." He paused. "You're saying to treat her the way you treated me."

"It's the benefit of being the lead detective. The difference in this case is, she'll submit much longer reports with fewer typos."

Leo breathed a sigh of relief. "Thanks, partner. It's time we moved on to find out if this is a homicide or not." He put Steve's hand on his arm. "We're going back through the great room. There're three steps before I open the door. Don't trip."

"I remember," said Steve as he felt with his cane.

Once in the great room, footsteps from what sounded like two men came toward them. Leo and Steve stopped at the same time.

"Are you the detective in charge?" asked a man with a voice that sounded like it came from the bottom of a barrel.

"Detective Vega," said Leo in a way that communicated he was leading the investigation. "And this is my former lead partner, Steve Smiley."

A second man spoke next. "I'm Lewis Crankshaw, attorney for the Green family. Why is Mr. Smiley here?"

Steve spoke up. "I'm a private investigator, invited here by Mr. Sid Green."

"Why?" demanded the first man.

The attorney spoke before Steve could. "Please, Howard, let me handle this."

"Mr. Smiley, can you tell me the purpose of Mr. Sid Green employing you?"

"You misunderstand," said Steve. "He hasn't employed us yet. We were exploring the possibility of looking into a matter for Mr. Sid Green when word reached us of Lucy Green's death. My partner went to see if she could be of any help."

"And your partner's name?" asked the attorney.

"Heather McBlythe. She's also an attorney. The elder Mr. Green wanted her to go to the crime scene to make sure the family interests weren't compromised."

"Heather McBlythe," said Howard Green. "Why is that name familiar?"

Mr. Crenshaw answered the question for his client. "She's heiress to the McBlythe fortune and runs her own investment company in The Woodlands."

Steve added, "She's also a great private investigator. Other than a maid, Heather was the first on scene and did a preliminary sweep of the bedroom. She and Detective Vega's partner are on the back patio if you want a first-hand account from Heather."

"What maid?" asked Howard Green with more volume than necessary.

"Sylvia Lopez," said Leo.

Steve added, "Ms. McBlythe also took photos and video of the potential crime scene."

Steve always liked the way he and Leo ping-ponged information to potential suspects. It made them listen closely and decreased the interruptions.

Despite the attorney's request that Howard Green remain quiet, he spoke again in the same demanding tone. "Where are you going now, Detective Vega?"

"Upstairs, to your wife's room."

"Why are you taking a blind man with you?"

Steve laughed out loud, knowing it would stun the prospective heir and his attorney into temporary silence. "Sorry. Detective Vega uses me like a bloodhound. When I lost my vision, other senses increased in sensitivity. I'm going to check for odors in your wife's room, such as perfume, cigarette or marijuana smoke, incense, a man's cologne—anything I can detect."

"What good will that do?"

Steve gave a mischievous grin. "You never know. I had a murder case not long ago where the wife used a fragrance by Estée Lauder. The husband returned from a business trip with his shirts infused with the odor of Chanel."

Steve took a step closer to Howard Green and sniffed the air. "Interesting," he said.

Mr. Crankshaw raised his voice. "Perhaps it would be best if Mr. Green and I spoke with Ms. McBlythe. She's on the back patio?"

Leo answered. "Heather and my partner, Ayana Keita, are both there."

Neither Leo nor Steve spoke until they were halfway up the stairs and Leo huffed out a smirking sound. "What kind of perfume did you smell on that overstuffed oil tycoon?"

"Do you have any idea how many women's perfumes, colognes, and body washes there are? It would take me the rest of my life to match the odor with a name. All I know is, it smelled sweet, inexpensive, and I'll buy you a steak dinner if it matches anything in his wife's room."

"Did you make up that story about working a murder case involving the guy coming home with a strange fragrance on his shirts?"

Steve stopped when the stairs played out. "It's called creative license to see how a suspect reacts. Now you have Howard Green at the top of your list of people to investigate. After all, family and friends commit most murders."

Leo started down the hall at an easy-to-keep pace. "Beside there being a murder, there's not much sign of Christmas, or cheer, in this place. Not like our house. Reindeer, snowmen, shiny balls... it's everywhere. The youngest thought we had to have one of those giant inflatable Santas for the yard this year."

Steve chuckled. "Well, they're only young once."

Leo stopped. "Are you ready to sniff around a crime scene?"

"Lead me to it. Let's see if my associative chromesthesia still works." The mention of the technical name for what Steve considered a gift brought to mind the many times in his career he'd used it to determine whether the crime was a murder or some lesser category of homicide, like manslaughter or negligence. If he had the impression of seeing bright red at the crime scene, it meant murder. As the shades of red declined from red to pale pink, it meant some other category of crime involving someone losing their life. If the darkness of his present world remained when someone spoke the victim's name, there was no crime. It really came in handy when people staged their death, usually to commit insurance fraud. Sometimes they simply wanted to disappear and assume another identity.

While Steve considered the cases he'd worked, Leo helped him put on gloves and cloth booties, led him into Lucy's bedroom, and exchanged greetings with the forensic crew. Steve's senses shifted to full alert. "Everything I'm smelling tells me only a woman and a cat live here."

"That fits," said Leo. "Heather told us there were no men's clothes in the closet. Can you smell the same perfume that was on Howard Green's shirts?"

"No, but that doesn't surprise me. If they changed the sheets recently and laundered Lucy Green's clothes within the last day or so, she may not have put on any perfume yesterday. Not all woman wear perfume every day, even the ultra-rich ones."

Leo whispered, "They already have Lucy in a body bag. They're strapping her to a stretcher, preparing to take her down the stairs."

"Let me know when we can get next to the bed, then say her name. Didn't Heather say her full name was Lucille Green?"

Steve heard Leo's notepad flip open. "Yeah. I'm not sure about a middle name or her maiden name."

"It shouldn't matter for what we're interested in today."

Steve waited, listening to voices give hushed instructions and imagining the scene. Leo's hand softly gripped Steve's arm and directed him to the bedside. His cane touched against what sounded like the bed's wooden frame.

Leo spoke in a soft voice with more elocution than normal. "The woman's name is Lucy Green or Lucille Green."

Steve didn't speak for several seconds. Despite the many cases he'd solved, murder always triggered a deep emotional response in him. This became more acute after his wife, Maggie, died so needlessly. He came out of what could be described as a trance and spoke two words to Leo. "Bright red."

The two remained silent for at least thirty more seconds until Leo said, "Let's find Lucy's perfume."

"No need. Heather searched the bathroom cabinets as she secured the rooms. She'll know what kind Lucy wore."

"Do you smell anything else?"

"Wine. Heather mentioned it. Also, a cat spends a lot of time in this room."

Steve straightened his posture. "Let's go rescue Heather from Howard Green and his attorney."

"Not yet," said Leo. "I'm curious about Lucy's perfume. I'll be right back."

Steve stood by the bed as he heard Leo speak to someone inside the bathroom. "Have you bagged the perfume yet?"

Another voice, that of a male spoke up. "It's taking us longer than usual to bag and tag everything. It's like taking inventory at Macy's cosmetic department. I'm coming to the perfume now. It's from some company named Roja and looks expensive."

"Bag it but don't seal it yet."

"Are you finished, Detective Vega?" asked Steve.

Leo walked up. "Almost. Take a whiff and tell me if it's the same one you smelled on Howard earlier. I'm checking the price on the internet." He let out a low whistle. "Holy smoke. Thirty-four hundred dollars for a three-and-a-half-ounce bottle."

Steve shook his head. "Nope. Not the same."

Steve didn't speak again until he and Leo were halfway down the hall, headed for the stairs. "You're right, old buddy. This may be a complicated case. You and Ayana have your work cut out for you."

"I might need a hand."

Steve stopped. "Quit underestimating yourself. You'll know a lot more in a week."

"You won't be working on the case?"

"We don't have a client. I guess the decision is up to Sid Green or his son Howard. If the younger of the two runs the show around here, Heather and I probably won't be involved. Howard impresses me as a blowhard who isn't above hiding the truth behind high-paid lawyers. If he rubs Heather the wrong way, she'll tell him what he can do with his oil wells."

Leo said, "I'm hoping old man Green still runs the show."

"My money is on Howard telling his father he'll hire another private investigator, not me and Heather."

When Steve and Leo arrived at the back patio, Heather and Howard Green were in a heated discussion about Steve's ability, or lack thereof, to solve crimes with his physical limitations. They'd worked themselves into talking over each other. It reminded Steve of two dogs chasing their own tails in tight circles while barking at each other.

The fracas came to an abrupt halt when Steve shouted, "We're leaving."

On the trip home Steve listened while Heather spewed venom directed at Howard Green. He finally cut her off. "If it's any consolation, Howard is the prime suspect."

The volume and pitch of her voice lowered, "I hope Leo leans on him extra hard. What did you find out when you went to Lucy's room?"

"I saw red and Lucy Green uses a perfume called *Haute Luxe*."

"That means Leo and Ayana can start doing background and interviews immediately."

Steve pulled his seat belt away from his chest and let it spring back. "He'll have to be careful with interviews until he gets the tox screen."

He could tell the refocus on the case had brought Heather's agile mind back on things other than Howard Green when she said, "You're right, Leo needs to hold off on the investigation. Ayana's computer of a brain won't process something like associative chromesthesia. Most people think it's pseudo-science, even though there've been hundreds of documented cases. She'd label Leo fit for a rubber room and the new chief of police might agree with her."

Steve remained silent as Heather continued to process the information he'd given her about the perfume. "What does Lucy's *Haute Luxe* have to do with her husband?"

"It's not the perfume I smelled when I first met Howard

Green today. Leo's looking for a younger woman who buys perfume at regular stores."

Heather slowed and pulled to the side of the road as a firetruck blew past her with siren and horn blaring. "What did you do to make Howard angry before he and Mr. Crankshaw came to the back patio?"

"I might have implied the perfume wafting from Howard didn't smell like something his wife would wear."

"No wonder he insisted the blind private detective only wanted to fleece his father out of money."

"Speaking of money; we need to find out who controls it in the Green family. If it's Howard, we may not be able to help Leo much." Steve paused. "Then again, we could get ourselves hired by the Webber family. If that happens, we'd have to investigate the Greens to be thorough."

Heather chuckled. "I'll see what I can do about that."

6

While lined up in highway traffic going nowhere, Heather turned to Steve. "There's a major accident a mile ahead and no exit we can take. Looks like we're stuck for the foreseeable future."

Steve had a practical side to him that shone through when a murder activated his mind. "I'm thinking about all the things I'd focus on if I were in Leo's shoes."

"Let's compare notes," said Heather. "I'd start with financial reports on everyone in the Green and Webber households. What about you?"

Steve rubbed his chin. "The wine. I'd want to know if it was a recent purchase and by whom. Or, was it already in stock in the Greens' household? If it was, then the chances of the Webbers being involved goes down."

It was Heather's turn to say what else she'd prioritize. "I'd want to talk with the domestic help in both households."

"That reminds me," said Steve. "What would be your plan for getting information from the employment agency if we were working this case?"

"I thought about buying it. Either that, or pretending I'm looking at buying and staffing a home in River Oaks."

Steve chuckled. "Buying it would be the easy way to give you an inside track to some of the wealthiest families in Houston." His voice took on a sinister tone as he spoke in an Eastern European accent. "You could recruit spies and plant them in every one of the homes owned by the capitalist pigs."

"On second thought," said Heather. "Buying a house in River Oaks might be a way to turn a few bucks and get information at the same time."

Steve chuckled and shifted in his seat. "Whatever you do, keep up with Sylvia Lopez somehow. I have a feeling she knows a lot more about Lucy and Howard Green. Also, she used to work for the Webber family."

Heather nodded. "Are you thinking she might know too much about the Greens for them to keep her on?"

"Yes, or they may think she's served her purpose. Lucy already pumped Sylvia's well dry of information concerning the Webbers. I wouldn't put it past Howard to have done the same. However, if they let her go, she'll talk, especially if it takes a while to get another good-paying job. The Green family may be in a Catch-22 situation with Sylvia."

The car's speakers announced a call from Heather's father, interrupting the back-and-forth between Heather and Steve about how to proceed on the case. She answered with a cheery tone. "Good afternoon, this is a pleasant surprise."

"How would you and Jack like to go on a short cruise with me?"

Thinking her straightlaced father had changed to a career in standup comedy, she asked, "What's the punch line to this joke?"

"There's no joke. I'm considering buying a substantial amount of stock in a cruise line and wondered if you and Jack could get away. I value your opinions on whether it might be a worthwhile investment."

Heather realized her mouth had hinged open. She swallowed and asked, "How long have you considered this purchase?"

"I've had my eye on the cruise industry for two years. The

companies burned through money during the last downturn and I think there's a chance for a tremendous upswing. I'd like to see for myself how the ships look and run by taking a few cruises. Would you and Jack like to join me?"

"Father," said Heather in a soft tone. "How are you coping without Mother?"

"Fine, fine. Do you think you and Jack can get away?"

"The last cruise you took was a transatlantic voyage on your honeymoon. Is this sudden interest in cruising about prudent investment decisions or something else?"

The excitement left his voice. "I'm trying to convince myself it's about business. It's the only way I can justify seeing something other than this empty house and my office downtown. People tell me not to make any rash decisions for a least a year, but—"

Steve interjected, "That's good advice."

"Is that you, Steve?"

"It is, Mr. McBlythe. I think the idea of cruises is excellent, especially if you're serious about a major stock purchase. There's nothing like seeing for yourself how a business is run. I understand there are a lot of cruise lines and they all cater to different demographics. Are you considering just one line, or multiple companies?"

"One in particular, but perhaps it would be a good idea to look at several."

Heather broke in, "There's no reason you can't run your business from a ship. You could even take a couple of staff members with you."

Steve added, "It will do you good to get away, work enough to keep the plates spinning, and see fresh sights."

"Tell us about the first cruise you have planned," said Heather.

"It's a repeat of the transatlantic crossing your mother and I took. I'll leave from Southampton, England and sail to New York."

"Please reconsider," said Heather. "Go someplace new and warm. There's nothing between England and New York but memories."

Mr. McBlythe sighed. "You're probably right."

"I'll do some research on the various lines and call you tonight."

Steve added, "There's a cruise out of Galveston in about three weeks I might be interested in going on."

Heather looked at him, "There is?"

"You might go on it, too."

Heather thought for a minute and she exclaimed, "Oh! You're right. We might both be going on that one."

Her father's next words had a lighter air to them. "That sounds intriguing. Are you two working another murder case?"

Steve handled this one. "We're on the way back to our condos from the home of Sid Green."

"The oil tycoon?"

"That's him. A maid found Sid's daughter-in-law dead in her bed this morning. It looks like foul play. Do you know if his son, Howard, runs things now?"

"Let me think." There was a three second pause. "Unless something has changed, that old buzzard Sid is still in charge. I'll double check and make sure that's accurate."

Steve then asked, "Are you familiar with the ongoing feud between the Green family and the Webbers?"

"It goes back generations. A real Hatfield and McCoy story, except it involved oil and two fortunes."

It was Heather's turn. "The cruise we were alluding to involves a destination wedding between the youngest generation of Green offspring, named Chad, and Anna Webber, great-granddaughter of the late Peter Webber."

"Ah. Karl and Ingrid Webber must be Anna's grandparents. He's not a bad sort, but that wife of his is the one who wears the pants in the family. Watch out for her. She's as ruthless as she is smart."

Heather's father stopped his narrative long enough to take a breath. "I can't believe either family would allow a wedding."

"It looks like it will happen, unless it's canceled because of Lucy Green's death," said Steve.

"Keep me apprised of how that case is going," said Mr. McBlythe. "A Christmas getaway combined with a few fireworks from the Greens and Webbers sounds rather intriguing."

Heather chuckled. "I'll keep you in mind. What about cruises between now and Christmas? There might be a short one you could squeeze in."

"Perhaps. I'm not really that interested in buying a cruise line, but I would like to experience the different classes from ultra-luxury, down to the cheapest cabin in the industry. Besides, my doctor told me I needed to increase my vitamin D. If I go to the Caribbean or the Mediterranean, I can work on a tan."

"You've never had a tan in your life," countered Heather.

"Not since you came along, Daughter. Call me tonight."

The car's computer announced, CALL DISCONNECTED.

Steve turned to Heather. "You gave him hope. I heard it in his voice."

Traffic moved and Heather wondered what else she could do to ease her father's loneliness. Nothing came to mind, so she drove without speaking, racking her brain for answers to a situation with which she had no experience—a grieving parent who wasn't getting any younger.

As they approached the Loop 610 interchange, Steve's phone announced an incoming call from Bella Brumley. He put it on speaker. "Good afternoon. This is an unexpected pleasure."

In her mind's eye, Heather saw the tall, statuesque beauty sitting in a lounge chair at her parents' hotel in the U.S. Virgin Islands. Bella's outburst of sobs took her by surprise.

"What's wrong?" asked Steve in a measured tone. "Talk to me. Are you alright?"

"No! I'm horrible. I'm coming to see you and wanted to know if Heather could put me up for a while."

Heather didn't wait for Steve to speak, "Of course I can. When are you coming?"

"Oh, Heather! It's so good to hear your voice." More sobs and a loud blow of the nose. "My life is over. You and Steve have to tell me what to do."

Steve, the ever-practical one asked, "Where are you?"

"At the airport." More sobs accompanied by hiccups.

"What airport?"

"Houston's airport. The big one, near where you live."

"Do your parents know where you are?"

"Uh-huh. I left home yesterday and made it to Miami. I was going to call you but my phone went dead and my charger was in my luggage. On top of that, I missed my flight last night." The crying returned with a vengeance. "They wouldn't let me on the plane because I couldn't stop crying."

"So you slept in the airport?"

"Uh-huh."

Heather said, "We're not far. Get all your luggage and go out to the curb. I'm driving a black Mercedes SUV."

"All right," came the timid, shame-laced voice. The phone call cut off.

Heather moved into the right lane so she wouldn't miss the exit to Houston's Bush Intercontinental Airport. She glanced to her right. "What do you think is wrong with Bella?"

Steve shook his head. "I was afraid this would happen. Bella has the body and brains of someone much older, but because she missed out on so much growing up the way she did, she's what I'd call emotionally stunted. With her adoptive father raising her in his shadow on his television hunting show, she never had the chance to be a teenager. When she told me she was considering marrying a pilot who did island hops in the Caribbean, I sensed she was in for a heartache."

"Did you warn her?"

"Not strong enough, I guess." He let out a huff. "In case you haven't noticed, I'm a little new to this quasi-parenting stuff.

Give me a murder to solve, and I'm right at home. Throw in a girl kidnapped as a child and trained to be a television personality, and I'm out of my league."

"I've never heard her cry like that."

Steve did a finger roll on his thigh. He stopped after six times. "Nothing hurts worse than a broken heart."

Heather shot him a longer glance. "Is that from experience?"

"I lost Maggie, didn't I?"

Heather grimaced. What a thoughtless remark. In her defense, Steve knew he was stretching the comparison. She lowered her voice, "You know I wasn't talking about Maggie. Did you ever get dumped as a teen?"

"Twice. Once in the seventh grade and again my junior year of high school. The last one told me I was a lousy kisser."

Heather tried to hold in the laugh, but there was no stopping it. "What did you do about that?"

"Nothing, until I got to college. After word got around that a dead fish had more zing in its lips than mine, I thought it best to wait until after I graduated high school before I tried again."

"Girls can be so cruel," said Heather.

"Everything turned out all right. All it took was one good woman who liked my fish kisses, and I was set for life."

"There's Bella," said Heather as she pulled to the curb.

"Load her and let's get home and order pizza. It may not mend her broken heart, but it won't hurt. She'll talk after she feels safe and loved."

"Speaking of love," said Heather. "I need to check in with Jack before he dumps me. It wouldn't do for you to have to deal with two distraught women at once."

"Three," said Steve. "Kate's been calling me all day and I haven't returned her calls."

7

The trip from the airport to Steve and Heather's bookend condos passed with few words. Every time Heather cast her gaze in the rearview mirror, Bella either had her head dipped or was looking out the window. Puffy red eyes appeared on the single occasion she momentarily looked forward.

As for Steve, he took his cue from Bella's silence and would wait until she was ready to talk. After all, she wasn't a murder suspect. Or was she? Heather's imagination kicked into high gear. She thought about the old saying regarding fools rushing in where wise men fear to tread, but took the plunge, anyway. "Was it a big fight?"

"Yeah."

"Is the relationship beyond repair?"

"It's over."

"Did you hit him?"

"Uh-huh."

"Good," said Steve. "I hope you broke his nose."

"It was only a slap, but it put him on his backside." The tears started again. "Can we wait until later to talk about it? I need a shower and a nap."

"A nap sounds good to me, too," said Steve. "I'll tell Max you need a bed buddy."

Heather thought about how her chubby Maine Coon cat had befriended Bella and helped her through a tough time. How long ago was it that the man who pretended to be Bella's adopted father was murdered while Bella looked on? Almost three years since Steve, with her help, solved the case and returned Bella to her birth parents. Since then, they'd been in regular contact with the girl who'd became a woman—and a drop-dead gorgeous one, at that.

The SUV eased into the garage. Steve made his way to his own condo while Bella slipped her long arms through the straps of a massive backpack and rolled a large suitcase into Heather's condo. She held the door open for Bella and said, "Nothing has changed since you were last here. Leave your door cracked if you want Max to join you. I'm going next door and work from Steve's kitchen table while you two take a siesta."

Bella nodded. Sobs came in quick bursts, accompanied by intermittent words. "Your ring. I just noticed it. I'm so happy for you and Jack."

Heather acknowledged her with a hug instead of words. As they separated, Heather said, "Take a long, steamy shower, and sleep. I'll tell you all about how Steve played matchmaker after you wake up."

This seemed to brighten Bella's mood a little. "I could use a good Steve story."

Heather went to the pet door in the dining room that allowed Max access to both condos. She bent over, pushed the plastic barrier open and hollered that she was coming over. After grabbing the satchel containing her laptop, she made the short trek next door and entered without knocking. A quick check proved that Steve wasn't in the kitchen, dining room, or living room. Muffled voices on the other side of his closed bedroom door told her he was likely checking in with Kate. They both claimed the successful author was his writing coach, but

Heather hoped something more would come from the friendship.

She retreated down the hall and set up her workstation at the dining room table. It wasn't long before she had the name, address, and phone number of Five Star Employment Services. The company's website stressed that they dealt only with trustworthy domestic, lawn, and general maintenance employees. It also emphasized their specialization in meeting the needs of discerning families in the River Oaks area of Houston.

The initial phone call went as Heather expected. The receptionist, who acted more like a gate master, must have had strict instructions to screen all calls from prospective clients and employees looking to work for wealthy families in Houston. Since Heather wasn't a resident of River Oaks, it took some convincing for the woman to agree to pass on her request for a return call from the company owner. What turned the tide was when Heather told the woman to do a Google search on McBlythe Investments and that she was interested in buying a home in River Oaks and wanted to discuss her potential staffing requirements.

Rapid-fire clicking of keyboard keys sounded. The woman came back with a more accommodating tone to her voice and said the owner would be out of the office until the next morning. "Ms. McBlythe, you can expect to receive a phone call from Mrs. Dubois by 9:00 a.m."

Heather smiled. That was one thing checked off her list, and it only took one tiny half-truth to get the ball rolling. She'd known about the River Oaks section of Houston and had already targeted homes there to purchase if her company found someone whose riches were turning to rags. Choice locations within the Hwy 610 loop of Houston commanded top dollar, especially if renovations were minimal.

Steve appeared over her laptop as she typed in notes. "Couldn't sleep?" she asked.

"Didn't try to. I've been on the phone with Kate. She's

excited about Leo's case. Wants me to keep a journal if we get involved."

"I thought we were involved already. I have an appointment to speak with the owner of Five Star Employment Services in the morning."

"We don't have a client."

Heather shook her head. "I've worked with you long enough to know some of our cases start out with no client. Then, everything hits the fan and we're up to our necks in a murder. On this one, we already know it's a murder. Besides, this involves Leo, who has a partner with no experience in homicides. I know you won't stay out of it."

A youthful mischievous smirk pulled up the corner of Steve's mouth. "I'm too predictable."

Steve asked if she'd like a cup of coffee. After her positive response, he set about preparing a full pot. This signaled the beginning of a full evening with the potential to stretch into the night doing background checks on members of both families. Also, they'd need to order the obligatory pizza for Bella.

Heather corralled her wandering thoughts when Steve asked, "Have you talked to Jack since we've been home?"

She shook her head in disgust. "Why is it you're always having to remind me to call him?"

No answer, so she sent her fiancé a text.

Steve felt the top of the coffee maker, lifted the flap, and drizzled in water. He'd already measured the coffee. "You don't call Jack because you focus intently on tasks. It's the thing that makes you such a successful businesswoman and a good detective. Maggie used to hit me over the head with a rolled-up newspaper when she talked to me and I ignored her."

"He may be busy with a client. I'll get an answer to my text when he gets a chance."

Fortified with coffee, the two private detectives spent the rest of the afternoon with headphones on, doing computer searches, making phone calls to people who knew the family members, and taking copious notes. Heather typed hers out and put them in neat files in her computer. Steve did the same, except he dictated his notes.

By five-thirty, Steve had a decent start on background for Sid and Howard Green, and the deceased, Lucy Green. Heather concentrated on the deceased patriarch of the Webber clan, Peter. She then moved on to Karl and Ingrid Schmidt-Webber. She also wondered about the woman who found Lucy Green's lifeless body, Sylvia Lopez. Curiosity about how the day went at the Green household after she and Steve left got the better of her. She looked in her notes and found Sylvia's phone number.

"Hello, Sylvia?"

"Yes. Who's calling?"

"This is Heather McBlythe. I was checking on you to see if you're all right."

"To tell the truth, Ms. McBlythe, I'm not doing very good. Mr. Howard fired me."

"I'm so sorry," said Heather. "Did he give any reason?"

Her voice caught when she spoke. "He said I talked too much to you and the police. He was furious."

"Some people strike out at others when their spouse dies."

She let out a huff. "You don't know Mr. Howard. He wasn't upset about his wife as much as he was mad at your partner, Mr. Smiley."

Heather looked at Steve but his headphones were over his ears so she didn't interrupt him.

"What did he say about Mr. Smiley?"

"Like I said, he blamed me for talking to you and thinks Mr. Smiley accused him of killing Miss Lucy."

Heather asked, "Would you be willing to meet me tomorrow so we can discuss this in greater detail? I'll make it worth your time."

"The only thing I need to do tomorrow is go talk to Mrs. Dubois at the employment agency. I hope she can find another job for me."

Heather always prided herself on being a quick thinker. "It so happens, I'm supposed to hear from Mrs. Dubois the first thing in the morning. I'll put in a good word for you if you want me to."

"That would be wonderful, but I don't know if she'll listen. She's almost as strict as Ingrid Webber."

"I'll call you tomorrow after I speak with her." She paused. "I feel it's at least partly my fault you lost your job. I'd like to help you over the hump before you get a new job. How much were you making a month working for the Green family?"

Sylvia hesitated, then reluctantly spoke a figure that seemed in line for a full-time maid in that area of Houston.

Heather responded with, "Let's meet tomorrow morning for breakfast and I'll bring you a check for a month's pay. You name the place."

"I don't... I don't know what to say, Ms. McBlythe."

"I believe you're a good employee, Sylvia and I'm in a position to help you. Now, where do you want to meet for breakfast?"

With tomorrow's meeting planned and her phone call disconnected, Heather heard the kitty door slap shut. "Hello, Max. Is Bella awake?"

Meow.

"Are you ready for your dinner?"

Meow.

As Heather scooped cat food from a can, Bella hollered through the pet portal. "I'm coming over."

Steve hollered back, "Good. I'm ready to order pizza."

Bella came in looking like a Scandinavian princess with her silvery-white hair braided into a waist-length rope. Heather always thought of Rapunzel when Bella braided her hair. Unlike the fairy tale character, Bella wore a cropped T-shirt and shorts that showed off long, lean, tanned legs. No wonder she was chosen to host a fishing show where she showed off her skills catching and releasing exotic tropical fish. She roamed the

Caribbean, and sometimes the U.S., fishing with celebrities and dazzling the audience with her skill and smile.

Yet, all was not well with the young princess today and it would be up to Heather and Steve to put her back on track.

Steve started off with, "Do you want your usual? A meat lovers with double cheese?"

"I suppose," she said in a forlorn voice.

"Get me a large salad," said Heather.

Steve nodded. "That's two large meat lovers with extra cheese, two regular salads and one large salad. Any bread-sticks?"

Both women gave a negative reply. Steve phoned in the order and closed his laptop. Heather motioned for Bella to take Steve's computer and headphones to his bedroom as she cleared her workplace and set her valise by the front door.

When Bella returned, he asked, "Did you and Max have a good nap?"

"It was the first decent sleep I've had all week. Max knows how to cuddle."

"I missed my nap, but I'll make up for it tonight." He rose from his chair. "We have at least thirty minutes to kill. Let's go to the living room."

Seven minutes of catching up with small talk followed, mainly about Bella's parents and how much Steve wanted to return to their ocean-side hotel. Heather agreed that a sun-drenched trip to the Virgin Islands sounded better than staying in the drizzle of late December north of Houston. Then came the pause that signaled the conversation would change.

Steve prompted Bella, "Are you ready to tell us what happened?"

She folded her hands together on her lap. "No, but it has to be done. I'm sure you've heard the story a thousand times, but I never thought it would happen to me. How could I not see it? He's tall, dark, and has dreamy brown eyes. He was the perfect gentleman with me. Well, at least he started off that way. About a month ago he got pushy, if you know what I mean."

"I certainly do," said Heather. "Isn't he a pilot?"

"Yeah," said Bella. "Remind me to never fall for another one of those. I thought it was sailors who had a girl in every port. It seems pilots in the Caribbean have a girl on every island."

"Ouch," said Heather. "How did you find out?"

Bella dipped her head. "You two may not realize this, but you're my heroes. I watched how you investigated the murder of the man who said he was my adopted father. Ever since then, I've read hundreds of detective stories, explored online courses, and even wanted to be a private investigator myself. Of course, my television show and modeling kept me super busy, but that's changed now."

Steve held up his hand as a stop sign. "This is news to me. What's changed?"

"The production company insisted I wear bikinis in almost every shot. They wanted an edgier show than I was comfortable with. Standing mostly naked in the tropical sun all day is a good way to ruin your skin. Everything came to a head when the producer arrived on the island to meet with me and my dad. Things got ugly and Dad threw him out of the hotel. Dad's my hero, too."

"Good for him," said Heather.

"I'll second that," said Steve. "Did losing your television gig happen before you found out your prince wasn't so charming?"

"Dad told the producer to take a hike three weeks ago. I should have called you."

Steve waved off her last comment, and summarized her present situation. "Three weeks ago, you lost your job. When did your love life fall apart?"

"Four days ago." Bella cast her gaze to Heather and then dipped her head. "I put into practice some things I learned about being a detective and paid one of the hotel maids to help me. She flew to three of the islands where the creep would stay overnight. At each island, he met a different woman for dinner followed by a night in his hotel room."

"He doesn't deserve you," said Heather as she clenched her fists.

"What made you suspect him?" asked Steve.

"Perfume. Like most men, he hates to wash clothes, but he came home with wet shirts. I saw them draped over the shower bar after one of his trips. I guess he thought there was less chance of the perfume staying in the fabric if he rinsed them out before he came home."

Steve chuckled.

"It's not funny!" snapped Bella.

"I'm not laughing at you, sweetheart. I find the coincidence funny. This morning I smelled perfume on a murder suspect that didn't match his wife's."

Bella's eyes opened wide. "A murder case? How cool. Maybe I really could become a private eye. Can you use me? I'll work for free."

Steve cleared his throat. Heather wondered if he'd unintentionally encouraged her too much. As usual, Steve's response took her by surprise. "You can help me by doing background checks. I'll teach you how."

"Are you sure about this?" asked Heather.

Steve flipped his hand, dismissing her protest. His next words went to Bella. "No field work. No interviews. Only what you can find on the internet with Heather or me supervising."

Bella's next words came out sounding more like her normal upbeat self. "It's a start. I'll be doing stakeouts before you know it."

8

The next morning, Heather's phone rang at eight thirty. She answered with her usual greeting.

"Ms. McBlythe? This is Mary Dubois with Five Star Employment Services. I received your message and wondered how I might help."

"Thank you for returning my call. I'm afraid my personal assistant jammed my calendar full this morning, but I was wondering if I could buy you lunch today. I've made reservations at Dominic's, which I believe isn't far from your office."

"That would be lovely."

"Fine. I'll see you at noon."

"Wow," said Bella, sitting at the table wearing a cut-off football jersey and sleep shorts. "You molded her like putty."

Heather smiled. "If you're wanting to be a detective, you have to speak the language of whomever you're talking to. Mrs. Dubois is used to dealing with wealthy people who have high expectations. Did you notice how I only gave her one option of when to meet me? That told her I was serious about doing business and she'd better make herself available. You can bet she's already looked at my background, and has a good idea of my net worth. Acting wealthy is easy for me. It took me a lot longer to learn how to talk to homeless people."

"I can talk like a hotel maid," said Bella with pride in her voice. "That's what my parents have me doing. Both of them work hard and it didn't take long after the television show fell through for them to tell me I could either pay regular room rates or earn my room and board. They want me to learn the hotel business from the ground up so I can take over when they retire."

"They love you very much."

"That's true. It didn't thrill them when I said I was coming here, but I really needed to get away. The island was closing in on me." She cocked her head to one side. "Did you ever have to get away from something?"

Heather thought back to a sterile existence growing up. "Everyone feels that way."

"Did you run far?"

"Very far. All the way from Princeton to working as a cop in Boston for ten years. I kept running until I got to Texas. My father chased me, trying to get me to come home and be a part of his world. Then Steve came into my life. He needed me. At the time, I didn't realize how much I needed him."

"What do you mean, you needed Steve?"

"He pointed me back to my parents. Now Mother's gone, but Father and I are closer than we've ever been."

"I guess some things take more time than others."

Heather rose and chuckled. "We dressed alike. Football jerseys and sleep shorts. If Mrs. Dubois could see me now, she'd turn and run."

"I think you're the prettiest woman I've ever met, and I know Jack thinks the same." She paused for a breath, then plunged ahead. "When's the wedding?"

Heather held up her hands. "Put the brakes on, young lady. Where did that come from?"

"You're engaged, aren't you? It seemed like a logical question."

"When were you and your prince going to get married?" asked Heather to deflect the uncomfortable question.

"He hadn't asked me, but I was sure he would. Anyway, I wanted to get married at Christmas. The best thing that ever happened to me came at Christmas when you and Steve found my parents. I think a Christmas wedding would be lucky."

"Jack and I are taking things slow," said Heather, to pacify the inquisitive young mind.

"Why wait?"

Heather turned. "You need to go next door and cook breakfast for Steve."

Bella bounded out of her chair. "You're making me feel right at home. Whenever my mom doesn't want to answer, she finds something for me to do."

With steamy water pounding her head, Bella's two-word question seemed to echo in the shower. "Why wait?"

Heather spoke out loud an answer that would satisfy no one, especially herself. "It's complicated."

STEVE SIPPED COFFEE AND LISTENED TO A REPEAT OF THE EARLY morning local news when the cat door opened and Bella hollered, "I'm coming over." He never imagined when he moved to this condo many years ago that there'd be a hole in the wall between his dining room and the one next door. After her inheritance came through and Heather decided to make her home beside him, the pass-through for Max seemed the perfect solution. It also worked well as an early warning system.

Bella flopped on the couch. "Anything good on this morning?"

"The freeways and major roads are reporting a slew of accidents, the normal blather by finger-pointing politicians, there's a thirty percent chance of light rain today, and only two murders last night."

"Sounds like a rinse-and-repeat sort of day."

Steve already had the remote in hand, so he clicked off the television. "What are you cooking for breakfast?"

"I'm not hungry. Do you want a couple of fried eggs and sausage?"

"Not yet. I need to do a couple of miles on the treadmill this morning."

"Me, too," said Bella and followed the words with pig oinks. "I stuffed myself on pizza last night and feel like a blimp." Her voice went up a note. "Let's take a walk instead of going to the gym."

Steve pushed a wayward lock of hair back in place. "We'll be wringing wet if we walk two miles outside. Our December weather feels a lot like September this week. Are you sure you don't want to go to the gym?"

Bella hesitated, and the cheerful tone left her voice. "It doesn't normally bother me when guys watch me working out, but if it's all the same to you, I'd like to walk where there aren't many people."

"No problem. Let's do three miles on the walking path around the complex. We'll sweat so much no one will want to look at either of us. A good cleansing of the body and mind will be good for both of us."

Steve pushed himself out of the recliner. "If we work that hard, there'd better be pancakes, sausage, and eggs as a reward."

Bella came off the couch like a Jack-in-the-box. "I'll race you to see who can get ready the fastest."

The front door slammed before Steve made it to the bedroom. The race was on and the two met outside the condos, with Bella only slightly ahead. He asked, "Does my shirt come close to matching my shorts?"

"Not really. Are you trying to impress some cute widow or divorcée?"

Steve held out his hand and Bella placed it on her arm. "Let's make a deal this morning. No talk about either of our crummy love lives."

A hint of mischief seasoned Bella's next words. "Can we talk about Heather's?"

"Not until we finish two miles. After that, I may need oxygen and won't be responsible for anything I say."

Bella took off at a quick pace. Steve's shorter strides made it difficult to keep up. It wasn't long before he gave his rendition of a steam locomotive while Bella's long legs ate up real estate like it was candy.

"No fair," said Steve, as he spoke in short sentences. "Your legs are too long."

"Do you need me to slow down?"

"Keep going," said Steve, even though his lungs felt like someone set them on fire. The calves of his legs were burning in sympathy with his lungs. Something that felt like a boulder had wedged in his left shoe, making the speed-walk even more miserable. He managed to get out a simple sentence. "Bring phone?"

"Sure. Why?"

"In case... I need... ambulance."

Bella patted his sweaty hand. "You're doing great, and we're almost to the two-mile mark."

He wanted to ask if she didn't mean the twenty-mile mark, but he was hurting so bad he didn't want to waste what little breath he had on a lame joke.

On they went until Bella said, "Two miles. Let's rest."

Steve crumpled to the wet ground, took off his shoe, and shook it. Bella took it from his hand. "Why didn't you tell me you needed to stop?"

"Was having... too much... fun."

He felt her put the shoe back on and tighten the laces. "There. We need to keep walking or your muscles will contract, and I'm not sure I can carry you. Let's take the pace down to where we can talk normally."

That was music to his ears. Her shorter strides were such that Steve used his cane to navigate the asphalt path without holding on. Eventually, his lungs stopped burning, and the rest of his body fell into line. He could even ask a complete question without panting. "What were you and Heather talking about this morning?"

"Girl talk. She was getting the scoop on my dumpster fire of a love life."

"Ah. We agreed not to talk about that. Do you want to renegotiate?"

"No, and thanks for not pressuring me to tell it again."

"Excellent decision. Sometimes you need to talk to someone you can trust, and other times silence is a pleasant companion."

They walked on for another three minutes before Bella said, "I'm worried about Heather and Jack."

"Oh?"

"I'm afraid she'll never get up the courage to marry him and she'll regret it the rest of her life."

"She's a complicated woman."

Bella stopped, so Steve did too. "That's almost the same words she used when I asked her why she was waiting."

Steve took a paper towel from his pocket and made it soggy by running it over his face. "I used up all my good will when I helped her see she wanted to be engaged. It was an elaborate scheme, but it pushed the boundaries of our friendship. That's as far as I'm going with matchmaking. Besides, I need to concentrate on solving a murder."

"More background information this morning?" asked Bella.

Steve nodded. "Until yesterday, there were seven members of the Green family living under one very large roof. Now, there's only six."

"How many in the Webber mansion?"

"Six, unless one or more got bumped off in the night."

"Let's see," said Bella. "Heather worked on three histories

last night, and you and I made files on two. That leaves seven and Heather's going to Houston today."

"You're not counting Lucy, the victim. We have to know her history, as well as the staff of both homes."

"Holy smoke. We'd better get to work."

"Breakfast first. The first rule of being a PI is to fuel up at the beginning of a day. If Leo doesn't solve this case, we'll need all the energy we can get."

9

The bistro Sylvia chose sat in a strip mall on a major street running through a middle-class neighborhood. Upon entering the ten-table restaurant, Heather scanned the patrons. The recently fired woman lifted her head and nodded a greeting. She wore jeans and a pullover sweater that accentuated broad shoulders and a nicely rounded figure. Heather guessed Sylvia's age to be early forties by the crow's feet etching the corners of her eyes.

"Thanks so much for meeting with me. By the way, my name is Heather. I'd like you to call me that instead of Ms. McBlythe."

"After looking you up on the internet, I feel like I should call you Ms. McBlythe."

Heather waved off the compliment. "I put my shoes on one at a time, just like you did this morning."

That drew a smile and a word of instruction, "The quiche is excellent here, but they make the French toast from day-old white bread."

"Thanks for the warning. I'll take whatever you're having as long as I can wash it down with good, strong coffee."

The conversation remained light while they waited for their orders. Heather guided Sylvia into an evenly timed information swap about family and children, or lack thereof in Heather's case. By the time only crust remained on their plates, the conversation flowed without effort.

Heather dabbed her mouth with a paper napkin and got down to business. "I'm meeting Mrs. Dubois for lunch. I'll do what I can to get you into another home as soon as possible."

"That would be wonderful. My middle child started college this semester, and we weren't expecting to be a single income family. And Christmas is just around the corner." She paused. "I wanted to thank you for your calm and control yesterday while I was blubbering and falling apart. When I looked you up on the internet, I saw that you're a private investigator. When you went into Lucy's room you gathered information and evidence, didn't you?"

Heather stacked the two plates and put them to one side. "My main reason for going into the room was to make sure no one was in there and to secure it. Sid Green had a premonition that the marriage between Chad Green and Anna Webber would reignite the feud between the two families. He was particularly worried that someone might die. I knew when I went in there was a possibility the room could eventually be named a crime scene. It appears now that Sid was right, but he called us too late."

Sylvia leaned forward and lowered her voice. "Mr. Howard and Mr. Sid had a terrible fight yesterday after you left."

"Do you know what it was about?"

"Not really, but Mr. Howard brought in a private investigator he knows quite well and Butch called in extra men to guard the house and grounds. By the time Mr. Howard fired me, the place was like the White House, complete with Secret Service."

Heather took a sip of tepid coffee. "Do you know the name of the private investigator or any of the guards?"

"I think the investigator's last name is Drake. He's done work for the family before. Mr. Howard seems to like him, but Mr. Sid doesn't."

"What about Lucy Green? Did she have any interaction with Drake that you know of?"

Sylvia's black hair had a few stray strands of silver in it that caught the light when she nodded. "They both talked to him like he was on old friend, but as far as I know, he only helped them discover a sticky-fingered cook's helper."

"When was that?"

"About a year and a half ago. I didn't work there then, but one of the gardeners told me about it."

"Was the helper arrested?"

Sylvia cast her gaze to the parking lot. "That's not the way they do things in River Oaks, unless it's something serious. If you're fired with cause, Mrs. Dubois blackballs you. You might as well leave the state and start over somewhere else."

Heather briefly considered the kitchen helper as a suspect, but just as quickly rejected the possibility. Even if the thief blamed Lucy for her dismissal, it occurred well over a year ago. Plenty of time to cool off. It was time to dig deeper into the victim's history.

"Did Lucy Green drink wine every night?"

"She'd have a glass with dinner, but preferred pills to help her sleep at night. She was an avid reader of romance novels, so her routine was to eat supper with the family, go to her room, read for a couple of hours and take pills to help her go to sleep. It surprised me when they found a bottle of wine in her room."

Heather wondered if she should press Sylvia for more details about the family. It might be too soon. If Sylvia clammed up, she'd lose her only source of inside information. Perhaps a more subtle approach would suffice.

"Can you help me get all the Green family members straight in my mind? Would you mind sketching out a diagram of the family tree for me?"

Sylvia tilted her head in apparent confusion. "I'm not sure what you want."

"Let's do it together." Heather wrote Sid Green at the top of a blank piece of paper. "Who were Sid's children?"

"His only son's name is Howard. He and Lucy had two children, Tim and a daughter named Carol. Carol married and divorced. She has issues."

"How so?"

"She has a tendency to slur her words by early afternoon."

"I see," said Heather. "And Tim's wife's name is..."

"Tammy Palmer-Green. Her parents live in River Oaks, too. Tim and Tammy's only child is Chad Green."

"The future groom," said Heather.

Sylvia cocked her head. "Have you ever noticed how rich people have fewer children than the rest of us?" Her eyes grew in size. "I'm sorry. Sometimes I speak before I think."

Heather held up a hand. "No offense taken. As I grow older, I'm finding I think more like my parents than I ever imagined I would. They only wanted one child and I'm happily childless."

Even though she tried to minimize Sylvia's remark about the economic chasm between the two of them, she knew a class barrier had gone up. Sylvia had let her guard down for a moment, but Heather sensed it was in place again. Instead of pressing her further about what went on behind the thick oak doors of the Greens' home, she shifted to a more general question.

"Did Detectives Vega and Keita interview you again?"

"Only Detective Vega. The other detective interviewed the kitchen staff."

Sylvia raised her chin. "Detective Vega said I could trust you. He also told me what happened to Mr. Smiley, and how rich you are."

"Did he also tell you I lived in an efficiency apartment in Boston for ten years when I was a cop? Believe me, I've eaten my share of ramen noodles. That's when I paid my own way through law school."

"Without your family helping?"

Heather nodded. "I'm annoyingly independent."

She smiled and got the conversation off herself. "Was the family attorney there when Leo interviewed you?"

Heather sensed Sylvia's guard drop a little when a chuckle preceded her answer. "He was there, but he doesn't speak Spanish. Detective Vega told me to follow his lead, so we both spoke extra fast, with heavy accents. I think that might have contributed to me getting fired."

Heather handed Sylvia an envelope. "If you agree to meet with me again, you'll receive another check for the same amount."

Sylvia hesitated, but took the gift. "I'll talk to you again, but I won't take any more of your money." She looked at the envelope. "My husband and I have always worked hard and paid for what we have."

"Expect a call this afternoon. Your vacation will soon end."

HEATHER WHEELED HER SUV INTO THE LANE MARKED FOR valet parking at the front door of Dominic's, an upscale Italian restaurant on the fringe of River Oaks. She checked her makeup and long auburn hair in the rearview mirror before getting out and running her hand down the silk dress she'd purchased an hour before at a nearby boutique. The clock on the dashboard told her she was ten minutes late. "Perfect," she whispered. The skinny jeans, plain blouse, and cross-trainers she'd worn to meet with Sylvia sat in a bag marked *Mimi's* in the back seat. For good measure, she'd also bought new heels and a scarf that draped across her shoulder.

Once inside, she checked with the maître d' and learned Mrs. Dubois waited in the main dining room. With shoulders back and head level enough to carry a book with a glass of water balanced on it without spilling, Heather strode to the table and extended a hand. "Mrs. Dubois, please excuse my tardiness. I hope I haven't kept you waiting."

"Not at all," said the woman in a way that communicated she'd mastered patience by working with the privileged few.

Heather lowered herself onto a high back chair covered in thick damask fabric. A tasteful miniature vase holding a sprig of holly adorned the table. The carpeted floor soaked up sound as wafts of garlic, bay leaves, thyme, and rosemary caught a ride on a gentle breeze from the air conditioner.

"I see you've already ordered iced tea," said Heather. "Would you like something from the bar?"

"No, thank you. I make it a rule not to indulge while discussing business."

"A wise rule, and one that I also follow. It's amazing how a small amount of spirits can cloud one's judgment."

Heather ordered unsweetened iced tea and took stock of Mrs. Dubois. She looked to be in her late forties but the lack of wrinkles and thick makeup made Heather reconsider. The plastic surgeon had done a good job.

Heather spread her linen napkin in her lap, smoothing out the wrinkles, then perused the menu and laid it aside. When the silence between them bordered on discomfort, Mrs. Dubois said, "Your phone call intrigued me. Are you planning to move into a home in River Oaks?"

"Not exactly," said Heather. "I'm considering purchasing one or more properties, but they must meet my needs. I've done research and found the people who purchase in River Oaks are very discerning. Much like those in other upscale areas of the country, and the world even. People make and lose fortunes everywhere. I'm interested in the homes owned by families in the latter category. What I'm hoping to find are homes that are down at the heels, owned by people who can no longer afford them. I'm running the numbers on homes I can purchase, renovate, and offer to the next buyer who's looking for something truly stunning."

"I don't think I've heard of anyone wanting to, pardon the expression, 'flip' a home in River Oaks." She knitted her eyebrows together. "It may very well work, but I don't see how I fit in your plans."

"I'm a bit of a maverick with real estate, and have a knack for thinking outside the proverbial box. Father says I'm reckless, but I assure you, I do my homework and go into things with my eyes wide open." Excitement peppered Heather's next words. "My plan is to fully update the home and grounds. Then, I'll host one or more parties that will introduce people to the phoenix-like home. Resurrected from the ashes, so to speak. Everyone loves to see updated styles and new gadgets. Word will spread. There are always customers willing to buy the best in the most exclusive neighborhood."

"You mentioned parties. Like an open house?"

"You could say that, but on a much grander scale. To make this work, I'll need groundskeepers and staff to clean and maintain the properties. Of course, I'll require temporary help when I host parties."

The server came to take orders, which put further conversation on hold. Heather carried on a brief conversation with the server in Italian and took his recommendation for a lunch selection.

Once they were alone again, Heather asked, "How much do you know about me, Mrs. Dubois?"

The woman didn't shy away from answering. "Enough to know you can pull this off and that I'll be happy to provide you with quality employees."

"Do you know I was in the home of Mr. Sid Green yesterday when they found his daughter-in-law Lucy?"

Mrs. Dubois squirmed in her chair, a sure sign of discomfort. "I heard Mrs. Green died, but I'm not familiar with any of the details, other than Mr. Howard Green called and told me he'd fired the maid."

"Did he tell you why?"

"I assumed it was because her primary duties were seeing to

his wife's needs. With the death, I assumed she was no longer needed."

"That could be true, but not entirely. The important thing for you to know is that Sylvia Lopez is a skilled and loyal worker. I had breakfast with her this morning and she hopes Mr. Howard's rash dismissal won't affect her good standing with you and her ability to move into a similar position with another family. I can't go into details, but I assure you, Sylvia Lopez did nothing to deserve dismissal on such short notice."

Mrs. Dubois put on her best poker face. "I'll need to look into the matter and make a determination. This was her third placement in a home. It makes me wonder about her."

"And all of the dismissals came about because of extenuating circumstances." Heather took a breath. "I'm not telling you how to run your business, and I'll understand if you decide otherwise, but it would be a personal favor to me if you'd find Sylvia a new employer."

The gaze of Mrs. Dubois went past Heather as she spoke. "Sylvia did last much longer with Ingrid Webber than anyone else, and I currently have a family that wants a bilingual maid. They live several streets away from the Webbers and the Greens. I believe Sylvia could be a good fit."

"Thank you, Mrs. Dubois." Heather smiled. "I'm looking forward to working with you on at least one project in the future."

Heather realized that the more she thought about flipping homes in the exclusive neighborhood, the more she wanted to try it. She came out of her thoughts when Mrs. Dubois leaned toward her. "I know you're an attorney and also a private detective. Was Lucy Green murdered?"

Heather matched the lean and whispered, "You can't say a word until the police announce it, but yes."

"Was it her husband?"

Heather leaned back and signaled to their server. "It's too early in the investigation to tell."

After giving her credit card to the server, Heather said, "Thank you for meeting with me today, Mrs. Dubois. You've been a great help."

"Thank you. I look forward to hearing from you again."

Heather pondered their conversation while she waited for her car to be brought by the valet. Once inside her SUV, she drove only as far as necessary to find a parking spot away from other vehicles and speed dialed the office. Her personal assistant picked up on the first ring.

"Joy," said Heather. "Get the acquisitions team together and tell them to research properties in the River Oaks neighborhood of Houston. I'm looking for something that needs a major renovation and is owned by someone who's overextended, preferably facing bankruptcy. The bigger the home, the better."

"I'm on it. Anything else?"

"I'll be out of the office for the rest of the day. Anything on your end?"

"Call your father. He sounded excited."

10

Heather took the time to see how many calls and texts she'd missed while having lunch with Mrs. Dubois, then dialed her father. It took three rings for him to answer.

"Hello, Heather. Are your bags packed?"

"Do they need to be?"

"I've booked me, you, and Jack on a cruise that sails out of Miami tomorrow afternoon."

Heather rolled her eyes upward. "How many days are we talking about?"

"It's a seven-day cruise, but I don't expect you to stay the entire voyage. The first two days are at sea. After that, your plane can meet you at the first port of call."

Heather racked her brain for an excuse to turn her father down, but the desire to continue developing a positive relationship with him weighed heavy on her heart. She considered the murder case. She and Steve agreed to help Leo, but that only went as far as doing background research and Heather's follow-up interviews with Sylvia. The simple fact was, they didn't have a client. More than anything, she didn't want to hear the disappointment in her father's voice if she turned him down.

"Jack has a trial that's scheduled to last four days, so I know he can't come. Count me in."

"Fabulous!"

"You said we sail from Miami. On what cruise line?"

"I booked us suites on a Seabourn Cruise Line ship. The first port of call is San Juan, Puerto Rico and the second is St. Martin."

"Seabourn. That's one of the upper tier cruise lines."

"That's how they advertise themselves. It will be fun discovering if they live up to their claims."

"It's been a long time since I've been to either of those islands." Visions of azure water and white sand beaches invaded her thoughts. "I'll decide after we're at sea if I can be away four days or five."

"Like you said, your office can be anywhere you have a phone and internet connections."

"You're right. Put me down for five days. I'll tell my pilots to drop me off in Miami and fly on to St. Martin."

"The ship sails at 5:00 p.m. tomorrow. Don't forget your passport."

A phone call to her pilots and a second one to Joy, her personal assistant, were all it took to get the working vacation with her father in motion. Next, she needed to call Steve and let him know she'd be gone the better part of a week. Her mouth opened to tell the phone to call him when his name came through the car's speakers as in incoming call.

"Did you finish your talk with Mrs. Dubois?" he asked.

"I did, and I believe everything will work out fine for Sylvia Lopez. She's a very likable woman."

"Where are you?"

"Outside a restaurant named *Dominic's*, close to River Oaks."

"It sounds expensive. Stay there. We have an interview with Ingrid Webber. She wants to hire us."

"Today?"

"Yeah." Steve paused. "If that's a problem I can have Leo meet me."

"It's not really a problem."

"Decide," said Steve. "Is it a problem, or not?"

"No problem. I'll go back inside and wait for you."

"I'm only about ten minutes from you. A very nice Uber driver will drop me off and we'll go to the Webber house."

Heather backtracked. "I may have messed up. I told Father I'd go with him on a cruise that will take me to the Caribbean for five days. Make that six days including the flights."

"When will you leave?"

"Tomorrow."

It took Steve less than a tick of the clock to reply. "That's no problem. You and I will pump the Webbers for information today and Bella and I will follow up on any leads we generate from both families. It will take at least a week to get complete histories on the members of both families, their staff, and anyone else who pops up."

"That reminds me," said Heather. "Sylvia told me Howard Green hired a PI named Drake to find Lucy's killer and Butch called in a commando team to guard the Greens' fortress."

"So much for us getting back in to interview any of the Green family members. We'll have to find a work-around."

"I'll see what I can think up when I'm whiling away the day in a lounge chair on the cruise."

Steve chuckled. "You might be in a lounge chair, but you'll have a laptop, a tablet, and your phone all going at the same time."

Heather thought of something else. "Is Bella with you?"

"Of course not. She was told from the start that her part in this investigation is restricted to working on a computer. No face-to-face interviews or even phone interviews."

"Right," said Heather with emphasis. "By the way, I looked at a photo of the exterior of the Webber home online. Imagine the

Versailles Palace washed in hot water, put in an industrial dryer, and shrunk to fit on five acres."

A SHORT TIME LATER, WITH STEVE BESIDE HER, HEATHER turned into a split driveway. She bore to the right and drove around trees that looked like cake decorations and a central fountain that should have shot water skyward. Marble cherubs played in lesser fountains in the elongated pool leading to the home. At first glance the home surpassed the Greens' Tudor-style home. On closer inspection, the driveway needed resurfacing, an urn that should have poured water was dry, and the hedges needed a trim. Chipped paint around the windows spoke of the need for scraping and a fresh coat.

"What's your first impression of this place?" asked Steve.

"It could use some love."

"That explains the smell of slimy pond water."

Heather glanced toward the row of cherubs. "Perhaps Ingrid Webber fired the person responsible for the lawn and fountains."

"I wouldn't doubt it," said Steve. "If it weren't for Leo needing our help..."

The front door opened and an ancient man wearing a butler's uniform with frayed sleeves stood as still as one of the marble guardians of the green water. He spoke with a German accent. "Frau Webber is expecting you. We should not keep her waiting."

Heather's gaze took in the two-story foyer. A sweeping double staircase emptied from the two wings of the second floor onto marble floors in what was once the centerpiece of the home's entry. The thin spots in the carpet runners descending the stairs not only detracted from its magnificence and beauty but served as further proof of the family's financial straits.

Like the Green home, there weren't any Christmas decorations to lighten the feel of heaviness.

The butler shuffled to a stop at a double door, knocked, and listened until a woman with a thick accent barked out a command to enter. He turned the handles of both doors and gave them a push. Heather wondered if the move was choreographed to give the impression of entering a royal chamber.

The room turned out to be a library, constructed of dark woods and shelves stuffed with leather-bound tomes. A woman with gray hair wound in a tight bun at the base of her neck stood at the mullioned window, looking out over the front lawn. She continued to stare as the butler stood in place, looking like a well-trained pointer locked on its master's prey.

Heather schooled her expression to a neutral gaze at the matriarch. She'd seen this power play more times than she cared to remember, especially among fading aristocrats who still held a title, but were generations away from the dynamic person who'd earned the fame, fortune, and glory.

"Sit," said the woman.

This was the butler's cue to direct Steve and Heather to a low-slung couch across from a tall chair whose oversize dimensions ensured the person seated on it would look down upon those on the couch.

While still looking out the window, the woman spoke. "I understand you two are private investigators and you were next door when Howard Green killed his wife."

Steve spoke up. "You're correct, up to a point."

The woman jerked her head around. "Up to a point?"

"Ms. McBlythe and I were not in the home when she died. The police announced a little while ago they're treating the death as a possible homicide. As for Howard Green being the killer..." Steve shrugged.

Frau Webber took her seat in the grand chair. "But she was murdered?"

"An autopsy is ordered, and the exact cause of death will be determined. It's too early in the investigation to label it murder."

Heather joined in. "Based on the totality of the evidence,

they'll hold off on making a final determination until they're sure. It could be death by natural causes, accidental death, suicide, or homicide."

"How long until they know?"

"It could take a day, or up to a week." Steve added, "I assume we're speaking with Mrs. Ingrid Webber, is that correct?"

The accent seemed even thicker when she said, "That is correct, Mrs. Schmidt-Webber."

Heather asked, "Will your husband be joining us?"

"Karl is busy."

Steve asked, "Have the police questioned you or anyone in your family?"

"Of course not. Why should they?"

"They will," said Steve.

"They have no right. No one in this family had anything to do with Frau Green's death."

It was Heather's turn. "Considering the multi-generational feud between the two families, the police will need to explore all possibilities."

Ingrid Webber lifted her chin. "I won't allow it. The Greens will do everything in their power to implicate us and cast suspicion away from Howard Green. They'll try to make us a convenient scapegoat, and I'll have none of it."

Steve asked, "Why do you believe Howard Green is involved in the death of his wife?"

"Perhaps you're not as good of a detective as I've heard, Mr. Smiley. It's common knowledge in River Oaks that Howard and Lucy Green's marriage has been on the rocks for years. He's had four affairs in the last three years that I'm aware of. The women get younger as he grows older."

"You're well informed," said Steve.

Ingrid's mouth cracked open in a crooked smile. "Knowledge means money, Mr. Smiley."

Heather wanted to squirm in her seat after seeing the self-righteous smile, but learned long ago how to hide her emotions.

Still, there was the feeling Ingrid had a lot in common with the pond scum in the fountain pool out front.

Steve carried on. "What are your expectations of us?"

"Quite simple," said Ingrid. "Protect the good name of the Webber family and help the police prove that one of the Green family members killed Lucy."

"What if the evidence points to someone in the Webber family?"

Any remnant of Ingrid's smile left. "It won't, but should the Greens plant evidence implicating anyone in this family, you're not to give it to the police. Bring it to me and I'll tell you how I want to handle it."

Steve nodded, not in agreement, but only that he understood her expectations. He loaded and fired another question. "One last question from me. What if the police determine Lucy's death is a homicide and there's no evidence to implicate Howard Green or anyone in his family?"

Ingrid stood, walked to the window, and seemed to mull over the answer to Steve's question. "There's no need to discuss that until we have an agreement that you'll work for me."

Heather jumped back in. "We require all clients to sign a formal contract that stipulates the terms of what we will and will not do."

Ingrid turned and laughed. "You'll do whatever I tell you. Those are my terms."

Steve and Heather both rose. He unfurled his cane and waited until Heather placed his hand on her arm. He did the talking. "There will be no charge for this meeting. I'm sure you'll have no trouble finding a private investigator better suited to fit your needs."

Heather added in German, "*Auf Wiedersehen, Frau Webber. Sie sollten etwas gegen Ihre Brunnen unternehmen.*"

"Get out!"

11

Steve buckled in only a second or two before Heather sped toward the front gate of the Webber chateau. As she wheeled out of the gate and onto the street, she offered an apology for not handling the matriarch in a more tactful manner.

"What did you say to Ingrid in German?"

"I told her good-bye and said she should do something about the fountains."

Steve erupted in a guffaw. When he brought himself under control, he said, "That's nicer than what I had in mind to tell her." He paused. "I'm afraid we've painted ourselves into a corner. We have no client and we've burned our bridges with both families. I did it by making a big deal out of the perfume on Howard Green's shirt."

Heather took over. "And I did it today by telling Ingrid she needed to do something about the nasty fountains in front of her home. The Webbers look to be on the downward slope of wealth and I fired a volley at her pride." Heather cast a glance Steve's way. "What do you suggest we do?"

"Nothing until I sleep on it. And speaking of, I think I'll take a nap on the way home." With that brief announcement of his intentions, he put the seat in full recline.

Steve remained in a horizontal position until they were almost home, and he brought his seat up to his usual position. "What time do you fly out in the morning?"

"Not too early. The ship leaves at five tomorrow afternoon, but I need to be on board at least an hour earlier. Father's meeting me at the airport and has arranged transportation to the cruise terminal."

Steve pictured a long, black limo snaking its way through Miami traffic with Heather and her father in the back seat. They'd both have a copy of the *Wall Street Journal* and would speak only if something caught their eye as a potential investment or a signal to dump a few thousand shares of an underperforming stock.

Heather's next statement reminded him there was a thrifty side to her. "I need to put a load of laundry in before I come over to discuss how we can proceed with helping Leo. I'm down to my last three pair of clean panties and I'm not about to pay what the cruise ship charges." She took a breath. "I need to pick up a new sun hat, but I guess that can wait until I get on board."

Once parked, Heather went her way and Steve entered his unlocked condo. Bella welcomed him and announced she'd made chocolate chip cookies.

"I smelled them the minute I walked in. We'd better hide them from Heather."

"Why? One or two won't hurt her. She's the perfect weight for her age and height and she works out like she's training for the Olympics."

"True, but I'm the proud owner of a pudgy belly. She knows I can eat my weight in chocolate chip cookies, especially warm ones. She threatened to buy me a smart watch that tracks things for my health if I get any heavier."

"They should be cool enough by now to bag them and put them in the freezer. We can get them out after she goes to work in the morning. Is she coming over soon?"

"She'll come over after she starts a load of clothes and calls

Jack. She's leaving tomorrow on a cruise with her father." He smiled. "We'll have five days to enjoy those cookies."

Sounds coming from the pantry told Steve that Bella was on task to hide the evidence of their cookie caper. While walking toward the stove, she asked, "How did your interview with Frau Webber go?"

"Not great. We came to a mutual agreement that we'll all sleep better if Heather and I don't work for her. She has a most disagreeable disposition."

Further discussion ended with dual interruptions. Max, Heather's massive Maine Coon cat, came through the kitty door followed by Heather entering through the front door.

"Is that cookies I smell?"

"Busted," whispered Steve so only Bella could hear him.

"I baked them, but I told Steve he could only have one after lunch and dinner," said Bella. "I'm bagging them to put in the freezer so I can ration them."

Steve wondered if Bella remembered to cross her fingers so the lie didn't count. He wanted to further deflect Heather from the truth by holding out empty hands. "Look. No crumbs on my shirt or on the bar. I remembered what you said about cholesterol and triglycerides. Two tiny cookies a day will be my limit."

Heather's footsteps went toward Bella. "They're as big as a saucer. Make sure he only eats half after a meal."

Steve looked for an honest loophole. If he had four meals a day... He quickly changed the subject. "How's Jack?"

"Busy. The client he's defending isn't making it easy on him. It's an assault charge, and the guy keeps beating up other inmates in the county jail. Jack's only hope is to have the judge block all testimony about subsequent assaults until guilt or innocence on the first charge is determined."

"Can he do that?" asked Bella.

"It's possible," said Steve. "There's a presumption of innocence on all criminal charges."

"But," said Heather, "it's also possible the prosecution could sneak in the information and influence the jury. Once the jury hears something, they can't un-hear it."

"I thought the law was more exact than that," said Bella.

"Law and medicine," said Steve. "They call them practices, not certainties."

"What about being a detective?"

Steve answered this question, too. "You train yourself to give the facts of what you've discovered to someone who makes a lot more money than you do and move on. A good detective will find the truth and leave it to others to decide what to do with it."

Heather spoke after a few seconds. "Bella's pondering what you said. What questions do you have?"

Bella hesitated. "Unless I missed something Howard Green told you both to hit the road yesterday."

"That's right," said Steve. "And Ingrid Webber told us the same thing today."

"So how will you discover the truth about Lucy Green's death?"

Steve couldn't help but smile. "One step at a time. Heather and I need to decide what our next steps are before she leaves on vacation."

Steve could tell by her voice that Heather faced Bella as she asked, "Were you able to map out the Webber family tree like we did for the Greens?"

"Uh-huh. I did searches in the society pages of the Houston newspapers, then took all the names and searched for them on the social media platforms. Unless I missed someone, there are only three generations of Webbers still alive. There's Karl and Ingrid Webber, who are in their seventies. They have one son, Kurt, who's in his fifties. His wife is Monica, and they also live in the family home part-time."

"Part-time?" asked Heather.

"They're involved in all kinds of causes. It's not unusual for them to be gone for weeks at a time. They drive a converted van and live a minimalist lifestyle."

Steve chuckled "When they're not living in a mansion. Do they work?"

Bella nodded. "They have a YouTube following that must be enough to get them by."

"Where were they when Lucy died?"

"At a PETA meeting in California."

Steve asked, "How many children do Kurt and Monica have?"

"Two. Adam and Anna Webber."

"Anna's the prospective bride," said Heather.

"Right," said Bella.

"Anything special about Adam?" asked Steve.

"Photos I've seen show deep dimples in his cheeks when he smiles." Bella quickly added, "I made a chart like you did for the Green family."

The sound of papers shuffling reached Steve's ears and Heather said, "This is excellent work. Now that we have a full listing of all the Webber family members, I'll go deeper into their finances."

"Before you get started," said Steve, "I'll call Leo and see if he's already put Ayana to work on doing that."

Heather came back with, "I'll have my acquisition team do research, too. I might be interested in purchasing that French chateau if the Webbers are hurting for money as much as the property showed."

Bella asked, "Isn't there something else I can do to help?"

Steve gave his head a nod. "There's one thing that you can help me with. There was wine found in Lucy Green's bedroom. The maid said it was Lucy and Howard's anniversary, but why would she break her nighttime ritual by drinking wine in her room? And alone at that. Why did she deviate from the norm? Her routine was to read and take pills to help her sleep. The wine raises other questions too."

"Like what?" asked Bella.

"What kind of wine was it and where did it come from? Was it a sparkling wine? If so, that shows a celebration of some sort, which would make sense if it had something to do with their anniversary. Was she really alone when she drank it? Did someone trick her into drinking it? Is it a rare wine, or one of the more ordinary brands? Was the wine already in the home's stock, or was it a special purchase? When and where was it purchased? Who bought it?"

The faint sound of Heather picking up her phone came to Steve. She said, "I have the video of the room. I'm sure I have a shot of the bottle. I remember looking at it, but don't remember what it was. Let me find the video and you can look it up on your phone, Bella."

Heather scrolled her phone for a moment. "Here it is. I'll read the label one letter at a time. K-R-U-G. C-L-O-S. D-'-A-M-B-O-N-N-A-Y 1995."

Steve imagined Bella's fingers flying over the key pad.

"Holy smoke! It's a champagne and it's twenty-six hundred dollars a bottle."

"Hmmm. Interesting," said Steve. "Someone spent a lot of money on a possible murder weapon."

"Where do we start?" asked Bella.

Steve lifted his eyebrows. "Where would you start?"

"Uh... I don't know. I'd probably start by questioning the staff."

Heather spoke before Steve could. "We can't do that. We're persona non grata in both the Green and Webber homes.

"Even if we could," said Heather, "the Greens' attorneys would insist on being present for all interviews. The police will have to jump over a bunch of hurdles if Howard Green tells his attorney to make things difficult for them."

"Which he likely will," said Steve as he scratched his chin.

"Then how do you gather evidence if you can't talk to suspects?" asked Bella with frustration seasoning her words.

Steve took his time responding. "The only things I can think of doing while Heather's gone is to continue to learn as much as we can about the family members, staff, and anyone who pops up with a motive for killing Lucy Green. I'll keep in touch with Leo and see how many roadblocks he and Ayana have hit. Finally, we can look around for places that sell expensive bottles of wine. You'll need photos of all family members and staff if we find a store that's sold a bottle of Krug whatever-you-call-it recently."

"Isn't there an easier way?" asked Bella.

"If this was easy," said Steve, "anyone could do it."

Heather's footsteps headed for the front door. "I'll get my pilots to pick me up here in the morning. You'll need my car if you're going to drive all over Houston looking for expensive champagne."

The front door opened and closed again.

"Quick," said Steve. "Get us each a cookie out of the freezer before they get hard as concrete."

The freezer door opened, then shut. The next sound Steve heard was Heather's voice coming through the pet door. "Bella, put the cookies back in the freezer."

12

Heather reached for the phone next to her seat as her twin engine jet raced across clear skies. Her thoughts alternated between the time she'd spent with her father and anticipation of seeing Jack again. In the seat facing her sat the new straw hat she'd purchased on the cruise. She looked at it and thought it should be Jack in the seat instead of a wide-brimmed hat.

The phone call to Jack was long and sweet. He counted the trial to be a partial success in that he worked out an eleventh-hour plea bargain with the district attorney, and the judge accepted the recommendation of a five-year probation. They both lamented that the decision didn't come until Heather and her father had been at sea for fourteen hours.

They agreed that Jack would pick her up at Conroe's airport and she'd go to his house, where he'd cook her a bunless hamburger. Then, he'd take her home in time to get a decent night's sleep. At least that was the plan.

Her plane was well over the Gulf of Mexico when she called Steve. He answered with a cheery, "Hello, stranger. Bella baked six dozen cookies since you've been gone and I ate every one of them."

Heather replied with, "They had an upscale watch store on

board. You'll love the Fitness-Pro I got you. It sounds an alarm every time you think of cookies. Once you put it on, it's impossible to take it off."

Steve chuckled. "Now that we've both told our lies, how was the trip?"

"We got our crying over Mother's death out of the way the first night. After that, it was clear sailing. The captain made sure we had full access to the ship and the crew. He wined and dined us in style. The rooms were amazing, but a suite can seem empty if that certain someone isn't with you."

"It's a shame Jack and the D.A. didn't reach a deal earlier. Did he tell you we went out for pizza the night the trial was supposed to begin?"

Heather couldn't help but smile. "Yes. He said it didn't matter how pretty Bella was, he would never want a woman who could pack away pizza the way she does. What did you and Bella do besides stuff yourselves with pizza and cookies?"

"I reconsidered searching for the bottle of wine. With online ordering, it seemed too big of a haystack to search in without narrowing the suspects first. Including staff, we'd be showing photos of about twenty-five people to shop owners. Instead, I showed Bella how to look for work permits pulled on the Green and Webber homes in the last forty years."

Heather sat up in her seat. "Good thinking. What did they reveal?"

The phone went quiet for a while, but she could hear Max's insistent meows and Steve's muffled voice. Steve came back on. "Sorry about that. Max was telling me it's time for his mid-morning snack. Where was I?"

"Pulling work orders."

"Oh yeah. It's what I expected. The Webbers have done no serious renovations in the last twelve years. We found the names of some plumbers, electricians, and small job contractors that worked with them. They all said getting money out of Ingrid was like squeezing wine out of a raisin."

"And the Greens?" asked Heather.

"They pay in full and on time. They also have a new roof and the old pool in the back yard was dug up and replaced seven years ago. What's interesting is that the Webber house has almost twice the square footage as the Green house with fewer people living there full time."

Heather looked out the window at an approaching cloud bank in the distance. She tucked Steve's comments away in her memory and continued with another question. "Has Leo given you any helpful information?"

"He's having to tip-toe around Ayana and all the brass that's breathing down his neck. The Greens' lawyer is like a guard dog, making sure the interviews are just enough for Leo not to demand depositions. They're lacking in substance, especially with Howard Green's peccadilloes."

Heather switched the phone to her other ear. "I'll call Sylvia Lopez and see if she can shed light on who Howard's latest love is." She paused to consider what she said. "If he's smart, he's lying low until all this blows over."

"If he was that smart, he wouldn't have a girlfriend, or a line of former girlfriends, while he's married. Ayana worked some sort of computer magic and cross-referenced Howard's old credit card receipts. It was enough for her and Leo to pound the pavement and get names for two of Howard's former girlfriends. Both cooperated, but nothing valuable came out of the interviews. Leo still can't connect Howard to his wife's death."

Steve had to sneeze. After blowing his nose, he said, "The mold count must be off the charts. It's been raining here like Noah may make a return visit."

"That explains the cloud bank we're about to fly over. How's Bella's broken heart?"

"She'll live to love again. She spent more time researching the Webber lad with the deep dimples than anyone else. I'm pretty sure she knows what size shoe he wears and what type of pizza he prefers."

Mistletoe, Malice And Murder

Heather groaned. "Great! Just what she needs. What's the scoop on him? Isn't his name Adam Webber?"

"It is. He's out of college, where he made top grades in business and finance. No criminal history. It seems the last generation of Webbers is fairly normal."

Heather took in a deep breath. "Well, that's something. Give me your overall view of how the case is progressing."

Steve cleared his throat. "We're boxed in on all sides. We can't talk to any of the Greens or the Webbers. Leo is being watched like a known shoplifter in a jewelry store. He now has two of the big bosses telling him how to run the investigation, so he's getting nowhere fast."

"Is there anything we can do?"

"Like I told Bella, if you looked plain and wore a terrific disguise that made you look like a homely housekeeper, you could get your buddy Mrs. Dubois to place you in the Greens' home as a maid. What we really need is someone on the inside."

"Wigs make my head itch. As for disguises, Sherlock Holmes might pull it off, but Howard Green and Ingrid Webber both know what I look and sound like. You'll have to come up with a better idea."

"Nothing's coming to mind," said Steve with a sigh. "Let's have breakfast in the morning and talk more about it."

Heather nodded in agreement, even though no one could see her. "Bella has a young, agile mind. Perhaps she can come up with some ideas."

The pilot pulled back the curtain separating the flight deck from the five leather seats in the main cabin. "You'd better buckle up tight, Ms. McBlythe. It's going to be bumpy from here on out."

"Thanks for the warning."

Heather lifted the phone to her ear again. "Bad weather ahead, Steve. I'd better go."

"Make it a late breakfast," said Steve. "I keep forgetting I have to share you with Jack. You two will need to talk about the cruise and his trial that turned out not to be a trial. Conversations like that can last into the wee hours of the morning."

Heather smiled. "A late breakfast sounds better, especially after a rainy night."

IT WAS ALMOST NINE THE NEXT MORNING WHEN HEATHER pushed back the covers, but only after Max let out a loud meow. She assumed it was his way of telling her she'd overslept by four hours. She reached and gave his wide head a thorough scratch, which seemed to placate him. Taking time to brush her teeth and throw her hair up in a messy bun, she hustled next door, hoping she wasn't too late for breakfast.

Instead of smelling bacon, ham, or the sage-rich sausage Steve liked so much, his condo was void of any odor except coffee. She made a path to the coffee maker and poured herself a full mug.

"Where's your roommate?" asked Steve.

Heather spoke through a yawn. "What do you mean? I thought Bella would be here cooking breakfast for us."

"Haven't heard her all morning."

"Is she out running?"

"In the rain?"

"She might have gone to the gym," said Heather, although that seemed out of character for the girl who loved the outdoors. "When did you last talk to her?"

Steve closed the top to his computer. "We had supper together last night, then she said she had things to do and left about eight-thirty. I heard her puttering around in her room until ten-thirty or eleven. I haven't seen or heard her since then."

"Not even this morning?"

"I would have heard her if she was stirring, unless she got up and out when I was in the shower."

Heather took her coffee cup with her as she headed for the door. "I'll go check. I hope she's not sick."

The holler of Bella's name after Heather opened her front door brought no response. Her pace picked up as she passed the dining room and kitchen and found nothing disturbed. She bolted to Bella's room, only to find the door open. She'd missed this in her rush to breakfast next door. An envelope leaned against a pillow on the neatly made bed. Ripping it open, Heather read once for speed and the second time to catch all the words.

Dear Heather and Steve,

I hope you don't get too mad at me, but the pace of the investigation was driving me nuts. Steve, you were awesome at teaching me stuff, but I can tell you both need help. You said you needed someone on the inside if the case was to be solved, so I took action. (That's something else you both taught me.)
While Heather was on her cruise, I submitted an application with Mrs. Dubois and completed a phone interview. I used you as a reference and told her I worked well with older, cranky women. (I didn't use the word cranky, but she must have understood what I was saying.)

I start this morning working for Mrs. Ingrid Webber. Mrs. Dubois doesn't know that I understand German and can speak it fairly well. My plan is not to tell Mrs. Webber either.

Hopefully she'll let her guard down and I'll find out all kinds of juicy things to help you solve the case. Everyone who doesn't know me expects me to be a dumb blond. That's what I'll be to Frau Webber.

Mrs. Dubois told me I can't have my phone during working hours, which is pretty much any time Frau Webber is awake. I'll relay what I've learned every night by text messages or emails. There are no days off until I've worked there four weeks.

Give Steve a hug for me and tell him not to worry. I've been in the ocean with every flesh-eating creature you can imagine. An old German lady doesn't scare me one bit.

Heather took a deep breath, counted to ten, and let out a brief scream of frustration. "If Frau Webber doesn't kill her, I may." She held the letter in a death grip and hustled next door.

Steve had moved to his recliner where he sat with hands folded on his lap. "I heard the scream. Feel better?"

"She's gone," said Heather as if that were earth-shattering news.

Steve remained as still as a monk with no sins to confess.

Heather tried again. "Do you know what she's done?"

"I can make a good guess. She's gone to work for either the Greens or the Webbers. I'm guessing the Webbers."

"You knew? Why didn't you stop her?"

"I guess she left a note?" said Steve instead of answering her question.

Heather smoothed out the note and read it aloud, which fueled her rage and frustration at Bella's impulsive decision. After pacing and spewing her intentions to drag the lass out of the Webber home by her thick rope of ultra-blond hair, Steve held up his hand for her to stop. "How old is Bella?"

"Twenty."

"That makes her an adult. Is she smart?"

"Of course, she is."

"I agree," said Steve. "She was smart enough to leave your condo this morning without either of us catching on to what she was doing. I only just now put the pieces together to what she's been planning to do even before you went on your cruise. We can trust anyone that crafty. She'll gather at least some of the information we need. Besides, if Frau Ingrid follows true to form, she'll fire Bella in two or three days."

"I can't believe you're allowing her to do this."

"If I thought she was in any real danger, I'd have Leo drag her out. But she'd never forgive me if I kept her from this chance to prove herself to both of us."

Steve motioned for her to have a seat on the couch. Once Heather settled on the couch and her mind slowed down, he continued, "Think about it. She'll be so sick of doing a stake out that involves non-stop cleaning and bowing to Frau Ingrid's every whim, she'll be ready to swim back to her parents' hotel."

Heather's tightly-strung emotions began to release their grip. "Is this what a parent feels like when a child grows up and makes a life of their own?"

"Probably. I'm the wrong person to ask."

"One more reason not to have children," said Heather.

"Look on the bright side," said Steve. "We can expect nightly reports from Bella. Things may get moving on this case."

13

After serving a breakfast of mixed fruit, yogurt, and granola, Heather cleaned the kitchen as Steve picked up his phone and called Leo. The first thing out of his mouth was, "Can you talk?"

Steve had his phone on speaker so Heather could hear both sides of the conversation. "Yeah, for a little while. Ayana is in some sort of worthless meeting with the bosses, so I'm flying my desk until this afternoon."

"What happens then?"

Leo sort of growled. "You know how I always put off firearms recertification until the last minute? Well, it's three weeks past last minute. Once again I'm in the dog house."

"What's Ayana going to do while you re-qualify?"

"She's to stick with me and do whatever I do, even though she just qualified at the academy."

Steve took a sip of coffee. "I'm glad it's you and not me."

"Me, too," added Heather as she placed a bowl in the dishwasher.

"How was the cruise?" asked Leo in a louder voice.

"Wonderful. You need to take your wife on one."

"I'll do it on one condition: You come stay with the kids."

"On second thought, you wouldn't enjoy cruising. Too much water, high potential for getting seasick, crowds, and nothing to look at but the sky and sea."

Leo chuckled. "Yeah, that's what I thought you'd say."

Steve added, "There's another reason he shouldn't go on a cruise. They already have six kids and that much time alone might add to the count."

"I just lost all interest in cruising," said Leo. "Now tell me what's on your mind."

"Good news," said Steve. "Bella decided on her own that the case wasn't moving fast enough to suit her, so she got hired to work for Frau Webber."

"It wasn't my idea," said Heather as she sat at the table across from Steve. "But I have to admit she might be an excellent source of information."

"I'm not so sure," said Leo. "Ingrid Webber didn't impress me as the type of woman who'd open up to anyone. She's not above telling cops she's too busy to talk and insists I give her three days' notice before I darken her doorstep."

"Bella's supposed to work day and night for four weeks without a break. She'll have a room there and not leave."

Steve took his turn. "How many staff members are there today?"

"Let's see," said Leo. "It's hard to keep up with the staff because Ingrid keeps firing them. There's the old butler that has to oil his joints to move and his wife, the cook. They're both German as sauerkraut and pretend they can't understand English. I had to call in a translator. What a waste of time and money, but I managed to learn two German phrases, so it wasn't a total loss. '*Ich erinnre mich nicht*' and '*Ich weiß es nicht.*'"

Heather parroted back the translation in English. "I don't remember, and I don't know."

Leo let out a huff. "I could have figured that out with Google Translate."

Steve set his cup down on the table. "We may be in luck.

Bella speaks German fairly well, but understands it even better."

"Now you have my attention. The butler never has much to say, but Ingrid and the cook seemed to treat each other more like sisters than that master-servant thing Ingrid does with the other help."

Heather added, "Bella is supposed to communicate with us every night through text or email. We'll keep you apprised if she finds out anything interesting."

"Interesting or not, pass on the information. I need all the help I can get."

"Anything new on the Green family?" asked Steve.

"There was a development yesterday. Sid Green hired Lucy's maid, Sylvia Lopez, back. I believe he's showing Howard who's boss."

It was Heather's turn to have her attention grabbed. "Now we have someone in each house who can give us information. Bella's a sure bet and Sylvia owes me a favor if we need to call it in."

Steve placed his palms on the table and rolled his fingers, making tapping sounds. "What about the wine? Has anyone thought to pursue that line of research?"

"Ayana is working on it," said Leo. "I'll ask her today if she's made any progress."

"With a person in each house," said Heather, "we should at least be able to find out if either family keeps that vintage in stock."

"Ayana checked credit card receipts for the occupants of both households, but came up blank."

"I guess they could have paid cash, but that seems unlikely," said Steve. "This was more productive than I thought. It may take days or weeks to put together a clear picture of suspects and motives, but at least we're moving in the right direction."

Leo said, "I like the idea of days much better than weeks. And speaking of days, Lucy Green's funeral is in four days. Ayana and I will be there."

Steve ended the conversation with a final word to Leo. "I won't be at the funeral, but Heather will. I'll send you a text tonight and let you know how Bella fared with her first day working for Ingrid Webber."

"I'll be looking for it, unless Ayana uses me for a target at the shooting range."

THE DAY PASSED WITH HEATHER REVIEWING THE NOTES STEVE and Bella collected on the two families and their respective members. It didn't take long for Heather to realize something happened in the Webber clan about thirty years ago that caused their fortunes to hit a sharp decline. She also pored over Leo's search of the Webber's bank accounts, a report from her acquisition team on distressed properties, and her own cursory research of publicly available stock and bond holdings. By putting together all the scattered pieces she determined the Webbers had enough residual income to pay the taxes and give the illusion of wealth.

She took her findings to Steve, who sat with his right hand cupping his chin, the pose he sometimes struck when he listened with extra intensity. After she finished her report, he stayed motionless and silent for at least thirty seconds. He finally allowed his hand to drop. "We need to find out what happened to their fortune. We know the Greens reaped the most from the oil partnership, but the Webbers had more than enough to live in luxury for generations."

The ring of Steve's phone put further discussion of a fortune, which was mostly lost, on hold. He told the phone to go to speaker and answer the call. The caller ID only gave the number of the person calling, not the name.

"Mr. Smiley," came a voice crinkled with age.

"Is this Sid Green?" asked Steve.

"Come back and talk to me. I don't like or trust the investigator my idiot son hired."

"Are you sure Howard and the bodyguards will let us in?"

"Don't worry about that. I still control most of the money around here. I'm paying for the bodyguards; they'll do what I say. As for Howard and that silly PI he hired... This is still my house. Nobody will stop you coming in."

He let loose with a phlegmatic cough and had to catch his breath. "I had another dream that someone else is going to die and the man looked a lot like me. As long as I get to see my great-grandson married to that sweet Anna Webber, I don't care. Until then, I need all the help I can get."

"When do you want us to come?"

"Time's ticking away. You'd better come today, and make sure that pretty lawyer lady comes with you. She's enough to make an old man's heart go giddy-up. I may get an extra day or two of living out of a visit from her."

Steve covered his mouth to suppress the chuckle. "Since she does the driving, I'll bring her along. We'll be there as soon as we can punch our way through traffic."

The phone call ended and Heather stood. "I'll take a quick shower and run a brush through my hair. Give me thirty minutes."

Steve made the sound of a horse whinnying. "Giddy-up, cowgirl. There's an oil baron that needs our help."

She didn't have a comeback, so she left.

An hour and ten minutes later, they pulled into the driveway of the Greens' mansion. Butch met them at the front door and ushered them inside. They passed two men dressed in khaki pants, collared shirts, and navy jackets. The snug fit of their blazers accentuated their broad chests and did little to hide the bulge of firearms. No one smiled.

As expected, Butch walked at a brisk pace with head erect, swiveling from side to side as if it were mechanical. Heather caught his reflection in a mirror and saw Butch's eyes darting like that of a bird of prey. He knocked on Sid's door and waited for the sound of two latches to click. She noticed on the way in that another dead bolt had been installed.

Once seated, Heather asked, "How long do you plan on keeping the bodyguards?"

"Until you two find who killed Lucy and get the police to lock him up and throw away the key."

Steve tested the water. "To accomplish that, we'll need access to all family members and staff. It's to be made clear to them we expect their full cooperation."

Sid ran a hand down his whiskered face. "Like a fool I already gave Howard too much of his share of the inheritance, which means I don't have as much control over him as I used to. He's independent and stubborn, so I can't promise much cooperation from him, but there's plenty Tim and Carol are still due to receive. You'll have their cooperation after I get through with them. Thankfully, I don't need to threaten Chad with changing my will for him to do the right thing. He's one of those rare Green men that's not looking for how he can get his hands on the next buck. Even rarer still, he's getting married for love."

Heather needed to make sure she had Sid's descendants straight in her mind so she drew out the diagram from her valise. "Speaking of your family, I want to refresh my memory. Howard is your son."

"I'm unhappy to say that he is."

"Why do you say that?" asked Steve.

"Howard acts like I'm already dead and can't wait until this place is in his name. The other day, he had no right to kick you out. He has money, but not the big chunk and he doesn't own this house."

Steve then asked, "Why did you wait so long to call us back to look for Lucy's killer?"

Sid pointed to Butch and motioned toward an oxygen tank. "Get me some clean air and tell them."

A plastic face mask covered Sid's mouth and nose. Once Butch finished his task, he stood erect. "Mr. Sid took the death of Lucy very hard, and he believes Howard is the prime suspect in Lucy's death."

"He did it," said Sid through the plastic which muffled his voice.

Butch continued, "The strain of the death was almost too much for Mr. Sid. His lungs filled and I thought we might lose him, but between the medicine and his desire to live to see Chad and Anna married, he pulled through."

Sid pulled the mask down. "Truth. That's what I want you to find. I think Howard is guilty, but I've drilled enough dry holes in my day to know I can be wrong."

"I believe Heather and I speak the same language as you, Mr. Sid. We brought a contract for you to sign that states what we'll do, and not do, to find Lucy's killer."

Sid waved the contract away and again pulled the mask from his face. "Give it to Butch. He has limited power of attorney and understands all that legal stuff."

Heather handed it over. For the second time since she'd met him, Butch smiled. "University of Texas School of Law. I used the GI bill to help pay my way after I discharged."

With the contract signed, Steve and Heather spoke with Butch and made plans to return the following morning. Their discussion of where to eat on the way home was interrupted when Steve's phone announced an incoming call from Leo. "Hey, Leo. What's up?"

A sheepish voice with a heavy accent spoke instead of Leo. "Mr. Smiley?"

"Yes."

"This is Ayana."

She said something else, but the words made little sense.

"Ayana," said Steve. "Where's Leo?"

"In ambulance on way to hospital."

"What happened?"

"I shot him."

The call disconnected.

14

Heather put on the emergency flashers and leaned on the horn to try to move cars out of her way. She escaped the freeway at the first exit and shoehorned her way through traffic until she wheeled into the parking lot of a fast-food restaurant. Meanwhile, it took Steve three phone calls to detectives and a lieutenant in Houston P.D. before he found someone who knew what hospital Leo was going to. Details conflicted about the injuries or their severity.

Heather spoke the name of the hospital to her car's navigation system and watched the map appear with a blue line plotting out the course they'd need to take.

"That's just great," said Heather with sarcasm dripping off each word. "We're at least ten miles away and it's rush hour."

Steve nervously tapped his finger on his thighs. "Do the best you can."

It took the better part of forty minutes before Heather pulled into a parking spot outside the emergency room and Steve uncurled his fingers from the passenger's armrest. She met him at the front bumper and they moved at a quick pace toward the emergency room door. A quartet of police cruisers sat parked in the fire lane.

Once inside, Heather led Steve toward a gathering of two uniformed officers and two in plain clothes. Snickers and guffaws punctuated their conversation. A man wearing slacks, a long sleeve shirt, and a lanyard around his neck with a gold badge dangling from it saw their approach and took a step away from the group.

"Hello, Steve. Have you come to finish Leo off?"

"Kirby? Is that you?"

"Yep. They haven't run me off yet. Don't worry about Leo, he's fine." The man paused. "Not really fine, but he'll be home and sleeping in his own bed tonight. You might say it's only a flesh wound."

The men overheard the remark and burst out laughing.

"What's so funny?" said Heather. "We heard he'd been shot."

"That's correct, ma'am, but it's nothing life threatening."

Steve interrupted, "Kirby, this is Heather McBlythe, my partner in our private detective agency."

The man didn't allow Steve to finish the introduction. "We've all heard about Heather McBlythe. Leo told us you traded him for the new and improved model of detective. I think he left a few details out." He held out his hand to Heather. "Nice to meet you."

Heather nodded as she shook his hand.

Steve cut to the chase. "Why don't you stop trying to score points with an engaged woman and tell us what happened and how serious his injuries are."

"Sure, Steve." He shifted his gaze to Heather and then back to Steve. "Leo and his new partner were at the range. As usual, Leo was late qualifying."

"Were you there?"

"Yeah. I was standing well behind Leo and that detective from South Africa. The range master was between us barking out instructions. You know. Just another day qualifying. It must have been a misfire in Ayana's pistol. Instead of pointing the muzzle downrange, she pointed her weapon at the ground beside her."

Heather could see in her mind's eye the scene and what happened next.

"The range master screamed at Ayana to keep her gun pointed level and downrange. She jerked her head around to look at who was yelling. Her hand followed her head and the pistol discharged. The round took off the tip of Leo's little toe."

Steve and Heather both released a sigh.

One of the uniformed officers added, "That's one little piggy that won't go to market again."

Perhaps it was relief from knowing that Leo's pride was injured more than his body that caused both Heather and Steve to start with a chuckle. It soon morphed into a full riot of laughter.

The mirth lasted until the group spied Leo's captain come through the door. He took one look at the gathering and said, "Kirby, stick around. The rest of you need to find something else to do."

Like a covey of disturbed game birds, the group flew from the captain's icy stare.

Once the group was out of earshot, the captain said, "I don't blame them for laughing, but this is a real mess. The big-wigs are looking at me to clean it up."

Kirby said, "Captain Donaldson this is Steve Smiley, a former homicide—"

The captain broke in, "I know who Smiley is. At least by reputation. It's good to be able to put a face to the name."

"And this is Heather McBlythe, his business partner."

"Pleased to meet you, ma'am."

Heather put out her hand to the captain. "I assume you're the one who corrals Kirby and Leo."

The captain nodded his head. "The best I can."

Steve rested both hands on top of his cane. "Kirby, how long before we can see Leo?"

"You know how hospitals and doctors are these days. Everyone's afraid of lawsuits, so they called in an orthopedic surgeon. She just arrived."

"That means we have plenty of time to get a cup of coffee. We had some recent developments in the Lucy Green case that will interest you, Captain."

Steve couldn't see it, but the captain's eyes widened when he said Lucy Green's name.

They left Kirby in the waiting room and a few minutes later, the trio sat in the hospital cafeteria sipping coffee. Steve added a bowl of peach cobbler to his order to stave off hunger pains. Heather filled the captain in on Bella going undercover and Sid hiring Steve and her to investigate the family and staff of the Green household. The lawman took in the information and seemed to be mentally chewing it like it was a tough piece of steak.

Long seconds passed before he said, "You two may be able to get me out of the pit I find myself in. Ayana is a special guest of this country and I'm under instructions to make sure she gets the credit for solving a murder before she ends her stay with us."

Steve gave his head a single nod. "She must be the daughter of someone special."

"Very special," said the captain. "I assume you've already done background on her, so you already know about her."

Steve gave his head another nod. "Some. I knew there was more to Leo's story of a simple exchange program when I learned she had no field experience."

"The good news," said Heather, "is that we still have plenty of time to feed information to Leo so he can solve the case and make it look like Ayana did the work."

"It's not that simple after what happened today. Leo will be laid up for several weeks before the doctors give him permission to come back to work. There's also the not-so-small issue of an officer-involved shooting."

"What about Ayana?" asked Heather. "It won't look good for her to return home with a stain on her record."

Steve faced the captain. "I know how you'll have to spin this, and I don't like it. The official report will say Leo accidentally shot himself and Ayana wasn't at the range. Am I right, Captain?"

"Sometimes you're too smart for your own good, Smiley."

Heather's Scotch-Irish blood heated to the temperature of her coffee. She opened her mouth to condemn the duplicity of the plan, but Steve had his hand up to cut off her words.

"Heather and I will stay on the case, but there can't be any blame put on Leo. It's bad enough he lost his toe without some politician trying too hard to save their skin. If anyone tries to play games with us on this, Heather and I will go public and you'll have a real mess on your hands."

Heather leaned forward. "You have no idea what grief we could bring to the department."

The captain swallowed. "I'd much rather have you two on my side than against me. How can we make this a win-win situation for all concerned?"

"This will take some massaging along the way," said Steve, "but here's a suggestion. Assign Kirby to take over the case. Unofficially, keep Leo in charge and we'll funnel information to him. We'll talk to Leo and make sure he understands the situation."

The captain rubbed his chin. "It might work. Are you sure Leo will go along with this?"

"I think he'll go along with it. Every now and then a situation requires a work around. Telling him if he doesn't do it, he'll be designated the official babysitter for future exchange detectives won't hurt either."

The captain chuckled.

Steve stood. "You have damage control to take care of. There are at least two uniformed officers, two detectives, and a range master with stories that don't match what you want the official version to be."

The captain took a step forward and lowered his voice. "I'm dropping that hot potato in the lap of my boss. I draw the line at falsifying witness statements." He extended a hand to Heather. "Thanks to both of you for being such a friend to Leo and the department. If you can solve this case and make it look like Ayana deserves a commendation, I'll owe you a big favor." He paused. "Make that several big favors."

Steve extended his hand. "Give the favor to Leo as a reward for his silence and half a toe."

The captain had his phone in his hand as he walked away. Heather could only imagine the intrigue being discussed to save some reputations.

"Let's go see Leo," said Steve.

It wasn't long before Steve had talked his way past a nurse and stood looking down on his former partner. "I thought I taught you better than to get shot."

"I prayed for a break from Ayana. The Lord has quite a sense of humor."

"Any pain?" asked Heather.

Leo grinned. "Modern medicine is wonderful. No wonder people get hooked on this stuff."

"We've been talking to your captain," said Steve. "I think I found a way for you not to have to worry about being late on your firearms qualification again."

Leo squinted his eyes. "I've heard that tone of voice before. It usually comes before you tell me about some harebrained scheme you've come up with."

Steve related the plan for Leo to fully recuperate at home while he, Heather, and Bella gathered information on the Green and Webber families. Relevant information would go to Leo, who'd pass it on to Detective Kirby. He'd slip it to Ayana and make sure the reports reflected her name before his.

Heather passed on the political reasons for the change in protocol.

Leo shook his head in apparent disgust. "Are you telling me that a careless cop blows off my toe and she'll take a commendation back to South Africa with her?"

"Something like that," said Steve. "But you're looking at this all wrong. There's plenty of upside for you."

"Like what?"

"As much recovery time as you need or want."

Leo shook his head. "That could be a two-edged sword. My wife will have me repairing everything broken or bent in the house. She's also been talking about painting all the bedrooms."

Steve rubbed his chin. "You won't be working with Ayana."

A grin came across Leo's face. "That's a definite plus. Keep going."

"The captain told us if we solved the case and made it look like Ayana is a female Sherlock Holmes, he'd owe you a stack of favors."

"What good does that do me?"

Heather patted him on the arm. "Think of all the silly meetings you can get out of."

Steve added, "All you have to do is go along with whatever story they come up with by keeping your mouth shut. Lie low and let the big boys and girls play loose with the truth."

"Ayana didn't shoot me? Is that what I'm supposed to say?"

"You'll find out soon enough what story they'll come up with. Don't lie, just don't contradict it."

"Is that all? I won't have to write a report on what happened? No internal affairs or pencil-pushers who'll say it was my fault she shot me?"

"That's the gist of it," said Steve. "The only thing you'll need to do is funnel information from us to Kirby. It's his and the captain's job to make Ayana look good."

Leo scratched his head. "It seems I don't have much choice if I want to keep my retirement."

"It's sure nice to get a check every month for not working," said Steve.

The nurse came in and handed Leo his clothes. "You're ready to go, Mr. Vega. You're lucky that lawn-mower didn't take off all your toes."

Once the door shut, Steve said, "Someone much higher than the captain has been busy."

Heather turned toward the door. "I'll get the car so we can take Leo home."

"Good idea," said Steve. "Leo needs to sleep off the good stuff they're giving him and we'll need to be alert when we see Sid tomorrow."

15

The next morning, Heather buttered whole wheat toast as Steve relayed the contents of Bella's brief text message. "She didn't send it until very late last night. It seems Frau Webber has been without domestic help for over a week. Between the backlog of laundry, cleaning, changing sheets, and vacuuming, Bella worked until she fell into bed after midnight."

Heather spooned and spread strawberry preserves onto the buttered toast and asked, "Did she overhear anything of use yesterday?"

"Not a word. She described the Webber's cook as an old bratwurst stuffed with a critical attitude."

Heather chuckled, "I commend her descriptive creativity, but that doesn't help much."

"As the British say, 'It's early days.'"

Heather delivered the toast. "Did she meet any family members?"

"She literally ran into Adam Webber, the prospective bride's brother. The stack of clean, freshly folded towels she carried rained down like confetti." He paused. "Those are my words, not hers."

"Did she talk to Adam?"

"Yes, and for too long apparently. She got a taste of Frau Webber's ire." Steve picked up a piece of toast but waited to take a bite. "The only thing she said about Adam was that he's much better looking in person than in the photo."

Heather groaned. "I have a bad feeling about this. Are you sure she should stay there?"

Steve took a small bite of toast and spoke with it squirreled in the side of his mouth. "In for a penny, in for a pound."

She looked at Steve. "Did you stay up late watching English detective shows?"

"I listened to one of Kate's audio books." He finished chewing the bite and chased it with coffee. "Before you ask, she's doing fine and sends her regards. She thinks it's awesome that Bella's doing undercover work. She said that type of thing is like fertilizer to her imagination."

As usual, Heather wanted to ask more questions about Kate to see if interest between the reluctant widow and widower had grown or waned. The problem was, neither party invited questions of that nature, so she changed the subject. "When did you say Lucy's funeral was?"

"The day after tomorrow. We'll need to restrict our interviews to the staff for the next several days and not bother the family members."

"It may not take that long to wrap up the case if we get lucky."

Steve dabbed his mouth with a napkin. "Slow and steady will win this race."

Heather thought for a moment. "I don't think that's a British saying."

With toast in hand, Steve said, "I spoke it in English. That's close enough."

THE FIRST CONVERSATION OF THE DAY PROVED TO BE THE shortest. It took place on the small front porch of the Greens' home and involved a near collision with Howard Green as Heather led Steve to the front door. The scowl on Howard's face intensified as he recognized the detectives. "Oh. It's you two again. I'll expect you to be gone by the time I get back."

Steve didn't hesitate. "We understand this is a difficult time for you, and we'll restrict our questions to the staff until after the funeral."

Heather wasn't as considerate as Steve. It was part of the good-cop, bad-cop routine they'd rehearsed if they found themselves confronted by Howard or any other family members. "We're here at the request of your father. Since we don't know where you're going or when you'll be back, we may or may not be here when you return. In fact, you can expect us to be regular visitors, and we look forward to your cooperation."

Howard squinted as he said, "Anything I have to say to you will be through my attorney."

"That's the type of response I expected," said Heather. "Perhaps we should tell the police to start formal proceedings to have you subpoenaed and deposed."

"Now, Heather," said Steve. "Let's allow Howard time to grieve the loss of his wife in peace."

Heather sighed. "You're right, Steve. There'll be plenty of time to depose him later."

Howard shouldered his way past Steve, bumping into him and turning him sideways. The car door slammed with a resounding thud. He laid a long ribbon of black on the driveway before the two-seater sports car gained traction.

"Interesting," said Heather. "He drives a new Corvette, a sure sign he's chasing his youth."

Steve added, "He'll never catch it, even in a Corvette."

Heather turned as Butch opened the door. "The boys called me when they saw you drive up. Did Howard try to run you off?"

"Let's just say he'd rather we weren't here," said Steve. He stepped into the foyer and immediately changed the conversation. "How is Mr. Sid today?"

"So far, it's a good day. He's excited about you two starting your investigation."

"Is he up to seeing us? There've been fresh developments since yesterday."

"It's still early in the day," said Butch. "He's always better in the mornings, but he tires easily. It's best if you could limit your time with him to less than thirty minutes. His mind is still sharp, but his body is another story. If you could bend the rule in your contract and give him something new to think about every day, it would bring him peace of mind that progress is being made."

"Will he be going to Lucy's funeral?" asked Heather.

Butch gave his head a nod. "I talked him into not going to the burial because heavy rain is in the forecast, but he insists on going to the church service."

With that, Butch extended a hand inviting them to follow him. The trio passed between two bodyguards who secured locks behind them. Fortress Green was still on high alert.

Heather asked, "Do you have someone trailing Howard?"

"Affirmative," said Butch. He pulled out his phone and pushed a couple of icons. "I put a tracker on Howard's 'Vette. He's following his usual route to his office, where he'll likely stay until noon. After that he'll meet his lady friend for lunch and spend the rest of the day with her at her townhouse. He usually stays well into the night and sometimes overnight. But since Lucy died, he's been coming home at five-thirty."

She asked, "Does Howard's attorney know he's being comforted by his girlfriend every afternoon?"

"He warned Howard not to see her until the police make an arrest."

"That seems to have fallen on deaf ears," said Steve.

Sid sat erect in his wheelchair as the trio come in. A boyish impatience seasoned his words. "I hope you have news. That fool of a private detective Howard hired won't tell me anything.

I don't think he knows anything; he only wants to pump money out of Howard until the well goes dry."

Steve took over. "We normally don't give our clients regular updates, but Heather and I decided you deserve to know what's happened in the last twenty-four hours." He then told Sid the short version of them landing an undercover operative in the Webber household without using Bella's name.

Sid slapped his knee. "That's more like it. What else have you done?"

Heather explained they'd done fairly extensive background checks on the family members in both households and had a good idea who had alibis. She didn't say who obtained the information or how.

"Also," said Steve, "there will be a new homicide detective added to the case who will take over for Detective Vega. Leo was involved in an accident and will be on medical leave for a while. The new detective's name is Kirby. I can vouch for him; he's an honest cop who's been around for a long time."

"Let me get this straight," said Sid. "You have someone in the Webber house feeding you information and you have contacts in the police department helping you fill in gaps with both families?"

"That pretty well sums it up," said Steve. "We'll interview as many of your staff as we can today. Don't expect us to come back every day with updates, but that doesn't mean we're not working on the case."

"Just like drilling wells," said Sid. "It takes time to drill down far enough to get past the dirt, rocks, and water. Many of the wells don't produce, but all it takes is one good one to make up for the ones that come out dry." He looked at Butch. "Make sure everyone knows they're to give Steve and Heather anything they need and I'd better not hear of them not cooperating."

Butch gave a quick, affirmative answer and nodded for a bodyguard to let Steve and Heather out of Sid's room.

Once in the hallway, Steve whispered to her, "Do you know

where the kitchen is? I want to start with their chef, and I'll need your expertise in questioning about wine."

They followed the maze of hallways back to the entry, where a man who looked too old to be one of Butch's body guards came from the great room. He walked toward them with an overconfident swagger, his silver hair and weathered skin confirming he was past being anyone's body guard.

"You're wasting your time," were the first words out of his mouth.

Steve responded with, "Aah. You might be one of Mr. Crankshaw's attorney buddies, but my money is on you being Henry Drake, the PI Howard hired."

"The latter," said Drake. "You've done your homework."

Heather asked, "Do you mind telling us why you believe we're wasting our time?"

"You should be next door. That's where you'll find Lucy's killer. Ingrid Webber may not have done the deed herself, but she knows who did. She's grown more and more bitter over the years as she watched her fortune melt away like wax in a very large candle. She probably made her husband kill Lucy to make up for all the poor business decisions he's made over the years."

"You're well informed," said Steve.

This earned a laugh. "Mr. Smiley. I started doing work for Howard before I left the force, but you already knew that. Don't worry, I won't do anything to get in your way." He opened his arms wide. "The house and everyone in it are all yours. Unrestricted access. I've already interviewed everyone and they all have legit alibis."

Steve stood with right hand on his cane. "Tell me Mr. Drake..."

"Just Drake. I dropped my first name a long time ago."

"All right, Drake. You're a good PI who was a good cop, just like me and Heather. You've worked for Howard Green off and on for years. Karl Webber, Ingrid's husband, is responsible for losing much of the family fortune." Steve took his time before he said, "I'm thinking you've stayed busy for about twenty-five years digging deep and finding out all kinds of information to help Howard make sure the Webbers' fortune dwindled."

"That's much better, Smiley." He pointed at Steve and wagged an index finger in a way that communicated admiration. "There's the quick mind I've heard so much about. In business, information means money, and Howard pays very well for the sort of information I can give him."

Drake turned to leave, but stopped and faced them again. "I know you won't take my advice, but you're wasting your time talking to anyone in this house. Like I said, the killer is right next door."

One of the bodyguards unlocked the front door and Drake walked into the sunshine. Heather looked at Steve. "I wasn't expecting that."

Steve didn't respond at first, then he held out his hand for Heather to lead him. After several steps he said, "Drake's right about one thing. We're not taking advice from him. The kitchen must be in the direction we're heading. I can smell the bacon they had for breakfast."

16

The lingering smell of bacon and baked bread led Heather and Steve through the formal dining room and into the kitchen. A man wearing a white chef's coat and black trousers met their arrival with a look of disdain. He looked to be in his late forties with a close-cropped salt-and-pepper beard and a belly that spoke of love for his own cooking.

Looking over glasses sitting half-way down his nose, the man gave a snort and said, "*Qu'est-ce que cest? Je suis tres occupe et je n'nai pas le temps pour toi.*"

Heather responded in English, even though she could have responded in French just as easily. "You've been instructed to give us your full cooperation. I can see you're busy preparing ratatouille, but it will take hours for that eggplant to cook or it will be tough as an old shoe. Surely a chef of your experience can step away from the stove for a few minutes."

"Ah," said the chef as his chest expanded. "This is not your first time to pick up the spoon and wear the apron. Were you trained in this country?"

Heather shook her head and spoke in French. "In Paris. My parents made sure I took classes during my breaks at boarding school. They were short courses, with some of the best chefs, mainly at the École de cuisine Alain Ducasse, but I also took a wonderful class on wine and cheese at La Cuisine Paris."

The man's face lit up as if he were a lamp. A conversation in French followed that lasted until Steve cleared his throat. The chef dipped his head. "I'm so sorry, sir. Please forgive Chef Aubert. I have so little opportunity to speak to someone in my two native languages, French and food."

Steve nodded. "Ms. McBlythe may want to spend time with you in the coming days, catching up on her skills, if that's possible. We won't take up much of your time today, but in our business, one question often leads to another and we frequently have to talk to people multiple times."

"My instructions are to cooperate fully. Ask anything you want. I prefer French, but in deferment to you, Monsieur, we will speak English."

Steve chuckled. "Thank you. I appreciate your consideration. Your English is near-perfect. I daresay if I ever tried French, mine would not be." He lifted his head. "Unless I'm mistaken, I'm smelling coffee. Is there enough for me to have a cup?"

"Certainly. Please have a seat at the table."

Heather led Steve to a small wooden table with four chairs at the far end of the kitchen. The chef came with two cups of coffee and went back to get one for himself.

"Thank you," said Heather. "We want to know if you stock Krug Clos D'Ambonnay 1995 in your wine cellar?"

"Ah. The wine that was delivered with the mysterious note."

Steve stopped the coffee cup from reaching his lips. "Do you remember what the note said?"

"It read, *Congratulations on another anniversary.*"

"Was it signed?" asked Heather.

"*Non.* We get so many deliveries each day, I'm not sure where the package came from or who delivered it. The bottle came to me already out of its box. I chilled it to the proper temperature for a Pinot Noir and sent word to Monsieur Howard and Madame Lucy that a well-wisher had sent the wine."

"Did either respond?" asked Steve.

"Only Madame Lucy. She sent word that she'd take it in her room after supper. Unfortunately, Monsieur Howard left the home after supper. I heard a rumor that poison was found in the wine. I can't believe anyone would abuse such a delicate vintage by putting poison in it. It's a crime against nature and the vintner to desecrate something so near to perfection."

Chef Aubert waved away the cloud of indignation as he seemed to recognize what he'd said. "Of course, the death of Madame Lucy is much more of a loss."

The words didn't match the tone. Heather wondered if the chef held Lucy in low esteem, or if he was like other French chefs she'd trained under. Some were so passionate about culinary arts that they placed them above life itself. She decided to spend more time with the chef. After all, he had the means and motive to inject poison into the champagne, or season a glass with something that would stop a heart.

Steve interrupted her musings when he asked, "Was Lucy a lover of wine?"

The chef's head shook side to side. "If she drank wine at all, it was a single glass at supper. Most members of the family, except for Monsieur Howard and Madame Lucy, prefer mixed drinks."

"All the family members?" asked Steve.

"Carol is a bit of a lush." He looked up. "Pardon the expression, but I have little patience with people who abuse food or beverages of any kind. As for the rest of them, their drinking is in moderation."

Steve leaned forward. "What about Howard? Does he emphasize quality, or quantity, when he drinks?"

"Quality," said Chef Aubert without hesitation. "He envisions himself a sommelier. I admire him for showing the proper respect to the history and art of making fine wine. He is the only person in the home who would appreciate the bouquet of a Krug Clos d'Ambonnet 1995."

Steve took a last sip of coffee. "Thank you, Chef. While I'm busy with the next interview, Heather may break away and you two can compare notes on the latest trends in fine dining."

"That would be most enjoyable."

Heather and Steve thanked the chef and made their way to the back patio to discuss the conversation and prepare for the next interviews.

STEVE GAVE HIS HEAD A NOD AS HEATHER WHISPERED, "A woman beat us to the back patio. She's wearing a sun hat and dark glasses. Unless I'm mistaken, she's drinking a bloody Mary."

"How old do you think she is?"

"Late thirties?"

"We might be in luck. That could be Carol Green, Howard and Lucy's daughter."

"Oh, yeah," said Heather. "She divorced and moved back home last year."

Steve considered the various ways to proceed and came up with a plan. "Why don't you park me in the shade close enough to Carol where I can carry on a conversation. You go back and see if you can pry anything else out of the chef. He seems to know everything that's going on."

Heather lowered her voice, even though double paned glass separated them from the back patio. "Are you sure you want me to leave you alone with the lush?"

"The day's too early for her to be too far gone. We should be on our way home before she makes a play for me."

He thought the absurd comment deserved a laugh, but all Heather could manage was a huff. "In your dreams."

The sound of the door opening almost noiselessly on its hinges reached Steve, as did the humidity of another day in Houston. It wasn't a warm day, but with the weatherman's prediction of imminent rain, the air felt like a damp blanket.

"Good morning," said Heather.

"Is it? I don't make judgments on the quality of a day until well after lunch."

"Do you mind if I park Mr. Smiley with you?" Heather didn't wait for an answer, which was a good idea since Carol didn't give one.

Steve took over, "Unless I'm mistaken, you're Carol Green."

"That's right. You must be the blind detective the old geyser's nurse told us about."

"Clever play on words," said Steve. "Instead of calling Sid an old geezer, you said 'the old geyser.' That's appropriate for an oil man."

"If you'll excuse me," said Heather. "Chef Aubert wants to give me pointers on what he does to ratatouille to give it his signature taste."

"He uses fresh rats," said Carol.

The laugh that came out of the divorcée was enough to send nearby birds to flight. Not only was it obnoxiously loud, but she followed it with a massive intake of air that sounded like the snore of a lumberjack with hay fever.

Heather made for the door while Steve played along and congratulated Carol on another comedic coup. "That's wit fit to print," he said.

On hearing his reply, she sputtered out another laugh and snort. "You're quite the cut-up, Mr. Smiley. I expected a sourpuss with no sense of humor. Would you like a toddy-for-the-body to get your day off on the right foot?"

"Not today. I'm the designated driver. Heather will practice her French on Aubert and that invariably leads to talk about wine and cheese pairings. The next thing you know they'll be three bottles down, singing The Marseillaise."

While Carol recovered from another bout of laughing and snorting, Smiley decided it was time to get as much information out of her as he could while she was still half-sober. "On a more serious note, I'm so sorry about your mother. You have our deepest condolences."

"Thank you, but you'll find I'm not a very sentimental person. I loved my mother while she was alive, but I believe wholeheartedly in seizing the day. Carpe diem, that's my motto."

"Don't you want to see justice done?"

He felt her hand on his forearm. "The person who did this needs to pay, but I like to keep an open mind. Perhaps they had a good reason to harm Mother, or perhaps they only meant to make her sick. We may never know the entire story."

"Do you think your mother is partially responsible for her death?"

He could tell by the sound of ice rattling in her glass, that Carol was taking a long drink. The ice shifted again when she placed the glass on the table. "Mother could be a real pain in the backside. She never wanted me to marry Eddy and when the marriage broke up, she was quick to tell me, 'I told you so.' She never thought he was good enough, nor bright enough, to deal with the amount of money I'll inherit."

"Ah," said Steve. "Did you blame her for the divorce?"

"Our divorce had a lot more to do with Eddy breaking two of my ribs and being arrested with drugs than anything Mother said or did."

"Where's Eddy now?"

"In prison. Daddy made sure he received a nice, long sentence."

"I would ask how he managed that, but I think I already know. Money can get people out of trouble or—"

Carol answered the second half of what Steve was about to say. "It can also put people in prison, and keep them there." She let out a sigh. "Oh well, easy come, easy go."

The ice shifted in the glass once more. "I'm going to freshen this. Are you sure I can't get you something?"

"A pine log float with ice would be nice," said Steve.

"What in the world is that?"

"A glass of water with a toothpick."

The laugh returned with a vengeance, louder and more boisterous than ever.

Once the door closed, Steve folded his hands on his lap. Carol seemed prone to mood swings and had all the markings of a spoiled rich girl who'd grown into an emotionally stunted rich woman. There was little doubt alcohol rehab would be in her future, but did she have enough of a motive to kill her mother? People did awful things when under the influence of drugs or alcohol. He'd arrested scores of people who'd killed in an alcohol-fueled rage.

Conversely, Carol didn't fit the pattern of someone who would premeditate such a complicated crime. She might get drunk and shoot someone, but going to all the trouble and expense of purchasing a special bottle of wine, finding a deadly poison, and injecting it into the bottle didn't jibe with a person intent on seizing the day. No, whoever killed Lucy Green was much more intelligent and cunning than Carol.

Steve whispered, "Everything keeps going back to Howard." He took in a full breath and let it out in a puffed cheek blow. "Perhaps Bella is having better luck at the Webber house next door, or Heather will get something more out of Chef Aubert."

17

Wealthy women who couldn't hold their liquor always rubbed Heather the wrong way. She offered a silent expression of thanks for Steve extracting information from Carol while she made her way back to Chef Aubert's domain of pots, pans, and all things culinary.

Chef Aubert looked up when she entered his space where copper and stainless steel gleamed. The smile on his face spread, then disappeared. "*Tout va bien?*"

She joined him in speaking his native tongue. "All is well, Chef. I came back to help you prepare lunch."

"Wonderful! There's an apron in the cabinet by the window. The baguettes are ready to take from the oven and the croissants can go in. It will be a simple lunch of soup, salads, and sandwiches. The bodyguards will come in here two at a time. The family, you, Mr. Smiley, and Mr. Butch will eat in the dining room."

Heather closed the oven door. "What else can I do, Chef?"

"Are you familiar with a *salade Niçoise?*"

Heather searched her memory. "Tuna, green beans, potatoes, tomato wedges, sliced boiled eggs, onions, and capers on a bed of lettuce."

"Excellent. Prepare two salads separate for Tim and Tammy Green. They're vegetarian, so substitute garbanzo beans for the tuna."

"How do you want the presentation?"

"Long plates with the ingredients separate for the family. They'll eat in the dining room." He waved a dismissing hand. "For the men who will eat in here, don't worry about presentation. Mix the ingredients in a large bowl. You could put the food in a trough and they wouldn't care." He pointed to one of three commercial refrigerators. "I did some of the preparation this morning, but you'll find everything in that one."

Heather looked until she found everything necessary to chop, slice, open, and have ready to plate when it was closer to noon. Frequent glances at her progress told her the chef was keeping a close eye on the progress. The absence of words showed he approved.

The chef took a large ham from the middle refrigerator and slapped it on a cutting board. Quick strokes of a knife against a steel preceded him slicing off paper-thin wafers of meat. While they worked on opposite sides of a large stainless-steel table, Heather wondered if he would talk and slice at the same time. Only one way to find out.

"Chef, you said Tim and Tammy Green are vegetarians. That seems odd if Tim comes from a family in the oil business. Oil men are known for their love of red meat, especially in Texas. I thought all the Greens would eat rare steaks at least twice a day."

He wagged his knife at her like it was an extension of his index finger. "That would be how Mr. Sid liked his before his doctors put him on a soft, mainly liquid diet."

"How about Howard?" she said. "Does he like steaks?"

"Medium rare." He looked up from the mound of shaved ham. "I never thought of it before, but Howard is the only big meat eater in the house." He shook his head. "There's also Carol. She enjoys Châteaubriand from time to time."

The flow of conversation encouraged her to dig deeper.

"Next in line is Tim; you said no meat for him. How did he get along with his mother? Were he and Lucy close?"

The chef held out his hand and wiggled it side to side. "I think you'll find none of the family are what you'd call close. Tim and his wife march to the beat of a different drummer. You'll see what I'm talking about when you have lunch with them today." He winked. "I wouldn't want to spoil the surprise when they all gather at the table."

"All of them are here today?"

"All but Howard and the youngest, Chad. He's a fine young man. You'll like him. He loved to help me cook before he went to college. Now he's getting married, and it feels like I'm losing a son, and a daughter."

"A daughter? Who would that be?"

Chef Aubert put down his knife. "Anna Webber. They grew up together and were constantly under my feet."

"What about the feud?"

Chef Aubert seemed to look back in time to fond memories. "No matter how hard the families tried, those two found ways to get together. Punishment only made their desire to be with each other stronger. Their mothers soon gave up, but not Howard. He hated little Anna and still does."

"What about Mr. Sid?"

A wide smile crossed Aubert's face. "Anna wore him down. She hugged him into accepting her. Now he's her biggest ally, even though he still can't stand Frau Webber."

Heather thought about what it must have been like to grow up surrounded by such bitterness.

"Did Anna get along with Lucy?"

"As well as could be expected. Lucy changed toward her over time, ignoring the rantings of Howard and their son, Tim. Enough talk," said the chef. Heather figured he must have realized the time and how much work remained to be done. "Check the croissants. If they're burned, you'll have to start over."

This was what Heather expected from a French chef. She'd

need to put any additional conversations about family on the back burner and focus on the meal before he banished her from his kitchen.

At ten minutes until noon, the chef instructed Heather to stop plating salads for the family. Her last act of service to the chef was setting the tables, both in the formal dining room and the kitchen. As she placed the silverware, Chef Aubert said, "Lucy made sure the home ran like clockwork, which included hiring and dismissing the staff. Sylvia Lopez, along with her other duties, is responsible for serving meals. She hasn't rejoined us yet, so I'm still responsible for three meals a day and snacks."

While Aubert finished the dishes, Heather took her seat in the dining room beside Steve. Sid was the first to speak. "Why isn't Sylvia here helping Chef Aubert?"

Tim Green spoke up. "I thought Daddy told you. She starts tomorrow."

Carol added with slurred speech, "And Daddy is grieving the death of his beloved wife Lucy so deeply, he couldn't trouble himself with telling one of the other maids to help Chef Aubert." The sarcasm sounded like it came from a 1930s melodrama.

Sid looked at Butch, who sat at his right hand. "Get one of your men to help serve."

Butch nodded, and pressed one of the bodyguards standing against a wall into service as an impromptu waiter to help serve salads. Aubert wasn't smiling as he had to cope with an untrained helper. His mood soured even more when Tammy let out a squeal at what the bodyguard delivered. "Is this some sort of dead animal in my salad?"

Aubert rushed to take the plate from her. "Sorry, Madame

Tammy. You received the wrong salad. I'll bring your vegetarian Niçoise and take this back to the kitchen."

"I'll skip the salad course," said Tammy with a flick of her wrist "All I can think about is how that poor tuna should swim wild and free in the open ocean."

"Bologna," said Sid. "The only reason you turned vegetarian is because you packed away so much pork your cardiologist told you to forget about outliving me."

"That's not fair," said Tim, coming to the defense of his wife.

Tammy took the last bite of a croissant and buttered a large slice of baguette. "Thank you, Tim, darling. It's just the ranting of a senile old man."

Carol took a drink from the glass she brought to the table. It looked like water with a slice of lime, but had the smell of gin. She looked at her sister-in-law. "Come on, Tammy. Tell us why you really went vegetarian. I heard it's because your spiritual adviser told you the tarot cards recommended it."

"That's enough out of you, sister," said Tim. "Spiritual enlightenment isn't something to be made fun of or toyed with. There's great power in the unseen."

"Double bologna," said Sid, as he let out a huff of exasperation. "I didn't come to the table today to hear a bunch of overgrown children take pot shots at each other. We have things to discuss, so let's all show some respect to each other and our guests."

Sid nodded to Butch, who stood and addressed the family. "The day after tomorrow, the limousines will arrive at one-thirty. They'll take us directly to the church. Howard, Mr. Sid, and I will be in the first limo. Tim, Tammy, and Carol will be in the second. Chad and Anna Webber will be in the third."

"I object," said Tim. "Chad is our son and he should be with me and Tammy. He may have received your permission to be tied to that Webber creature, but I never consented to it. I know my father doesn't want her at Mother's funeral, and neither do I."

Sid slapped his hand on the table so hard it rattled the dishes. "This isn't up for discussion. On Christmas day, Chad will marry Anna and there's nothing you or Howard can, or will, do to stop it. Consider this an opportunity to put the past behind us."

Tim stood and threw his napkin on his plate. "How can you say that when my mother's killer is living next door? We all know who sent that bottle of poisoned wine, and the police aren't doing anything to make the Webbers account for killing her." He pointed a shaky finger at Sid. "I mean it, Grandfather, I'll not have any of the Webbers at Mother's funeral."

Sid glared at Tim. If it took a lot to wind Tim up to speaking his mind, it took less for Sid's emotional kettle to shriek. Years of negotiating deals and managing wildcat oil rigs showed when he lowered his voice. "Sit down, little man. You have granola between your ears instead of brains. Karl and Ingrid Webber had no reason to kill your mother. It's me they're after, and have been ever since Peter Webber shot me. He thought he'd killed me, but I was too mean to give him that satisfaction. They've never forgiven me for making the deal that made us all rich. " Sid struggled to catch his breath.

Tammy spoke up. "Ignore him, darling. Like I said earlier, the rantings of a senile old man. Sid's mental acuity isn't sufficient to decide who should attend Lucy's funeral."

Carol joined the fray. "Let's forget about the funeral for a while. I think Christmas would be the perfect time to get an increase in our stipends. Tim and Tammy agree, don't you?"

Sid shook his head and his face reddened. "It's always about money with you three. More is never enough. Keep pushing me and I'll teach you a lesson about greed you'll never forget."

Carol spoke into her glass as if it were a microphone. "He's bluffing. We've heard this speech before, but he probably doesn't remember giving it."

Butch reached behind Sid, turned on the oxygen tank and moved to place the plastic mask on the patriarch. Sid pushed the device away and spoke around halting breaths. He fixed his eyes on the family members one at a time. "Listen close, because I'm only going to say this once. You'll act like perfect ladies and gentleman to Anna Webber at the funeral, or I'll cut you off without a cent." He turned to Butch. "Call my lawyer and tell him I want a new will prepared in case anyone doesn't believe me. I'll cut you off and send you all out to earn a living."

"You wouldn't dare," said Tim.

Sid slumped over and Butch put the oxygen mask on him. "I need to get Mr. Sid back to his room. Call his doctor."

Sid's head lolled to the side as Butch picked him up without effort and another bodyguard grabbed the oxygen bottle off the back of the wheelchair.

Heather scanned the faces at the table. Steve sat perfectly still, his expression giving up nothing. Tim had his eyes closed, massaging his eyebrows. Tammy took out her cell phone and announced she'd call the family's doctor.

Heather wondered if Sid meant what he said about cutting off anyone who didn't live up to his expectations at the funeral.

Steve asked, "Is that the first time Sid has threatened you with your inheritance?"

"What business is that of yours?" asked Tim.

Heather could tell by Steve's sudden change of posture that Tim made a mistake in giving a surly answer. "Ms. McBlythe and I are here to find out who killed your mother. To do that, we must get to know each of you. We answer to Sid, not to anyone else. We just witnessed each of you push a sick, elderly man to the brink of death, and you don't seem sorry about it. It makes us wonder if this family isn't eager to see another member of this household pass on, especially since Sid announced his will might change."

"That's crazy talk," said Carol, whose words came out as if the only thing she'd had to drink all day was orange juice. "We may hiss at each other, but we rarely scratch and never enough to break the skin."

Heather added, "You'd better hope Sid's condition isn't fatal.

The police could arrest each of you on a charge of involuntary manslaughter if he dies. At the very least, you could be arrested for elderly abuse."

Steve stood and added, "Heather and I will meet with each of you individually the day after the funeral. As for now, we'll leave you to grieve Lucy. And to consider how foolish you are in pushing Sid to his grave. We're in daily contact with the police and will file a full report on your conduct today."

Once in the car Steve fastened his seatbelt and turned to Heather. "How 'bout we stop and get a hamburger, fries, and a shake? I'm not sure what ratatouille tastes like, but I wasn't looking forward to finding out."

Heather chuckled. "What about the rest of the day?"

"We'll do what we said we'd do. Write a full report and email it to Leo. He'll probably call us and ask for details."

"It seems one of the most important things we learned was the wine came from an outside source. Perhaps Kirby and Ayana can track it down." Heather hesitated. "What else can we do today?"

"Think, rest, and wait for Bella to send us a text tonight. I hope the Webber household isn't as crazy as this one."

18

Heather knew better than to order the fish sandwich at the restaurant Steve suggested. If it had been up to her, she would have turned around and walked out as soon as she caught the first whiff of old grease. But Steve had an affection for a certain brand of cheeseburger, fries, and chocolate milkshake that needed monthly satisfying. He ate every bite and savored the shake until the last slurp.

As for her meal, the breading on the fish did nothing but soak up old vegetable oil and weigh like a boat anchor in her stomach. Taking it off the bun did little to minimize the sensation that someone had stuck an air hose from a mechanic's shop down her throat and filled her gut.

They arrived back at their condos with both of them wanting to go their separate ways for the next several hours. Heather to search for the plastic container of antacids at the back of her medicine cabinet and Steve to do the only thing that could improve his meal—take a nap. It pushed five o'clock when Heather hung up from speaking with her personal assistant. All was well at her office, but her acquisitions team wasn't having much luck finding homes with potential upside in the River

Oaks neighborhood. So far, they'd only identified the Webber home as a possible candidate, but they needed photos of the interior to give them a better idea of needed repairs and updates. "A job for Bella," said Heather to herself.

She hollered through Max's cat door she was on her way and scurried barefoot to Steve's front door. She let herself in and spotted him in his favorite chair. "Brrr. I should have put some shoes on."

"Is it raining yet?"

"Only a light sprinkle. It's supposed to pick up tomorrow and be a deluge the day after."

"Nasty day for a funeral," said Steve.

Heather started to ask if he thought it wise to have Bella take photos of the interior of the Webber's home when her phone announced an incoming call. She pulled it out of a back pocket and announced, "It's Father. He probably wants me to go on another cruise."

She punched a button on her phone. "Hello, Father. Was it a profitable day?"

"Not particularly, but there's a cruise line that will soon announce they're building two new ships with a capacity of over six-thousand passengers and crew on each." He gave her the name of the stock ticker and said, "They currently have two ships that sail out of Galveston. Are you and Jack available for a four-day cruise in the not-too-distant future?"

"What about me?" asked Steve in a voice loud enough to be picked up by the phone's microphone.

"Is that Steve?"

"It is, and we might accomplish more than one thing on the cruise."

Steve came closer so he wouldn't have to shout. "We told you about a case earlier that might involve us going on a cruise."

"Yes, I remember."

"We're helping the police with their murder inquiry and it's slow going. To make a very long story shorter, the case involves a longstanding feud between two families. Progress is slow and there's a good chance we'll still be working on it when the youngest members of the feuding families get married in Cozumel, Mexico on Christmas Day. It's a destination wedding and instead of flying, the families are cruising on the line you mentioned."

Mr. McBlythe said, "That's a couple of days shy of two weeks from now."

"Right. If the case is solved by then we can have a nice vacation. If not, Heather, Jack, and I can keep working. It could be our only chance to speak to some of the family members on somewhat neutral ground."

"Count me in on your investigation," said Mr. McBlythe. "If you give me the questions to ask, I'll do the rest."

"Father," said Heather with misgivings punctuating the lone word. "You don't know the first thing about interviewing suspects."

Mimicking her emphasis on the first word, Mr. McBlythe replied, "Daughter, I've done business deals with everyone from Las Vegas casino moguls to heads of state. It's all about knowing their weaknesses. Have you done thorough background checks on them?"

"Not complete, but I'd say we're ninety percent there on all but one or two."

"I can put my people on it, too, if you send me an email with the names."

"One question," said Steve. "Who will book the rooms?"

Heather and her father answered at the same time with a resounding, "I will."

Mr. McBlythe settled the question when he said, "I've already spoken with the owner of the cruise line. He told me to let him know when and where I wanted to cruise and he'd roll out the red carpet."

"I think that settles it. We'll let you take care of the bookings," said Steve.

Small talk about her father's latest business deals and how Heather and Jack's relationship was progressing occupied the next ten minutes until Mr. McBlythe received another phone call.

After Heather wished him a pleasant evening and the phone sounded its disconnection, Steve said, "We need to discuss the room situation on the ship."

"Why? Everyone can have a room to themselves."

Heather's phone vibrated and sounded a musical riff. "It's Jack," she said.

"Hey, beautiful."

"Hey, handsome. I'm here with Steve."

"Is anyone over there hungry?"

"Not yet," said Heather. "But we might be by the time you get here."

"You sound in a good mood. What's up?"

"Father called. We're all going on a Christmas cruise. That includes you and Steve. Don't even think about telling me you can't come."

"I'll enter a plea of guilty for every one of my clients if I have to. How long will we be gone?"

"It's a short, four-day cruise. Father's still stuck on the idea of investing in a cruise line and he's looking at one that sails out of Galveston."

"Hold on," said Jack. "Aren't the feuding families you're investigating taking a cruise around Christmas?" Jack's voice had just enough hesitation in it to give her pause.

"Yes," Heather drew out the one-word answer. "It's the same cruise, but we might finish the case by then. If not, Steve just recruited my father to glean information from the members of the Webber family." She paused. "Don't worry, by the time we leave, Steve and I will have identified the killer."

"And if you don't, you'll be working on the case." He let out a breath that sounded like a combination of uncertainty and disappointment. "We'll talk more about it when I come over.

It'll take me about an hour to get cleaned up and drive to your place."

The phone went dead and she continued to look at it. "He didn't sound nearly as excited as I thought he would."

"He'll be fine if you play your cards right."

"What's that supposed to mean?"

Steve hung his head and wagged it. "On our tenth anniversary I told Maggie we'd go to the beach in Galveston, rent a nice hotel room, and spend the weekend walking, talking, and eating out."

"That sounds wonderful."

Steve raised his head and gave it a tilt. "It should have been. The problem was, it sounded good to the guys in the office, too. Before I knew it, four other detectives had booked rooms on either side of ours. They were up before dawn with fishing reports blaring from a radio on one side and a television yapping on about the news on the other. That was after they played poker until one o'clock in the morning. What Maggie and I thought would be a romantic get-away turned into thirty-six hours of noise and frustration."

Steve summed up the experience. "What I'm trying to say is, Jack has expectations for what the cruise will be. What are your expectations? Do they align with his?"

Heather closed her eyes, trying to think of an appropriate answer to his words and what he'd left unsaid. "You have a way of drawing things to a sharp point, Detective Smiley. Part of me wants to tell you to butt out of my personal life, and another part tells me you're the wisest person I've ever met. I'll take your comments under advisement."

Steve held up his hands. "I'll leave the room assignments to you and your father. All I need is a bed and a bathroom. Don't waste money on a view for me."

Heather rose and said, "I'll be back when Jack gets here. I have a couple of things to do."

Once back in her condo, she curled up on the couch with

Max while her thoughts went round and round considering what she took to be a warning. She mindlessly stroked her beloved cat while giving thought to what Jack's expectations for the cruise might be. She then made a mental checklist of what she wanted to accomplish. First on her list was solving the murder. Next, to spend time with Jack. Her father came in third on her list of priorities.

The diamond in her engagement ring caught the light from a lamp and seemed to blink its own warning. "Priorities, Max. Why did I think of Jack as a pleasant addition to the trip, instead of putting him first on the list? Is it fair to Jack to ask him to come on a cruise and then ignore him? Will there be time to do all three? Perhaps Jack shouldn't go if he's going to be disappointed." She looked down at her cat and scratched behind his ear.

Max yawned.

"Then again, we might solve the murder before we go. That would eliminate one thing on the list and move Jack up." She let out a huff of exasperation. "Is that the way it will be from now on? Life was so much easier before I fell in love with that wonderful man."

THE OPENING OF THE FRONT DOOR BROUGHT MAX TO HIS FEET and off the couch. It also jolted Heather out of a meaningless dream. She sat up straight and rubbed her eyes.

"Wake up, sleepy head," came the voice from the front door.

"Bella? Is that you?"

The young woman came into the living room. "It's me, and your supper is getting cold."

"What time is it, and what are you doing here? Did Ingrid Webber sack you already?"

"It's a little after seven, I'm here to get more clothes, and

Ingrid Webber is a slavemaster, but I didn't get fired or quit... yet."

Bella reached out her hand to help pull Heather to her feet. "Jack wants you to get a move on. He said time and moo goo gai pan waits for no man, or woman."

"Yum."

The two were out the door in less than a minute. Bella went to the dining room, but Heather had to give her fiancé a full hug first. "I'm sorry I hit you with the idea of the cruise out of the blue. It's a lot to ask you to play second fiddle if we haven't solved the case by then."

He looked at her and smiled. "I've been thinking. Even if you haven't solved the case, it will be good to be there with you. Who knows? I might be of some help, too."

Heather gave him a quick kiss. "You're the best." She grabbed his hand and started toward the dining room. "Sorry I'm late everyone. I guess I dozed off on the couch with Max." She pulled out a chair. "A veritable Chinese feast and I'm starving."

"There's hope for you yet," said Steve. "Naps are an essential part of living a full and rewarding life."

Bella dug white rice from a cardboard carton and heaped it on her plate. She then studied the selections of main dishes to top the bed of rice, and spoke as she considered the options. "Steve and Jack have been telling me about the cruise. I want to go with you."

Heather scooped fried rice from a carton as she asked, "Will Ingrid allow you to go?"

Bella flicked away the question. "I'm planning to quit before then, so it won't matter about her. I might stay to help Anna and Adam, but Ingrid and that husband of hers can pack their own bags."

"Tell us about Anna," said Steve.

Bella made room for General Tso's chicken beside her rice. "Anna's really cute and sweet as she can be. Adam is different in so many ways, much more serious."

"How cute is he?" asked Jack.

"Anna's the cute, bubbly one. Adam is dark, quiet, and he has no idea how gorgeous he is, even dripping wet."

Heather raised her eyebrows. "Could you elaborate?"

Bella swallowed her first bite before answering. "I thought I was going to die when he came out of the pool."

Steve chuckled as she continued, "I'm glad I was inside looking out a window and not standing near him. I'm sure I'd have stuck my foot down my throat trying to say something."

Heather sat back. "Does Adam have anything to do with your sudden desire to go on this cruise?"

Bella grinned. "It's therapy. I need to get over losing the man I thought I was going to marry. Tomorrow I'm going online to buy my ticket."

"No, you're not," said Heather. "I'll let Father know to add you to the cruise list. You can stay with me in either a connecting balcony room or a suite."

"Cool," said Bella as she stabbed another piece of chicken.

"I was wondering about the sleeping arrangements," said Jack. "Why don't Steve and I get adjoining rooms close to yours? That will give us each plenty of flexibility to do what we need or want to do."

Heather wondered what Steve had said to Jack to assuage his disappointment about the cruise. Perhaps Jack would tell her later. Then again, he and Steve should have a secret or two.

Heather looked at Jack and gave a wink. "It's a good thing we won't spend all our time solving a murder." She grabbed her phone and sent a text to her father that read:

Need 2 balcony cabins with connecting doors for Steve and Jack.
2 more connecting cabins for me and Bella.

The reply came back as dishes were being loaded into the dishwasher.

2 balcony plus 2 inside connecting cabins reserved. Sorry couldn't do better.

"Now that we have the rooms sorted out," said Steve. "We need to hear from Bella about the Webber household. What have you learned in the short time you've been there?"

19

Heather scooped coffee into a press pot while Bella put a kettle on to boil and relayed what she'd learned in the brief time at the Webbers. "We've already established Ingrid runs the show in that family. At first, I thought it was only the house, but it turns out she spends a lot of her time in her office. Phone calls come in for her all day."

"Can you tell who they're from?" asked Steve.

"They're not all from the same person. I'm certain of that, by the tone and volume of her voice."

Steve nodded. Heather filed the tidbit of information away. It might mean something, and then again, it might not.

She took her turn with the next question. "What's the condition of the home?"

Bella gave a scoffing grunt. "It's cleaner than it was when I started, but it would take several full-time people to keep it looking the way it should, and that would be after a deep clean. That place must have a hundred rooms."

"Not quite," said Heather. "But it has twelve bedrooms, most with their own bathrooms."

"It seems like a thousand when you're vacuuming. She gave me a daily cleaning schedule for the common rooms that aren't locked off, told me to clean her bedroom every other day and make sure everything that's in plain view is dusted."

"What about the other bedrooms?" asked Steve.

"That's the only good news. The doors are to remain closed at all times and each family member keeps their room clean. Of course, I have to do all the laundry, except for Anna and Adam's. They do their own."

Heather settled her coffee cup on the table as Bella rose to look in the refrigerator.

"You can't still be hungry," said Jack.

"Thirsty. Are there any soft drinks?"

"Look in the pantry," said Steve. "You'll have to pour it over ice in a glass."

While Bella fixed herself a drink, Heather asked, "What's the furniture like in the Webber home?"

"Old," said Bella as she took out her phone and gave it to Heather. "I took pictures of the rooms that aren't locked. You can see frayed material on some of the chairs and stains on couches. Frau Webber tells me to make sure I keep the best side of the cushions facing down unless she's expecting company, but Adam told me I needn't worry about it. They quit having guests several years ago."

Jack took a break from blowing on the scalding coffee long enough to say, "It sounds to me like the Webber family has fallen on hard times."

Heather added, "I'm thinking many of the calls Ingrid receives are from bill collectors."

Bella gave her head a firm nod. "That's what I thought, too. In fact, they're in such a bind that Frau Webber asked Adam to loan her enough money to pay for the cruise."

"You've been busy," said Steve. "How old is Adam and how does he have that kind of money?"

"Twenty-three, but he acts much older. I'm not exactly sure what he does, but it involves a bank of computer screens in a room with no windows. He's in there all day from six in the morning until four in the afternoon. No break for lunch, other than the sandwich I take him."

Heather thought for a minute. "He could be playing the market with swing trades. It's risky unless he knows what he's doing."

Bella snapped her fingers. "I did catch one phrase when I asked him what all the graphs and charts were for. He's shy so I was surprised he answered me, but he said, 'Selling short on commodity derivatives.' Whatever that means."

"It's complicated," said Heather. "Adam and my father would get along fine."

Jack tilted his head. "Day trading is too deep for me. I bill by the hour and leave the high finance and risk-taking to others."

The conversation died down until Steve brought it back to life. "One thing we need you to find out, Bella, is about the wine found in Lucy's room. I'm sure the Webber home has a wine cellar."

Bella shrugged. "It might, but I don't think there's much of anything in it."

"Why not?"

"Frau Webber is the only one who drinks, and it's only one small glass of schnapps with the evening meal. There's wine in the fridge, but I don't think it's anything special."

"What makes you say that?"

"It comes in a box."

Steve followed the thread. "Tell us about the cook."

"Frau Schultz," said Bella. "She's married to the butler and she has arthritis. That old woman is a wonderful German cook, but like Frau Webber, her face might crack and fall off if she ever smiled. She also sneaks a glass of wine every evening. I think she's the only one who dips into the boxed wine."

Bella downed her soft drink, rinsed her glass and put it in the dishwasher. "I need to call Uber and get back to my slave quarters. Five-thirty in the morning comes early."

"No need to call," said Jack. "Heather and I will take you."

"Are you sure?"

"We're sure," said Heather. "That will give Jack and me alone time on the way back. After all, a woman and her man should have private time."

Bella raised her eyebrows. "That's what I told my parents when I dated that playboy pilot. They told me there better be a lot more talking going on than anything else."

Jack rose from his chair. "We'll take their words under advisement. Let's get you home. I'm overdue for a long conversation."

"Max and I will stay here," said Steve. "He's going to help me solve this murder after I call Leo."

STEVE STARTED THE DISHWASHER AND SETTLED IN HIS recliner in the living room. Leo answered his call on the third ring. "Don't ask about the toe. What's left of it hurts, and if you have anything smart to say about a lost piggy, I'll put laxative in your coffee next time I see you."

"Have the boys and girls at the office been hard on you?"

"Brutal. They sent me a pair of those stupid socks that look like gloves for your feet. Each toe fits in its own slot."

"Let me guess," said Steve. "They cut off the material on the little toe and sewed it back. Now you have a nine-toed pair of ugly socks."

"They didn't even do a good job sewing the hole shut. Stupid sense of humor. Needless to say, they're in the trash."

Steve remembered the pranks fellow detectives played on him and how much he enjoyed the payback. It was especially satisfying if they couldn't prove he'd done it and blamed someone else. In a twisted way, cops show they care without using words.

"Any sympathy from your wife and kids?"

"The boys think it's cool that I got shot, but not in the foot. My daughters say it's gross and that I can't ever go swimming with them or walk around the house without shoes on. I told them I'd wait until they brought a boyfriend over and I'd trim my toenails in front of him. As for my wife, she's ready for me to paint."

While Steve chuckled, Leo said, "Enough small talk. Give me an update."

"We had an interesting morning and lunch with the Greens. Carol drinks way too much. I thought Tim and his wife Tammy were limp noodles, but they both gave old man Sid a hard time at lunch. They might play the game of wanting to save the planet, but they insist on doing it in style. Heather spent the morning with the chef. They hit it off and I'm convinced we can take him off the suspect board. The only way he'd have killed Lucy was if she tried to tell him how to cook. Best we could tell, she stayed out of his kitchen."

"What about the wine?"

"It's not something they keep in their wine cellar. It arrived as a delivery and no one could remember who brought it. Howard Green is the only person, beside the chef, who knows a Chablis from a Chianti. He's a self-proclaimed connoisseur."

Steve took in a full breath. "Speaking of wine, I'll switch gears and tell you what Bella found out at the Webber house. It seems they're in worse financial shape than I imagined and the only wine anyone drinks comes out of a box."

"Hold on a minute." Steve could hear Leo holler for someone to get the dog who was licking his foot. "Sorry about that. It doesn't surprise me about financial problems. I'm surprised they can pay the taxes on that run-down castle, but no one in the family seems concerned enough to get out and work."

"There is one exception," said Steve. "The youngest, Adam Webber. He's bankrolling his parents and grandparents with enough money to go on the wedding cruise. I'm willing to guess he's paying for his sister's wedding, too. Have you run a financial statement on him yet?"

"Ayana did. That explains the sudden inflow into Ingrid Webber's bank account. Kirby told me about it today."

Max jumped on the couch and meowed permission to join Steve on the chair. He patted his lap, soon had company, and refocused. "It seems Adam is close to his sister, but is letting the rest of the family sink or swim."

Steve considered the cost of a destination wedding and cringed. "Is he doing that well as a day trader?"

"Ayana's report says Adam was making six figures a year in high school. He's into seven figures now. The young man knows his way around the stock market."

"I wonder why he's still living at home?"

"That may be something Bella could help us find out."

"She'll need to do it in less than two weeks. Bella's planning on quitting before Frau Webber can fire her. She's also going on the wedding cruise with us."

"Hold on," said Leo. "Who's *us*?"

"That would be Heather's father, Heather, Jack, Bella, and me."

"Why don't you take Max and clear out both condos?"

"Don't give Heather any ideas."

Leo partially covered the phone and hollered something in Spanish. He came back on and asked, "What do you want Kirby and Ayana working on?"

"Full background on Adam Webber. At least he has the brains to plan a murder like this one."

"Anything else?"

"Go back to basics. Keep looking for motive, means, and opportunity. Right now, there's at least four in the Green house that are ready to see Sid join Lucy: Howard, Tim, Tammy, and Carol. Also, have Kirby call tonight and again tomorrow morning to make sure Sid is recovering. Butch had to carry him out from lunch after the family pushed too hard."

Steve remembered one more thing to tell Leo. "Another thing. Sid was talking about changing his will and cutting out any family member who misbehaves at the funeral. The big dust-up at lunch was over Sid's insistence that Anna Webber accompany her soon-to-be husband in the limo."

Leo stayed quiet for a few seconds. "Do you really think Sid would cut blood kin out of his will?"

Steve had pondered this question ever since he saw how Sid reacted at lunch. "Butch is more of a grandson than any who carry the Green name. Sid can be as unpredictable and dangerous as a West Texas tornado. I wouldn't put anything past him."

"I'll tell Kirby to dig deeper on Butch too. That could be motive," said Leo.

"Be sure Kirby and Ayana go to the funeral and intervene if anyone gives Sid a hard time. He can't take much more, and there are people in his home, as well as next door, who'll dance on his grave when he's gone."

20

For once the weather forecast was accurate and rain pelted down in a steady cadence. Heather's funeral attire included black, knee-length boots and a black umbrella large enough to cover her and Jack. It was good Steve decided to stay home with Max and wait for her report.

Jack arrived in plenty of time for them to slosh their way through Houston's wet streets and make it to the church well ahead of the crowd. Once they arrived, she told Jack to go inside and save her a seat on the third row, behind those reserved for family. She wanted to see the limos as they arrived because Sid made a big deal of the number of limos and who would ride in each one. The family might have had other ideas, but she'd bet Sid got his way.

Jack shook his head. "You save the seats and I'll monitor who gets out of each limo."

"What difference does it make?"

He pointed to the windshield. "It's pouring rain, and we only brought one umbrella. I'm wearing a full-length raincoat and brought a cowboy hat with a plastic cover."

"I forgot you were an Eagle Scout."

He smiled, "Be prepared is the motto."

Heather tried to give him a peck on his cheek, but he turned his head at the last second and they both got their money's worth from a full kiss on the lips. She pulled back to catch her breath. "I enjoy the way you surprise me."

"My pleasure."

"Not exclusively."

Heather grabbed the umbrella, opened the door enough to stick it through the crack and pushed the button. It sprang open like a huge, black mushroom and allowed her to slide out and make it into the church with only her boots shedding water. She found the pew she wanted and waited. People filtered in at first then, like the rain, poured into the sanctuary designed to seat upward of a thousand people.

When the church was about half-full, Jack slid in beside her. He leaned over and whispered, "They arrived like Sid arranged except there was one additional guy in the first limo and another in the last. The extra with Sid and Howard looked too old to be a bodyguard, but I guess he is."

Jack cut off his sentence and motioned for Heather to look by cutting his eyes. "That's him. He and another bodyguard are coming in before the family."

Heather recognized the older of the two stern-faced men. "That's Henry Drake. He's the PI I told you about. The other is Butch, the medical guy and head of security."

Jack continued his report on the occupants of the two remaining limos which matched Sid's original instructions.

"No guard in the middle limo?" whispered Heather.

The answer came as a shake of Jack's head.

The church continued to fill as the family entered with Howard Green leading the way. Sid followed in his wheelchair, followed by Butch with the train of family members looking like so many boxcars. Each took their seat and waited.

It proved to be a standard service with a recounting of birth, education, marriage, surviving husband and family members. The pastor recited civic organizations and other notable accomplishments followed by two eulogies from Lucy's sister and a friend, a short sermon, and an invitation to pay last respects. Row by row, ushers invited attendees to rise and take a last look at Lucy while the family looked on.

With all the friends out of the pews, the usher motioned for the family to come forward.

The top third of the casket was opened and Howard was the first to view Lucy with Henry Drake close enough to be Howard's shadow. He placed his hand on Howard's shoulder as the two took a last look at the woman Howard married more than forty years ago. The widower broke away, but Drake lingered longer than Heather thought he would. A sharp word from Carol Green was all it took to prompt Drake to keep moving. The rest of the family slowed a little to gaze into the casket, turned, and exited through the same side door they entered.

Heather leaned toward Jack. "Go to the car and look for anything unusual. Steve wanted us to give a full report of everything that takes place from the time they arrived until they pull back into their home after the burial."

Jack left without question or comment.

Heather was caught in the crowd of mourning friends and acquaintances gathered on the covered portico as the organ continued to play hymns in the background. Once through the mass of people, she rounded the side of the church and dodged puddles until she joined Jack.

She gazed at the waiting hearse and counted the limos. The first limo in line was missing.

Once in her SUV, Jack explained, "Things happened fast. Butch put Sid in the first limo. I got a little too close and a bodyguard showed his displeasure by pulling out his pistol. He never pointed it at me, but it looked like he wouldn't hesitate if I hadn't turned away. He jumped in the back seat with Sid and they wasted no time in leaving."

What happened next took Heather by surprise. The side door to the church opened and Howard Green came out accompanied by a blond woman who looked to be thirty years his junior, perhaps more. Heather couldn't see clearly through the rain-streaked windows.

"That's Howard's girlfriend," said Heather. "If Shayla Daniels gets into the limo, she's going to the cemetery with that creep."

"No way. They're not that brazen," said Jack.

"Look," said Heather as she pointed. "There's Tim and Tina and Carol coming out of the building. It's a good thing we can't hear what those three are shouting."

The second limo left the church with Howard, his girlfriend, and Drake.

"Guess I was wrong. Appears they're pretty brazen," said Jack.

Heather had to clamp her teeth together to keep from littering the air with curses directed at Howard. Her gaze locked on the remaining family members and a bodyguard thrown in for good measure. She then noted the remaining black Lincoln Town Car. It wasn't a stretch limo like the other two. The math didn't work out. "There's six people left to fit into the back seat."

"I wonder what they'll do?" asked Jack.

"I have an idea. Pull up behind them. I recognize the bodyguard. He was standing during the service, checking the crowd for anything suspicious."

Jack did as instructed. Heather hopped out with one hand raised and the other carrying her umbrella high. "It's me, Heather McBlythe and my fiancé. He's an attorney helping Mr. Smiley and me."

"Put that gun away," said Tim to the bodyguard. "What do you want, Ms. McBlythe?"

"To help. There's room for three in my vehicle. It's a black

SUV and will blend in well. Why don't I take Chad, Anna, and Butch's friend? We'll follow you to the cemetery and then to your home."

Tim looked at his wife who nodded. "That's fine. Thank you."

The bodyguard said, "I need to call Butch and get this approved."

It wasn't long before the young couple and a burly man wearing a tight suit piled into the back seat. They looked relieved to be away from Tim, Tina, and Carol, who continued their conversation accompanied by hand gestures and loud voices. Thankfully the closing of the car door deadened all sound except the patter of rain.

Heather played hostess with an introduction to Jack and offered her condolences in an effort to ease the young couple's embarrassment. When she saw Chad offer a small smile to Anna after she whispered in his ear, she realized there was no need to be concerned about their embarrassment.

"I understand wedding bells will soon ring for you two."

Anna sat in the middle and Chad behind Jack, so Heather could see them by swiveling in her seat. The countenance of the petite woman with almond eyes came to life. "It's going to be a perfect wedding. We're getting married on the beach, no shoes allowed, at an exclusive resort as far away from the cruise ships and crowds as possible."

Chad chimed in, "We're staying at Cozumel and flying back a week later."

Heather tried not to show her surprise. "What do the two families think about you not returning on the ship with them?"

The two looked at each other and laughed. Chad was the first to speak. "This may sound like we're uncaring about our families, but the feud stops with us. When we were seven years old we agreed to marry and never live with our families."

"In fact," said Anna, "we're moving to Costa Rica."

Heather tilted her head. "What do your parents say about that?"

"They don't believe us," said Chad. "They can't imagine living a life outside River Oaks." He paused. "This may sound morbid, but the only reason we haven't moved yet is because of Grandfather Sid. We promised him we'd wait until after he passed"

Anna's next words seemed to complete her fiancé's thoughts. "It won't be long before he's gone. We hope he can make it through the wedding."

Chad added, "And we hope the two families stay away from each other on the cruise."

"And no one else dies," said Anna.

The words struck Heather as ringing true, something like a reliable prophecy. Would there be another murder before this couple could formally bind themselves together? Who was the most likely candidate? Howard Green? Ingrid Webber? Or could it be someone else?

In due time men wearing dark suits wheeled Lucy Green's casket to the waiting hearse and the funeral procession began.

Upon arrival at the cemetery, pounding rain made the occasion a miserable affair. Heather and Jack squeezed inside the white tent with family, pall bearers and the few friends brave enough to come. When Howard escorted his girlfriend to sit with the rest of the family, Carol wasted no time in insulting her with every term in her vocabulary to describe a woman of questionable morals.

Howard stepped between the women and said, "Carol, you will sit down now and shut up."

Heather was close enough to smell gin on Carol's breath as she continued her tirade, even louder this time.

Howard's guest proved to be no pushover. As the second round of insults started, she unleashed a slap across Carol's face that brought the tirade to a sudden stop.

When no reprimand came from Howard, Carol sat down in her assigned seat and sobbed.

The burial service was mercifully short. Heather added one more name to the family members who might face death in the near future—Carol Green's future stepmother. If Howard Green had the gall to bring his mistress to his wife's funeral, he'd surely take her on the cruise, perhaps as his wife, which meant one more person with a claim on an inheritance.

21

Steve sat in his recliner with his laptop resting on his thighs and earbuds plugged in. Ten days had passed; the only thing that changed was that Heather came down with a stubborn cold after braving the weather at the funeral. She sat on the couch and blew her nose.

"Did the tea with lemon and honey help?" asked Steve as he took out the earbuds.

"I think the only thing that will help my sinuses is sunshine and clear Caribbean saltwater. I may stay in Cozumel until my nose doesn't look like Rudolph's."

"Jack and your father wouldn't enjoy cruising home without you."

"Hopefully this drainage will clear before we leave for Galveston. If not, I may sleep in the ship's sauna and bake my sinuses into submission."

Heather took another sip of sweet, tangy tea. "I'm sorry I've been so little help to you this past week."

Steve flipped the apology away with his hand. "I'm not sure what else you could've done. We're missing something. I can feel it."

"But what? We've gone over every potential suspect for motive, checked alibis, and we still keep coming up with the same people."

Even though it might be a waste of time, Steve knew if they kept at it, they'd discover the key that would unlock Lucy's murder. "Let's go over the suspects again."

Heather let out a sigh. "My money's still on Howard Green. When he brought Shayla to the funeral, he displayed his true colors, and he has more motive than anyone else because he's the oldest male heir. A divorce could have taken half his fortune. I can see attorneys lined up to the street wanting to represent Lucy in a messy divorce trial. He's also the only one interested in wine. That's not to mention his questionable business practices, especially in his dealings with the Webbers. All that speaks to a corrupt character. I believe he'll do anything to get, and hang on to, the family fortune."

"No evidence," countered Steve, "And Shayla Daniels gives him an alibi for the time of death and most of the day leading up to it."

"But not the delivery of the wine," said Heather.

Steve puffed out his cheeks. "I'm not saying it's not Howard, but we both know there's not enough evidence to arrest him, let alone get a conviction. Until we can tie the bottle of wine to him, or anyone else, we're at a standstill."

Heather sneezed and gave her nose another blow. She added the tissue to a pile beside her. "At least Ayana tracked down the guy who purchased the wine and sent it to the Webber home through FedEx. Whoever is behind Lucy's murder was smart enough to pick a full-blown alcoholic for the purchase, someone he knew wouldn't remember the guy who hired him. It's a shame the Webbers' cook doesn't remember anything but taking the gift next door."

"No description," said Steve. "Any self-respecting prosecuting attorney couldn't put a guy like that on the stand. Talk about an unreliable witness. Let's move on. Who's your number two suspect?"

"Ingrid Webber. She has motive, means, and opportunity. After her husband, Karl, lost most of their fortune, she's taken over their remaining investments. She could have taken some of it and bought a very expensive bottle of wine for Howard and Lucy's anniversary. The alcoholic who sent the package to the Webber home said it might have been a woman who paid him to mail the package. All he remembers is gray hair."

"And that could have been a wig," said Steve.

The front door opened before Steve could play devil's advocate any longer. "I'm home, and never so happy to get fired," said Bella in a voice that sounded very cheerful for seven-thirty in the evening after a full day's work.

"Fired?" asked Heather.

Steve put his laptop on the table next to him. "I was wondering how long it would take."

"She fired me with just cause, but it was worth it. I waited until the markets closed in New York to tell Adam I was going on the same cruise with him. Up to today, he'd been super shy, but all that changed when I told him I was going on the cruise. He gave me the best kiss I've ever had. Wow! That guy has at least one hidden talent. I was enjoying seconds when Ingrid walked in."

Steve chuckled. "That may be the most enjoyable way of getting fired I ever heard."

Bella flopped on the couch next to Heather. "I was going to quit tomorrow so it's no big deal."

"Any reports for us on the investigation?" asked Heather.

"Ingrid told her husband, Karl, he should stay home. Adam told her his grandfather was staying with him on the ship and if she didn't like it, she could stay home."

"I'm liking Adam more and more," said Steve.

"Me, too," said Bella.

Heather groaned, then sneezed again.

Bella rose. "I'm going next door, wash clothes, and order a pizza to celebrate. Who wants to help me destroy a meat-lovers?"

"We had our supper," said Heather.

The words had barely left Heather's mouth when Steve said, "Count me in. I'm getting in shape for the all you can eat buffet."

He held up his hand as a stop sign for Bella. "Did Ingrid pay you for the work you've done?"

"Are you kidding? She stiffs everyone she can. No worries. My fishing shows are in syndication, and I'll keep getting residuals for years to come. I'm set until I take over my parents' hotel."

The front door opened and closed, bringing in a blast of winter air. "Where were we?" asked Steve.

"Wondering if Ingrid Webber killed Lucy Green."

Steve tented his hands. "I can see motive, but once again we run into that pesky thing the courts are so fond of—evidence." He shook his head. "Who else is on our list?"

"Tim and Tammy Green. I lumped them together."

Steve shook his head. "Not likely. Boys rarely kill their mothers and Tammy impresses me as a follower."

"There's Carol Green," said Heather, "but I don't think it's her. If it was a crime of passion, I'd seriously consider her because she stays inside a bottle of gin most of the time."

"You're right. This took too much brainpower for Carol to pull off."

"That's all the Greens except Chad, but he seems the least likely of all the family members. He and Anna have already abandoned both families."

"I still say we're missing something that's right in front of us. Let's call Leo and see if he has anything new."

Steve gave a verbal command for his phone to call Leo Vega.

He answered and immediately said, "Let me go outside where I can hear you. The family is watching *Elf* for the hundredth time." The sound of a door closing changed the background noise from riotous laughter to quiet.

"What's up?" asked Leo.

"Heather and I were calling to find out if you had anything new from Kirby and Ayana?"

"Did you know Howard Green and Shayla Daniels were married this afternoon?"

Heather responded before Steve had a chance to. "Why did I give that man the benefit of the doubt? Is there anything Howard Green won't do?"

Leo and Steve remained quiet, because Heather kept going. "Even if Howard didn't kill Lucy, he deserves to go to prison for being a scumbag."

Steve countered with, "I don't believe that charge has made it into the penal code yet."

"It should be," said Heather in a huff.

Leo took his turn. "Having a new stepmother on board should make your cruise even more interesting. Are your bags packed?"

"Not yet," said Steve. "The only fresh development we have for you is that Bella got fired today. She told Adam Webber she'd be on the same cruise as the wedding party. From the way Bella told the story, Adam was so happy he couldn't restrain himself from giving her a kiss that had her wobbling. Ingrid caught them in a full embrace and told Bella to hit the road."

"I'm glad she's out of that house," said Heather.

Steve changed the subject. "How's the toe?"

"Almost healed. The stitches are out and my wife made a list as long as my arm of things for me to do. We need to solve this case and give Ayana credit so I can go back to work and get some rest."

"Why don't you tell your wife you need to go on the cruise with us?" asked Steve.

"I already tried. She told me if I went on a cruise without her, it would cost me a new car of her choosing. I've never bought a new car in my life and I'm not about to start now." Leo then said, "Hold on a minute, there's a call from Kirby coming in. Keep your fingers crossed for good news."

Almost a full minute passed before Leo came back on. "I need to go. Howard Green arrived at Methodist Hospital thirty minutes ago with a gunshot wound to his arm. Kirby said it wasn't life threatening, but Howard will have his arm in a sling on the cruise."

Steve's phone announced an incoming call, "Sid Green is calling me. Let me or Heather know what else you find out."

Steve told his phone to answer Sid's call.

"Smiley. Get down to Methodist Hospital and find out how bad off Howard is."

"It's not life threatening. A gunshot to the arm."

"How old and reliable is that report?"

"Thirty seconds and it came from a homicide detective."

Sid let out a breath of relief, then stiffened his words. "It probably serves Howard right for acting such a fool. Still, he's my son, and I'd hate to go to my grave knowing the Webbers are still shooting at us. What do you recommend?"

Steve shrugged his shoulders. "Your home may be the safest place in Houston. Tell Butch to get Howard to your fortress as soon as possible and keep him and his new wife inside."

Sid's next words came out like a stick of dynamite exploding. "New wife? Did the fool marry that Shayla Daniels woman?"

"Sorry to break the news to you. We found out less than five minutes ago."

"Should have known. Howard always was a sneaky little cuss. Now he's a sneaky grandfather with a wife younger than his children. I may have to die on the way back from the wedding so I won't have to take another meal with the idiots in this house."

The phone told Steve the caller disconnected. He slipped it back in his pocket. "This may be a cruise we'll never forget."

Heather asked, "How many more deaths are you predicting?"

"Not more than half a dozen. Let's go to your place and have pizza with Bella. I want to find out more about Adam Webber."

22

Heather spoke loud enough for her voice to carry to Steve in the back seat of her SUV. "I'm trying to save you from coronary heart disease. Yogurt and fruit are all you needed for breakfast. Once on board, you and Bella can go to the buffet and stuff yourselves."

Jack looked over at her as he pushed a button and started her Mercedes. "Isn't this supposed to be a nice, pleasant, working vacation? What's wrong with you this morning?"

Heather told him to wait a minute. She opened her door, stepped out, and walked around the car. Once back inside, she said, "Everyone, please forgive me. Especially you, Steve."

"No problem," he said.

Bella spoke up. "What just happened? Why did you get out and circle the car?"

"I needed to change my attitude and leave the old one in the driveway. It's a trick I learned when I was a cop. After dealing with a nasty subject, I'd make laps until I could act like I was supposed to. One night it took thirty minutes to get my emotions under control."

Jack reached over and took her hand. "I promise never to give you more than an hour's worth of aggravation."

Steve said, "Mark me down for thirty minutes. Let's start now. What's really going on with you?"

Heather's seat belt tightened as she took in a deep breath. "I'm aggravated that I'm not feeling better. I thought this head cold would be over by now. Father flew in a day early and I forgot he told me he wanted us to come to Galveston last night. He even booked rooms for us."

"I didn't know," said Steve and Jack at the same time.

"See? I'm so out of it, I forgot to tell either one of you," said Heather. "I took a double dose of medicine and spent the evening with fuzzy-brain syndrome."

"Colds make my brain foggy without medicine," said Bella.

Jack released her hand. "Do you know what forgetting things tells me about you?" He didn't wait for an answer. "You're human."

Bella said, "Put some Christmas music on and let's pretend we're already on board."

"I'll start the conga line," said Steve, who pretended to walk in place, stop, and kick.

The image caused Heather to shake off the slate-gray clouds and misty rain that darkened her day. Her mood brightened with every mile as Jack skillfully wove his way down I-45 through the heart of Houston and past Pasadena.

They all held their noses as they passed the oil refineries in Texas City. Once clear, Steve asked, "Did your father fly into Scholes Field yesterday, or Houston Hobby airport?"

Heather shook her head. "I didn't ask."

"I flew in to Galveston once for a fishing tournament," said Bella. "It's a nice long runway, and no commercial flights."

Heather answered Steve's question with more detail. "I assume he flew into Galveston. He said his plane will fly on to Cozumel and be at our disposal if we need it. If not, the pilot and copilot brought their spouses and they can have a Christmas vacation. I bummed-out my aircrew when I told them I didn't need them."

"We can blame Sid for that," said Steve. "He wants us all to be on alert for anything that might spoil Chad and Anna's wedding. He was adamant about us staying for the full cruise. Butch is the only real bodyguard going."

Jack asked, "Do you still think something might happen on the ship?"

Steve waited a few seconds before he said, "I'm certain something will happen, but I'm not sure what, and that's what has my mind tied in knots."

Bella leaned forward, directing her words to Heather, but plenty loud for all to hear. "If that creep of an ex-boyfriend of mine were on the ship, I guarantee there'd be a disturbance."

Jack glanced at Bella in the rearview mirror. "Old grudges can get too heavy to carry. I have a client that held on to a memory of something that happened his freshman year of high school. It festered for years until his kid was playing pee-wee football. The guy came unglued when a kid decked his son with an illegal blindside block the refs didn't see. They allege my client went ballistic and broke the nose of the head official."

"Did he do it?" asked Bella.

Jack chuckled. "It's the jury's job to decide guilt or innocence. But my client won't have to worry about a jury. I'll cut the best deal I can, and settle out of court. The moral of the story is: don't hold on to anger and old grudges, even if you were in the right. You never know how it will fester and come out later."

Bella nodded her head. "I'll take it under advisement, counselor."

By the time they climbed up and over the bridge that spanned the bay and inter-coastal canal, Heather noticed Steve had dropped out of the conversation. She knew him well enough to know when that happened, his mind had locked on something important, or at least potentially important. As they dropped onto Galveston Island, Steve had his phone in hand and instructed it to call Leo.

"Yeah, Steve," said Leo.

"We haven't dug deep enough yet. Get with Kirby and have him put Ayana to work going back all the way to birth on the major players. Start with the primary suspects, but don't limit her search to the two families. Include the staff and anyone else who's a regular in either house. If we're ever going to solve this case and get you back to work, we also need to look at everyone outside the family members who might have had a grudge against Lucy or anyone in the Green family."

"We've already done that," said Leo with a hint of hopelessness in his voice.

Steve didn't join Leo's pessimism. "After Ayana finishes with the two families, give her the entire list of people working for both families in any capacity. Look for a link between the past and what's happened in the last couple of months."

"What about attorneys and CPAs?" asked Leo.

"Everyone," said Steve. "Things changed when someone tried to kill Howard. I believe the key to Lucy's murder and the attempted murder of Howard lies in the past."

Leo chuckled, "You sound like a hound that caught a fresh scent."

"Keep me posted on your progress. We're supposed to have good internet connections on this ship. If Ayana doesn't come through on this, I can almost guarantee we'll deliver a body back to Galveston."

The tingle in Heather's nose started in Texas City but waited until the cruise terminal was in sight before it matured into a sneeze that blew a hole in her tissue. She mopped up the mess with two other tissues and moaned.

"Awesome," said Bella. "I thought I was the only person who sprayed the dashboard when they sneezed."

Heather turned to Jack. "If you can't find me later, look in the sauna."

"Don't take anymore head medicine," said Steve. "We need you to be able to think clearly. You and Jack need to monitor the

Greens. Sid arranged for you to sit at the same table with them in the main dining room."

"What about me?" asked Bella.

"You're going to be with Adam so you'll be our spy with the Webber family."

"What about you, Steve?"

Heather answered Bella's question. "He and my father will go snooping on their own. Father's more excited than you about being part of a murder investigation."

Jack pulled into the luggage drop off area. He and Bella unloaded the cargo in short order. Once back in the SUV, Jack pulled forward to where vehicles of all shapes and sizes discharged passengers. "I'll park and be back as soon as I can."

Heather led Steve inside the terminal while Bella's thumbs flew over the face of her phone. It didn't take long before it sounded with a reply to the message she sent. "Adam brought his sister, Chad, and his grandfather. They're already on board."

Steve replied, "Did he say anything about Ingrid or his parents?"

"Let me ask."

Once again, her thumbs tapped out a message. Less than a minute passed before Bella's phone chimed.

"He says there was a big fight this morning because Ingrid's car wouldn't start. She blamed it on his grandfather."

Another incoming text sounded and Bella put a hand over her mouth to muffle her chuckle. "It seems Adam's grandfather Karl found his backbone and told Ingrid she could swim to Cozumel."

A third notification chimed. Bella scanned it and gave her interpretation of the message. "Adam saved the day and called an Uber for his parents and Ingrid. They should arrive soon."

Heather looked away from Bella in time to see Sid Green rolling fast through the terminal with Butch jogging to keep up with him. He pulled to the side when he saw Steve, Heather, and Bella. "Good. You're here in plenty of time."

"Where's the rest of your crew?" asked Steve.

"I travel in a special mini-van that's modified with all the fancy gadgets. There's no room for passengers. None of them wanted to ride with Howard and his new wife." He paused. "Can't say that I blame them. Come to think of it, I can't blame Howard for not wanting to ride with Tim, Tammy, or Carol either. They'll show up if they can keep Carol sober."

All the while, Butch scanned the crowd for any sign of trouble. Heather asked, "No additional bodyguards on the voyage?"

Sid shifted in his chair as Butch answered, "They do a better job scanning and checking luggage here than at airports. Mainly because they don't want people bringing their own liquor on board, or anything that might start a fire. Me and your crew will be plenty to protect Sid. As for the family, Sid says they're on their own."

Sid motioned to Butch, who leaned over to hear him. He spoke in a volume that didn't carry far enough for a passerby to hear. "Don't forget about the will."

Sid nodded and Butch stood up straight. "Ms. McBlythe, I understand you and your fiancé are both excellent attorneys. Sid has few people he trusts these days and that includes his lawyer, Lewis Crankshaw. He wants you and Jack to draw up a new will before we leave port."

Heather looked at him. "I'm meeting my father and the ship's captain as soon as we get on board."

Bella said, "Jack's supposed to take Steve to the buffet."

"There's too many people there," said Butch. "And I need to get Sid to his room as soon as possible "

Steve rested both hands on top of his cane. "Jack and I could come with you and order room service. That would allow Heather and her father to meet the captain, have some time alone catching up, and Jack could write out the new will."

Heather felt a hand on her shoulder. She smiled as she turned. "Jack, this is Sid Green and Butch."

All three nodded a greeting as Jack asked, "Did I hear my name mentioned?"

Heather put an arm around his waist. "There's been a slight change of plans. Sid needs a new will written before we leave the harbor. If it's all right with you, I'll spend an hour or two with Father and the captain while you and Steve go to Sid's cabin."

Sid didn't give Jack a chance to respond. "The deal includes anything you want from room service, and I'll triple your hourly rate."

Jack rubbed his chin. "A nice steak sounds good, but I'm on vacation. That means you'll get the will without charge."

"It's a deal on the steak," said Sid. "And you earned yourself a producing oil well. If you don't want it, give to Heather as a wedding present."

Sid looked at Butch. "Get me on board before the rest of my crazy family gets here and I lose my good mood."

Bella added, "Chad, Anna, and Adam are already on board. I'll be with them."

Sid gave Bella a hair-to-shoes slow scan. "You must be the girl that pretended to be a maid for Ingrid Webber. Your name is Bella Brumley?"

Bella nodded.

"Adam's a fine young man. Stake your claim on him as soon as you can."

"I plan to."

Heather groaned, sneezed, and groaned again.

23

"What are we waiting on?" asked Steve. Heather responded with, "I hope everyone has all the documents they told us to bring."

"You sound like my mother," said Bella. "No matter how many countries I travel to, she always makes me show my passport, tickets, and everything else required before I leave home."

It didn't take as long as Steve thought to go through security, complete the process, and walk across a long gangway. "I'm surprised at the size of the terminal. We must have walked half a mile already."

Jack spoke from behind him. "Add another mile for me. The parking lot is massive."

"How big is the ship?" asked Steve.

"Pretty darn big," said Bella.

"Can you be a little more exact?"

Heather took over. "Fifteen stories tall, plus everything below the water line."

"How many passengers?"

"Almost four thousand if she's sold out, and a crew of over a thousand."

"How long?"

Bella put her hand on his shoulder. "It goes all the way from the bow to the stern."

Steve pulled Heather to a stop. "Is Bella performing tonight at the comedy show?"

They started walking again to the sound of Bella's laugh and Christmas carols drifting overhead. "I couldn't help it. It's what my dad told me when I asked him about a cruise ship that docked in St. Martin."

"A dad joke. I should have known."

"Watch your step," said Heather. "We are officially on board."

Bella gave Steve a quick kiss on the cheek. "Adam's waiting for me with Anna and Chad at the buffet. I'll catch up with you later, Heather."

"Don't wait too long. We lose cell service once we're several miles from shore. Remember to put your phone on airplane mode or you'll owe roaming charges."

Bella didn't respond.

"Ms. McBlythe?" The voice had an accent Steve couldn't identify. The man gave his name, which sounded like a mixed salad of consonants and vowels, heavy on the consonants. "I'm the senior security officer on board, and I have instructions to take you to the captain."

Heather slid her hand down Steve's arm. "You boys behave yourselves. I'll send you a text when Father and I are in his cabin."

Jack placed Steve's hand on his arm. "Are you ready to take a ride on the elevator?"

"I sure don't want to walk up to deck ten. I'll save that for when I need to walk off a steak."

Seasonal music changed from a stringed quartet to recordings coming from speakers in the elevator's ceiling. As they ascended, Jack described the view from the glass-enclosed elevator. The cruise line had apparently spared no expense in giving the ship a holly-jolly face lift.

"Here we are," said Jack. "I studied the deck plans and various rooms last night. They call Sid's room a junior suite, but it's bigger than it sounds. It's over-sized because it's wheelchair accessible. His room connects to a standard balcony cabin for Butch."

The elevator settled as the sound of doors opening overpowered the music. "Where are our cabins?" asked Steve.

"On this same floor. They're smaller interior cabins."

Jack took off at a good clip. Steve counted his steps before they came to a stop approximately seventy-five yards from the elevator. "This is a big ship."

"There's still plenty of rooms toward the bow. The elevator dropped us off near midship."

"Bella was right," said Steve. "The ship goes all the way from the bow to the stern."

"At least it isn't as far from starboard to port." Jack knocked on the door which cracked open enough for Butch to verify the visitors.

"Come in," said Sid in an unusually strong voice.

Butch stepped into the hallway. Steve heard the door click behind the bodyguard/medic. "Mr. Sid wants me to wait out here until you're finished. You'll find a copy of his current will on the desk. That's where he wants you to sit, Mr. Blackstock. Mr. Smiley, there's a couch for you. Call if Mr. Sid needs anything, and please, make your visit as short as possible. It's already been a full day for him and it's barely noon."

Steve whispered to Jack, "We'll need to wait to order that steak."

Jack kept his words at a low volume. "I'll make notes of the changes, take the current will, and Heather and I can knock out the new one before we leave port."

"That's acceptable," said Butch.

The door clicked open and Steve followed the sound of Jack's soft footsteps into the cabin. With minimal help from Jack, he located the couch with his cane.

"There's no time to dilly dally," said Sid. "Steve, have a seat. Jack, open the door to the balcony and let me smell something besides stale air conditioning. You don't realize how much you miss fresh air until you're cooped up inside all day for months."

As Steve settled on the couch and folded his collapsible cane, a loud click sounded and a door slid open on its tracks. The wheelchair moved toward the door and Sid took in a large breath. "That's more like it."

The motor of the electric wheelchair whirled as Sid came away from the door. "Jack, there's a copy of the current will, a fresh legal pad, and a pen on the desk. I'll tell you what I want in the new will."

"I'm ready when you are, sir."

"The first change has to do with my sleazy son, Howard. I've done some bad things in my life, but nothing compared to the embarrassment he caused the family at Lucy's funeral. It's bad enough watching him be a terrible father, a crooked businessman, and a cheating husband, but I draw the line with disrespecting the memory of someone wearing the Green family name. I'm cutting him out of the will altogether."

Jack cleared his throat. "That might not be a good idea. Sir."

"Why not?"

"It's my understanding Howard is currently in charge of making many of the everyday decisions for your company. Is that true?"

"What of it?"

"If you allow him to continue to run the company until you die, but you cut him out completely, he's likely to challenge the will. His lawyer will parade a team of psychiatrists into the courtroom who will testify your actions were not those of a rational man, given you placed him in charge of the company while you were alive. If you want to control his inheritance, I recommend you take steps now to get him out of the decision-making role as soon as possible. If you do that, we can talk about a modest inheritance for him."

Sid waited several long seconds as he moved his wheelchair forward and back. Steve realized this was the mobility-impaired version of pacing the floor.

"I see what you mean, and it makes sense," said Sid. "That weasel has siphoned the cream off the top of my companies for years, and I turned a blind eye. The first thing I need to do is tell Howard and his new wife they need to go somewhere on their honeymoon and stay gone for at least two weeks. I'll make it my wedding and Christmas presents to them. While they're gone, I'll have one of those forensic audits done on the company. Believe me, there'll be so much dirt on him whatever I do will be justified."

Jack cleared his throat. "You're on the right track, but throw him a bone of some sort to prove you aren't vindictive because of some sort of mental imbalance."

The advance and retreat of the wheelchair continued. Steve wondered if Jack might have overstepped, but then again, it sounded like shrewd legal advice.

On the third return to his original place, Sid came to a stop. "I've got it. I'll give all of them the same amount, even though they don't deserve a thin dime. That will show I'm not throwing them out in the cold, but giving them an opportunity to become self-reliant. It's high time they learned to pull their own weight. Does a million dollars each to Howard, Tim, and Carol sound like enough?"

Steve piped up. "If I was on a jury in a trial of this nature, and the petitioner complained about receiving a million dollars, I wouldn't have much sympathy."

The sound of Jack's pen scratching paper preceded him saying, "That's one million dollars to Howard, Tim, and Carol."

Steve asked, "What about Tammy, Tim's wife?"

"Give her a million for putting up with that idiot she married," said Sid.

More scratching on paper. "What's next?" asked Jack.

"The bulk of the estate, except for the house, is to be divided equally into thirds with one portion going to Chad Green. A second chunk goes to Karl Webber, and a third goes to Adam Webber."

Jack lowered his voice. "Are you sure? You want two-thirds of your oil wells, stocks, bonds, cash—everything you worked for all your life for to go to the Webbers?"

"It's called making amends. I cheated Peter Webber out of a good portion of his wealth. Howard almost ruined them when he followed my lead and swindled Karl out of almost all his wells. I'll sleep better knowing I'm doing what I can to make things right. Have the will read right after my burial. My chances of making it through the pearly gates aren't too good; I'd like to hedge my chances the best I can."

Sid paused. "By the way, I told Karl what I was doing. Only Butch, Karl, and you two know about it. You can tell Heather, too, but that's all."

Steve asked, "Why are you giving a third to Adam Webber?"

"He's good, like his sister Anna. There's not a dishonest bone in his body, and believe me, I tried my best to find it. He used to come over when he was a boy. I taught him the difference between investing and day trading. He said he liked day trading better because he could get in, make money, and get out before someone manipulated the price. He wanted nothing to do with the schemes I tempted him with."

"You mentioned your home," said Jack. "Who gets it and all the furnishings?"

Sid grinned. "I hear Ms. McBlythe is looking for real estate in River Oaks to fix up and sell. I'll give the house to her with a provision she gives half the profit to Mr. Smiley."

"That's not necessary to include me, Sid," said Steve.

"I know it isn't, but that's the way it's going to be," snapped Sid. "Those vultures living there now won't want to move, but they'll tear each other apart if they stay under the same roof. It's time for them to get out and see what the real world is like. I know neither you nor Heather need the money, but you're both people of integrity. You'll put it to good use."

Steve immediately thought of the meager college fund for Leo's children. "Thank you, Sid. I promise we'll do right by you."

"Any special bequests?" asked Jack.

"No. I've already settled with Butch. He has my collection of gold bars and coins. He took them out of the house one at a time in his backpack right under everyone's nose. He's like me, not a big fan of paying taxes. We make up our minds on what a fair amount to pay is, and then find ways to make it look legal."

Jack said, "I didn't hear that."

Sid chuckled. "I think that's all, unless you two can think of something else."

"Who do you want to name as executor of the will?" asked Jack.

"You'll do."

"I was afraid you'd say that."

Papers shuffled and Steve rose to his feet as Sid asked, "How close are you to finding Lucy's killer?"

Steve unfurled his cane. "If all goes to plan, we should know who killed Lucy by the time we return from the wedding."

"What about Howard? Are you any closer to finding who shot him?"

"I believe it's the same person."

24

Heather slid her arm around her father's as they left the bridge of the ship. "That didn't take long," she said as they made their way to the nearest elevator. "What do you want for lunch?"

"Nothing too heavy. I had a large breakfast at the hotel."

"I know just the thing," said Heather. "There's a Japanese restaurant on deck five. I'll send a text to Jack and tell him to meet us there if they're finished with Sid Green."

"Is your head cold any better?"

"It will be after I cauterize my sinuses with wasabi."

"I remember the first time I tried that green dynamite. Your mother and I flew to Tokyo the year after we married. No one warned me about its potential to set your nasal passages ablaze." He chuckled. "Your mother never let me forget it."

Heather squeezed his arm. "You're not alone in missing her."

He nodded. "I know, and things are getting better. Taking these cruises with you has given me something to look forward to, not to mention the excitement of looking for a killer this time. The captain took the news in stride, but I wasn't expecting such a powerful reaction from the head of security."

"It was right to tell them. They'll do what they can to keep the two families separate, which shouldn't be difficult considering the Greens' cabins are near the top of the ship while the Webbers' booked in cabins on deck three."

They walked down a long hallway with cabin doors on each side. Heather stopped at the elevator, took out her phone and tapped in a text.

Meet us on deck 5 at the Japanese restaurant.

Jack's reply came in as the doors closed. She pushed the button for deck five.

On our way. Work to do this afternoon.

Shops and restaurants lined both sides of a wide walkway as Heather and her father made their way to the restaurant that boasted a wide variety of made-to-order sushi and sashimi, as well as stir-fry dishes. Jack and Steve arrived several minutes later and she received Jack's standard greeting of a quick kiss. She looked at Steve who stood with lips pushed tightly together.

Heather placed a hand on his forearm. "What's wrong with you?"

"Nothing. It's too noisy out on the walkway for my taste. Hundreds of people and loud Christmas music."

"People are excited. They're checking out the ship."

"If you can, find us a seat as far away from the crowd as possible." Heather led him to a back corner of the room and placed him facing the wall.

"Much better," said Steve. "Everything was echoing."

Jack gave an explanation. "It's quiet in here because you have to pay a la carte. Many of the people on board are working class and on a budget. The first thing they do when they get on board is drink the complementary drink of the day and head straight for the buffet. I'm sure they saved a long time to take this Christmas cruise and want to get their money's worth."

"Is this the same ship you took earlier in the year?"

"The same cruise line, but a different ship. The restaurants are the same."

Heather snapped her fingers. "I know what's bothering Steve. He wanted a steak for lunch, not rolled up rice with tiny chunks of vegetables and meat." She patted his hand. "Don't worry, you'll have four days to eat whatever you want."

"Get me whatever you're having," said Steve with a touch of resignation in his voice.

After they settled, Jack turned to her. "You and I will be busy for the next few hours. Sid wants a new will with major changes, and he wants me to be the executor."

"Do we have time to get it finished and signed before we leave port?"

Jack winked. "If we don't get distracted."

Heather's father chuckled, but said nothing. He didn't need to. His grin spoke volumes.

"When you say major changes, how major are you talking about?"

Steve answered this time. "Sid better not come back from the dead. His family will likely kill him again."

A low whistle came from Heather, as she scanned the room and stiffened. "Karl Webber just walked in and is at a table by the walkway."

Steve didn't hesitate. "Is he alone?"

"There's no one else at his table. I almost didn't recognize him. The only time I've seen him was when we went to the Webber house and Ingrid told us to leave."

"What does he look like?"

"Fit and trim for a man in his seventies. A full head of gray hair, leathery skin, but spry." Heather waited a few seconds and added, "He seems to enjoy watching people pass by."

"Ask him to join us. Let's see if he knows if the rest of his people are on board."

Heather walked to his table and cleared her throat to catch

his attention. "Excuse me, Mr. Webber, you probably don't recognize me."

Ice-blue eyes inspected her. "You and a blind man came to the house the day after Lucy Green died."

"You're very good at remembering faces. My name is Heather McBlythe. I'm here with my fiancé, my father, and my business partner."

He turned in the direction she held out her hand.

"I remember the man wearing sunglasses. I asked Ingrid who you were, but she told me to mind my own business."

"Steve Smiley and I own a private detective firm. Your wife requested an appointment with us, but we couldn't come to agreement on the terms." Heather smiled. "We noticed you're alone. Would you like to join us?"

"Why not? All I'm doing is watching pretty girls walk by." He paused. "By the way, you more than qualify."

His response caused her to take a small step back. "Thank you." Heather quickly added, "Shall we join the others?"

Karl rose from his chair. "Lead the way."

Heather passed out introductions then she and Karl took their seats. He was the first to speak. "Before things get too awkward, I'll tell you what you and Mr. Smiley want to know. I didn't kill Lucy, shoot Howard, or know who did."

"Thanks for being so direct," said Steve. "Do you mind if Heather and I are also direct?"

"Go ahead."

"What about your wife? Do you think Ingrid could have hired someone to commit either of the crimes?"

Karl let out a long breath, which bought him time enough to either plan a good lie or give a genuine answer. "There's no doubt Ingrid is mean enough to do it, but she didn't."

"Are you sure?" asked Heather.

On this response, he didn't hesitate. "If Ingrid was to kill someone, she'd have a real good reason, would do it herself, and she'd enjoy watching them die. Lucy did nothing to our family other than marry Howard. As for shooting that worthless piece of humanity named Howard Green, Ingrid couldn't have." He paused. "Ingrid has cataracts and refuses to have the surgery she needs. I'm not sure she could hit an elephant at fifty yards."

A worker behind the counter hollered out Jack's name, saying their order was ready for pick up. Jack responded with a quick, "I'll be right back."

"As for the rest of my family," said Karl without being asked. "There's my son, Kurt, and his wife. They're overeducated underachievers. All that hogwash they swallowed in college and graduate school made them allergic to work. They think money is evil, but they have no problem spending it. There used to be plenty until Sid and Howard swindled it away from us."

"You sound bitter," said Steve.

"I am, but I'm getting over it."

"Oh?"

"Bitterness has a way of sucking the life out of you." He shook his head. "I've carried it a long time; ever since a slick guy talked his way into our home and convinced me he was a telephone repairman. That was back in the days before people worried about computer security. I had a meeting downtown and left him there to install a separate phone line, dedicated to the computer. He stole all my log ins and passwords, which were then relayed on to Howard, giving him access to everything. That included bank accounts, stocks, oil wells, taxes, you name it. He took his time, but eventually used every trick in the book to steal almost everything."

"What about your home?"

"That's still in my name."

"Didn't you report it to the police?" asked Heather.

"Of course I did, but not until it was too late. That was in the early days of computers and not many people used them. I was what they call an early adopter. The police hadn't caught up with the technology and all my money was taken out of my accounts, or frozen in the few banks they didn't get to. They converted everything to cash and moved it offshore. What they didn't get in the first haul, they had access to because all my records were on the computer. Knowledge is power. Howard got by with it until I finally changed all the sign-ins and passwords. By that time, I couldn't afford to hire the attorneys needed to go after him."

"Are you sure Howard Green did that to you?"

Karl's blue eyes were the color of a glacier, and just as cold. "I know he did, but I couldn't prove it. It was that private investigator buddy of his who pretended to be the telephone line installer. Besides, who else would want all the wells I had, even the poor producing ones? Look at the Greens' portfolio of oil and gas. Half the leases used to be Webber wells."

Karl glanced out to where throngs of people walked by. He didn't seem to see them and said, "I've been around a long time. Things have a way of changing when you least expect them to."

"Speaking of change," said Steve. "I'm not really in the mood for rolled-up sticky rice with pieces of bait in it. Karl, how would you like to help a blind guy find a steak you can cut with a fork? My treat."

"I can watch people in a nice restaurant as good as I can sitting here."

"Perfect." Steve rose. "After we eat, you can either give me a tour of the ship or lead me to my cabin where I'll take a nap."

Karl smiled a toothy grin. "I say we tour the ship. I'll describe all the pretty women."

"That will take you all afternoon," said Heather.

"Only until four," countered Steve. "That's when the sail-away party starts on the pool deck. I plan to lead the conga line."

"I'll be right behind him," said Karl. "Someone needs to make sure he doesn't fall in the pool or go overboard."

"By the way," said Steve. "That maid Ingrid fired this week named Bella? We had her in your home snooping. She's with your grandson, Adam, along with the bride and groom."

"Another private investigator? I knew she was too good to be true. I hope you're not going to tell me she's going to break Adam's heart."

It was Heather's turn to take over. "She's not a private investigator, and if we have our way, she never will be. Search Bella Brumley online. She's been a popular sports celebrity the last few years. I'd say there's a better chance Adam will break her heart than her breaking his."

"I doubt that. She reeled him in before he knew he'd been hooked."

Karl's gaze shifted from Heather, to Jack, and back. "Anything else before we leave for parts unknown?"

Steve asked, "Do you know if Ingrid, Kurt and Monica are on board yet?"

"Don't know and don't care about Ingrid. Let me send a text to Kurt."

It wasn't but a few seconds before the response came and Karl read it out loud. *In terminal. Mother on warpath. Hide.*

25

"This is more like it," said Steve as he settled into a chair that seemed to wrap around him like a warm hug. A piano softly played a torch song in the distance and the aroma of flame-kissed meat played hit and run with his nose.

"It reminds me of the places I used to go for lunch," said Karl. "Today, instead of looking out over Houston, there's a bank of windows overlooking the ship channel. It's quite a view and brings back a lot of memories. Have you ever noticed that people with big money like to go up high? My life of wealth and privilege was gone before I knew what hit me, and now I work in the dirt."

Steve hoped this wouldn't turn into a pity party. Karl soon showed it wouldn't. When the server came around for drink orders, Karl ordered iced tea instead of calling for a top-shelf whiskey or a mixed drink.

"You're not a drinking man?" asked Steve.

"When I lost the money and wells, I quit pretending I liked the way scotch tasted and how it made me feel." He kept talking before Steve could respond. "I mentioned working in the dirt. A broken man can find peace working with his hands tilling the soil, mowing grass, and trimming hedges. I used to keep the fountains in good shape, but money doesn't stretch as far as it used to and I'm slowing down now that I'm in my seventies."

The tone and volume of Karl's voice changed, "Of all the places and people."

"What is it?" asked Steve.

Karl all but spit out the name like a foul taste. "Howard Green. He's with his new wife and the guy I told you about earlier. Until now, I've only seen his wife from a distance. She could be his daughter."

Steve had a good mental image of Howard and his new wife, Shayla, but who was the guy they were talking about earlier? Steve leaned over the table and whispered. "Do you know the name of the guy that's with Howard?"

"Henry Drake. He's the one who pretended to be a telephone repairman. He wore a fake mustache, mutton-chop sideburns, long sandy-colored hair with a phone company baseball cap. I didn't recognize him the day he came to the house, which made my charge against him sound weak to the police. All it took was Howard giving him an alibi and he was in the clear."

Steve kept speaking in a low volume with elbows on the table. "What can you tell me about Howard working with Henry Drake?"

"I heard they met through Lucy. If I remember right, Drake was a childhood friend. Howard has used Drake for years to provide information."

"Are they seated yet?" asked Steve.

"Yeah. All the tables next to the windows are full, but they're at a table for four about fifteen yards away."

Steve stood. "Point me in their direction and tell me if there are other tables that I might run into."

"Do you want me to take you to them?"

"That would be helpful."

"I'll drop you off on my way to the restroom."

"Gentlemen," said a male voice with a foreign accent. "My name is Miko, your server. I hope you're not leaving."

Steve waved his hand. "We're here for thick steaks, but there're some people I know and need to say hello to. We'll be ready to order in a few minutes."

"Excellent, sir."

The carpet muffled the server's footsteps as Steve held out his left hand for Karl to place on his upper arm. After only a handful of steps, Karl came to a halt and said, "Don't worry, Howard. I'm not here to cause a scene. Steve wanted to talk to you while I go to the restroom."

The voice of Howard Green dripped in sarcasm. "I'm surprised Ingrid allowed you out of the flowerbed. I guess you saved your allowance so you could afford to come to this joke of a wedding."

"Honey," said the voice of a woman Steve thought to be Shayla Daniels-Green, Howard's new wife. "You promised you'd be nice to the Webbers."

"You haven't changed a bit," said Karl. "You're still a sore winner. By the way, how's the arm? I hope it won't interfere with your honeymoon."

Shayla ignored his sarcasm and said, "We're making the best of the situation. Thank you for your concern."

"Concern?" snapped Howard. "The only concern he has is being arrested for shooting me. Better luck next time, Karl."

Karl came back with, "You need to be careful making false accusations. I hear you're lying low these days as the police tighten the noose around your neck for killing Lucy."

A chair scooted against the carpet. The voice belonged to Henry Drake. "Mr. Webber, you'd better move along before Mr. Green has you thrown off the ship."

Steve held up a hand. "So far I've heard three threats and we all know they're bluffs." Steve turned to face Karl. "Stop by on your way back to our table and I'll hitch a ride. I'd like to offer my congratulations to the newlyweds."

The piano player moved from a torch song to something

more upbeat. A small hand took Steve's. "I'm Shayla. There's a fourth chair at our table. Let me help get you seated."

"Thanks, Shayla, and again, congratulations on your recent marriage. Karl wasn't very tactful in teasing Howard about the honeymoon. The delay will only make it better when you get to go on one."

"Thank you, but if I had it to do it all over again, I'd wait to get married. I didn't know our marriage would be so upsetting to the family. Howard can be rather impulsive, and he's certainly persuasive. "

Howard spoke in a grumble. "This is none of Mr. Smiley's business."

"Howard's right," said Steve. "I didn't come over here to cause trouble, only to wish you well and tell you Sid is in his room and resting comfortably."

"Is Butch with him?"

"In the adjoining room."

"Where's your partner?" asked Howard.

"Eating sushi with her father and fiancé. She'll introduce you to them sometime on the cruise, or at Anna and Chad's wedding."

Howard grumbled again, then asked, "Shayla, is it time for another pain pill? This arm is killing me."

"Not yet, honey. And remember, no wine or alcohol of any type."

"How am I supposed to eat a steak without wine? It's sacrilege."

The sound of Shayla's chair scooting across the carpet caused Steve to listen intently. "If you'll excuse me," she said, "I need to powder my nose."

After a few moments of silence Henry Drake whispered to his boss, "If you can sneak next door after lunch, I brought two bottles of the good stuff. You can chase the steak with Château Mouton Rothschild, Pauillac 2000."

"What's the other one you brought?"

"A Krug Clos d'Ambonnay 1995."

"Save the d'Ambonnay for after the wedding. I'll not drink the swill they call champagne at the reception. Sneak the bottle off the ship and have the hotel staff chill it for Shayla and me. I'll lay off the pain pills that day so I can have a decent glass of bubbly."

"What about the Château Mouton?"

"Save it for the cruise home. I'll have it with another steak."

Steve made sure he faced Henry Drake. "I'm a little surprised you're on the cruise, Drake. But then again, you've known Howard for quite a while."

"He's worked for me more years than I can count," said Howard. "Sid has Butch to watch over him and since someone shot me, I figured Drake needed to earn his retainer."

"You're here as Howard's bodyguard?" asked Steve.

"More like another pair of eyes and ears," said Drake. "He has more important things to do than worry about what he's eating or drinking, or who might come up on his blind side. I'm not as young and tough as I once was, but I'm like you, Smiley. I figure things out."

Steve thought about Drake's response. The PI was like Steve in some ways, but not all. He seemed to have some holes in his conscience. Confronting him now would serve no useful purpose. Or would it? Only one way to find out.

"Tell me, Drake, do your duties include tasting Howard's food and drinks? Are you willing to sacrifice your life for your king and new queen?"

Howard laughed, but Drake's voice took on a hard edge. "I heard you like to push people's buttons to see how they'll react. It won't work on me, Smiley. I learned that trick a long time ago. Let me show you how I do it. Do you still have trouble sleeping at night because you didn't protect your wife?"

Steve came back with a somber, "Yes. I think of her often and regret I wasn't more aware of the people coming up behind us. What about you? Do you wish you would have protected Lucy?"

Drake snapped back. "Howard didn't ask me to protect her."

Howard spoke next, "I don't like where this is going. I can't tell Smiley what to do, but you work for me. Shayla's having a hard enough time relaxing on this ship knowing my family hates me and the Webbers want me dead. When she comes back, there better not be another harsh word out of you. Understand?"

"Yeah," said Drake. "No more sparring with the blind guy."

Dishes rattled as a server cleared a table behind Steve, probably one next to a window. Steve faced Howard. "I hope you're making more progress than we are."

"What do you mean by that?" asked Howard.

"Isn't Drake looking into who shot you?"

"He is, but the cops aren't cooperating. It seems Detective Vega is directing the show from off stage. Detective Kirby and that woman from South Africa seem to be in over their heads. Are you making inquiries?"

Steve shook his head. "We're working for Sid and his interest is on who killed Lucy."

"Are you any closer to naming the killer?" asked Drake.

"I'm having a hard time coming up with a motive," said Steve. It was true, but purposefully incomplete. He knew Drake wouldn't give him information on a silver platter.

Sometimes it's more effective to answer a question with one of your own, so that's what Steve did. "You must have known Lucy pretty well, Drake. Who had motive enough to kill her?"

The response seemed to catch somewhere in the top of Drake's throat. His reply came out as a low whisper. "I don't know, but whoever hurt her needs to die."

Karl and Shayla announced their arrival back at the table with her projecting a full laugh in response to Karl making the sound of a squirrel barking. "My daughter-in-law's worthless toy dog, Poopsey, ended up in doggy therapy after those three squirrels ganged up on her and stole the ribbons out of her fur."

Steve rose. "Thanks for allowing me to join you."

"Before you leave," said Howard. "Why are you and Ms. McBlythe on this cruise? I know it's not to keep an eye on Sid. That's what Butch is for."

"Several reasons. First, Sid invited us to come along. He's convinced someone else will die. Heather's father is interested in buying stock in a cruise line and he's testing out various cruise companies to see if one might be a prudent investment. He's also getting over the loss of his wife. As for Heather, she gets to spend time with her fiancé and her father, plus get out of the office."

"What about you, Smiley? You don't seem like you're much into the whole cruise vibe."

"This is the first time for me. Who knows, I might enjoy cruising so much I do it regularly when I'm between solving murders."

Drake asked, "Do you plan on gathering us all in a room and naming the killer Agatha Christie style?"

"Of course not," said Steve. "I'll name who killed Lucy, who shot Howard, and who the other man on the grassy knoll was who shot President Kennedy at the same meeting. Also, I want to try singing karaoke."

Everyone laughed, which was a good way to leave them. Once settled at their table, Karl asked, "I know you were kidding about who shot President Kennedy, but what about the other two crimes? Are you getting closer?"

"Closer, but not close enough."

Miko arrived at the table and asked if they were ready to order. "Steaks," said Steve. "The best you have."

26

Heather's cross trainers slapped the moving belt of the treadmill as she watched the sun peek its golden head over the horizon. The bank of windows in the ship's exercise room gave her a lofty view of seemingly endless calm seas in the Gulf of Mexico. She mopped her brow with a towel and looked down at her progress on the digital display. Mile two was almost complete. Beside her, Jack kept a steady pace on an identical treadmill. He preferred to listen to an endless stream of upbeat music as he ran, while she did some of her best thinking in the quiet of the otherwise mindless activity. She couldn't imagine a better way to spend the early hours of the morning on this full day at sea. Tomorrow they'd dock in Cozumel, a tropical paradise island off Mexico's Yucatan Peninsula.

She glanced to her left, where Steve walked at a good clip on his treadmill. "How are you holding up?" she asked.

His words came between breaths. "I can't believe... you talked me... into doing this... every morning."

"Most people gain a pound a day when cruising. This way you can reward yourself with full meals and not have regrets when we get back home."

"How much longer... before I'm finished?"

She glanced over at the display on his machine. "Three more minutes then we'll go to our rooms, shower, and go to the main dining room. Eggs Benedict sounds good to me."

"I thought you'd order... room service."

"Bella told me Ingrid Webber plans to eat a proper sit-down breakfast at eight o'clock every day. I thought we might try to have a chat with her this morning."

"Will Bella... be there?"

"Not a chance. She and Adam were out dancing until the wee hours of the morning. They plan on having brunch together at ten thirty."

"What about... your father?"

"He's having a light breakfast in his cabin. If he follows his normal pattern, he's been up for two hours checking the foreign markets. He'll make phone calls until noon. We'll meet him for lunch at a specialty seafood restaurant."

"Where's the off button... on this thing?" asked Steve. "Between the treadmill... and you making me walk... up and down stairs instead of taking the elevator, I'll be skinny as a toothpick... by the time we get home."

Heather turned off her machine and did the same for Steve. Jack took notice, followed suit, and took out his earbuds. "The sunrise was spectacular. I could get used to this."

An hour and five minutes later, the three walked into the main dining room. Heather nodded to the maître d' and gave her name.

"Yes, Ms. McBlythe, the captain spoke to me about your request to be seated with Frau Webber. I'll take you to her table."

"That's unnecessary. I prefer our encounter appear random. Point out her table and I'll make sure the captain knows how helpful you are."

"Of course. She's on the starboard side of the dining room, bottom floor." He pointed with an outstretched hand. "It's difficult to see from this angle because the support pillar is blocking her. You'll see her after you've made it halfway to the staircase leading to the second floor."

Heather's words of thanks earned a bow. She led Steve on a circuitous path through the tables until she spotted Ingrid, facing a window. Her unblinking gaze focused on the horizon. She held a coffee cup, but wasn't drinking.

Heather cleared her throat once she arrived at an appropriate distance to begin a conversation. *"Guten morgen, Frau Webber."*

Ingrid came back from wherever her mind had taken her. "Oh, it's you. I see you didn't come alone."

Heather ignored the caustic tone and jumped in with introductions. "I'm sure you remember Mr. Smiley. This handsome gentleman is my fiancé, Jack Blackstock."

The most gracious response Ingrid could muster was a nod of her head. Then, she launched an accusatory question. "Have you come to gloat about inserting that detestable creature into my home to spy on me?"

Heather knew better than to shy away from a bully. "Do you mean the successful and beautiful young woman named Bella Brumley?"

"I don't know how you measure success, Ms. McBlythe, but failing at domestic work isn't my idea of it."

"Perhaps that's because Bella is a television personality, model, and a businesswoman who's in line to inherit a high-end hotel in the U.S. Virgin Islands. Besides, she succeeded in getting into your home."

Heather kept talking. "We're not here to cause you distress, but to give you some information you might find interesting. Do you mind if we have breakfast with you?"

The three didn't wait for a response. Jack positioned Steve as Heather continued the rather one-sided conversation. After all, the worst that could happen would be Ingrid telling them to leave, or leaving herself.

"Since you're already here, you may as well join me."

Even though the tone didn't match the welcoming words,

Heather counted the invitation as a minor victory in breaking down Ingrid.

Steve asked, "Have you ordered yet?"

"Not yet. I always have two cups of coffee before breakfast."

"Me, too," said Steve. "At least two cups and sometimes three, if I had a sleepless night."

"If you suffer from insomnia," said Ingrid, "I can suggest a doctor I know. Her pills are magic. I believe she's the same doctor who treated Lucy Green."

Heather wondered if Ingrid had inadvertently revealed her source of poison for Lucy. She opened her mouth to ask for clarification, but retreated when Steve said, "I hope you're not referring to the 'sleep of death' that Shakespeare spoke of in Hamlet."

A malevolent grin parted Ingrid's lips.

With a change of subject, Steve said, "Your husband and I shared a wonderful meal yesterday, and we even ran into your neighbor, Howard Green, and his new wife."

"Mr. Smiley, it's obvious you've mistaken me for someone who cares about what you and my husband did yesterday. Furthermore, I'm not interested in what either of you are doing tomorrow, or any other day in the future. As for Howard Green, I care even less about him and try my best to ignore him."

Steve tilted his head in a way that brought to mind a confused puppy. "I can understand you not caring about me, but I thought you might be interested in what I learned from speaking with Howard and his private investigator, Henry Drake."

The muscles in Ingrid's jaw flexed as she ground her molars. "What makes you think that either Howard Green or Henry Drake would have anything to say that might interest me?"

Steve scratched his head. "You're probably right. It was only idle chatter, but it did concern how Howard knows what goes on in your home."

"That's impossible. My grandson, Adam, is a genius with computers. He's taken steps to make sure we're not monitored."

"That's good to hear, but there may be something you haven't considered."

"And what would that be?"

The server chose that moment to arrive at the table to take drink orders. Ingrid sat with lips pursed together until she could get back to her home leaking information. "Continue, Mr. Smiley."

"Continue what?"

Playing dumb was a ploy Steve sometimes used on suspects to tease them into showing how much they wanted information from him. Ingrid's huff of exasperation and the words that followed confirmed she wanted all the facts and speculation she could accumulate against the Greens, especially Howard.

"Your sight is impaired, Mr. Smiley, but there's nothing wrong with your brain. I'll not allow you to tell me my home is the victim of unwanted intrusions and then not elaborate. I insist you tell me how you believe I'm being spied upon by Howard Green."

The server returned with coffee for three and took breakfast orders. Once he was out of earshot, Steve leaned forward. "This much I know for sure, Bella Brumley isn't the source of information leaking from your home to Howard."

"Then who is it?"

Steve leaned back. "Bella never found out, and because you summarily dismissed Heather and me, we couldn't do a full investigation of your home. If allowed to question you, family members, and the staff, I'm sure we could have ferreted out who's passing along information to Henry Drake, who then gives it to Howard Green."

Heather broke in, "I can understand why you didn't cooperate with us, but we know you've been less than cooperative with the police also. We have a good working relationship with them, and from what we've heard, your memory fades every time they try to question you. That type of behavior only makes them suspicious of you."

Ingrid stiffened. "It's absurd to think either me or my family had anything to do with Lucy's death."

"Perhaps," said Steve. "But what about someone shooting Howard?"

"More wild speculation."

It was Jack's turn. "As a defense attorney, I'd say that keeping silent is usually the wisest thing a suspect can do. However, there comes a time in the investigation when a strong, truthful alibi can save people a lot of grief."

"The police call it eliminating suspects," said Steve.

Ingrid dismissed the talk of cooperation with a wave of her hand. "I subscribe to the belief that if I did nothing, then I don't worry or waste my time. Let's get back to something that does concern me. If I'm reading between the lines correctly, Mr. Smiley, you are suggesting there's a spy in my house who feeds information about our family to Howard Green through his lackey."

Steve nodded.

"Again, Mr. Smiley, who is this person?"

Steve raised his shoulders and let them fall. "You're a smart woman, Mrs. Webber. There're only so many people living or working in your home. Go through the list. I'm sure you'll find the culprit, or culprits."

"It would be easier if you'd tell me."

Steve smiled. "I could, but you wouldn't believe me."

Heather moved on with a complete change in the conversation. "I don't know about the rest of you, but I'm looking forward to a massage, spending time in the sauna, having a pleasant lunch with my father, and lounging with Jack by the pool this afternoon. What about you, Ingrid? What are your plans for the day?"

"I haven't thought of anything but how much I'm dreading the rehearsal dinner tonight. Such a waste of money. I still can't believe Anna is so foolish as to marry a Green. I hope she doesn't take his last name. The marriage is bound to fail."

"That's odd," said Steve. "If there's one thing that Sid Green and your husband agree on, it's that Anna and Chad are a perfect match."

"Ridiculous," said Ingrid. "I say it will end in failure."

There was something about the certainty of Ingrid's last statement that sounded a warning in Heather. This bitter woman was a schemer. She'd brow beat her husband into being a gardener when he'd once been an oil executive. She was a manipulator who demanded her way and would take action to see it through, no matter who she hurt along the way. Something had to be done to make sure she didn't ruin the rehearsal dinner and the wedding.

The server arrived with a tiny elongated shot glass of clear liquid and placed it in front of Ingrid. She raised the glass to her lips and threw back the drink in a single gulp. With her head held high she turned the glass over and placed it on the plate on which it was served.

Heather and Jack stared as she completed the strange ritual. They didn't have long to wait for the explanation.

"It's a custom in my family to begin and end the day with a shot of peppermint schnapps. I've never been sick a day of my life and I attribute it to the medicinal power of schnapps."

"I can smell the peppermint from here," said Steve. He added, "Heather, why don't you try it on your head cold."

Heather shuddered. "No, thanks. I'm almost over it and the sauna will complete the job."

27

Heather slid into a cobalt-blue evening gown her personal assistant had chosen for her to wear at Anna and Chad's rehearsal dinner. The black-tie affair would be the only time on this short cruise she planned to subject her feet to high heels. But just in case Jack had a special surprise planned, she brought a second gown and stiletto heels.

The knock on her door was Jack's, a syncopated rhythm of taps used only by the two of them. She took a last look in the mirror and nodded her approval. The dress accentuated her trim figure, and the ship's beautician earned a sizable tip by giving her hair an elegant updo. The cut of the dress was deep enough to suggest the curves it concealed, while a silk shawl covered her bare shoulders, giving a conservative balance to the overall look. A platinum necklace with a single sapphire, the size of a robin's egg, with matching earrings, completed the look she hoped to achieve. She spoke to herself, "Sophisticated, yet not overdone. After all, the bride should be the center of attention." She picked up her bag and went to the door.

"You're right on time," said Heather as she opened the door to two of the three most important men in her life.

Jack didn't disappoint when he stood with mouth hinged open and offered a one-word comment, "Wow!"

"You smell good," said Steve. "Let's go before Ingrid throws a wrench in the gears."

The threesome stepped into the elevator and rode it down until a mechanical voice announced they'd reached the lower floor of the main dining room. Steve asked, "Will the dinner be where we had breakfast with Ingrid?"

"Not exactly," said Heather. "There's a staircase that leads up to a balcony. There's also a private room on that level. We're to be treated to a five-course meal, each paired with an appropriate wine."

"Sounds fancy," said Steve. "A word to the wise: go easy on the liquor before the meal begins. I spoke with Adam Webber and his grandfather, Karl, about our problem with Ingrid wanting to derail the dinner. They're going to offer a series of toasts to start the festivities. Karl told me Ingrid only drinks peppermint schnapps. With any luck, she'll be mellow by the time the meal starts."

Heather wanted more information about the plan Steve put in place, but their arrival at the main dining room prevented her from asking. With a snap of his finger, the maître d' summoned a waiter, who gave a stiff bow and led them through the dining room, up an elegant stairway and into a private room. Glasses shimmered, plates sparkled, and the silverware shone bright against snow-white tablecloths.

Heather turned to Steve. "We're the first ones here. Each place setting has an embossed name card identifying who is to sit where. Here's your seat. We're going to do reconnaissance and see where everyone's sitting."

She and Jack made a lap around the table capable of seating twenty and reported back to Steve. "As expected, the bride and groom are in the place of honor at the head of the table. Sid put himself next to the groom with Butch next to him instead of the groom's parents."

"That sounds like something Sid would do," said Steve. "Who's next?"

"Tim and Tammy Green, the groom's parents, with Carol Green next."

Heather looked toward the middle of the table. "Next is Shayla and then Howard."

"Not Howard and then Shayla?" asked Steve. "That puts Shayla and Carol sitting next to each other. Sid must have done it to see how tough Shayla is."

"Finally," said Heather. "Henry Drake is to sit next to Howard."

"That's eight on the groom's side. How many on the bride's?"

"Let me check again." She walked around the end of the table and began talking as she walked. "We're going in reverse order. You're at the very end, then me and Jack."

Heather kept walking. "Then there's Bella and Adam."

"And next to Adam?" asked Steve.

"Ingrid."

"Ah," said Steve. "That doesn't bode well. Karl told me he rearranged the seating to show Ingrid he's still the head of the family. So, I'm supposing Karl is next to the bride."

"Yes."

Steve rubbed his chin. "That means Anna's parents, Kurt and Monica, are between Karl and Ingrid. Karl and Sid are sitting across from each other?"

"Yes, they are." Heather walked back to where Steve sat. "Judging by the number of forks and spoons, this meal is going to be a long, drawn-out affair. I'll make sure you don't get confused." She paused. "Why did you warn us earlier about the toasts and drinking?"

Multiple people in the wedding party came into the room, which caught Steve's attention. "You'll find out soon enough. If you and Jack don't want a tremendous hangover tomorrow morning, take small sips during the toasts."

Sid and Butch were the last to arrive. The wheelchair rolled into place and Sid cast a slow, lingering gaze at the men dressed in tuxedos and the women whose gowns twinkled in the soft light. He nodded his approval to Butch, who acted as master of ceremonies.

"If everyone would take their seat. Sid and Karl had a friendly talk this afternoon and decided the best way to start the evening's celebration was to toast the happy couple. The drink of choice for the family members will be served. For the rest of the guests, the staff will take your orders. This is to be a celebration of the marriage of two exceptional young people."

Servers returned with rolling trays topped with cocktails in a variety of glasses, serving each side of the table. The bride and groom sipped champagne while Howard had an amber liquid in a highball glass with ice. Ingrid looked at, but didn't touch, the slim glass placed before her.

Adam rose to his feet. "To begin, I'd like to offer a toast to the bride and groom. May they have a long and happy marriage." To show the way he expected the toast to be followed, he drained a glass that looked like sparkling wine.

Howard followed suit, as did everyone on the groom's side of the table, except Sid and Butch. Ingrid took in the scene and hesitated with lifting her glass until she saw Sid and Butch challenging her with crooked smiles. In response she took her nightly dose of medicine in a single swallow and repeated the show of turning her glass upside down with a flourish.

Servers appeared with seconds for everyone. Heather noted Steve returned an almost full glass of an amber liquid to the server.

Carol stood next. "I'm not about to let a Webber out-toast the Green family. Here's to the happy couple. May they live long and prosper." It took her several swallows, but she downed the tall, slender glass of clear liquid. This time it was Carol who challenged Ingrid with a haughty stare and fake smile.

Ingrid downed the schnapps in a single swallow and the empty glass rested upside down on a plate. The ritual kept going through four more rounds. With each round the toasts got longer. Well-wishers of note were Howard Green and his daughter, Carol, whose words now had a distinctive slur. On the bride's side of the table, Karl and Ingrid evened the score. One other person caught Heather's eye. Henry Drake, who should have been acting as Howard's body guard, downed six whiskey sours in the thirty-minute binge of toasts.

After Ingrid slurred her way through another toast in German, Sid thanked her and everyone who had wished the couple well. He then nodded to the head waiter, who signaled the serving of the first course, along with its wine pairing.

Steve leaned into Heather. "I called Karl while you were getting your hair done today. He told me that after three drinks Ingrid is prone to start singing."

"That explains the loud humming," said Heather. "I wonder what happens after four?"

"Karl said she used to get frisky, if you know what I mean, but that was thirty years ago."

Heather covered her mouth to hide a smile.

"With five, she reverts to only speaking German, and after six shots, there better be a bed or a couch close by because she's going down for the count."

When Heather glanced down the table, she saw Ingrid slump in her chair, her chin resting on her chest. "It looks like she's hit her limit. She's all but asleep in her chair."

Adam and Bella were on their feet. Each took an arm and lifted the German grandmother to her feet. "Come on, Grandmother," said Adam, "Let's get you to your cabin."

The lead waiter motioned to a stout server. "Escort Mrs. Webber to her cabin and have someone from the infirmary check on Madame."

The only people who looked concerned were the bride and groom. Heather turned to Steve. "This looks like one of your schemes."

"It worked, didn't it?"

Across from Steve, Henry Drake laughed out loud. "Well done, Smiley. You got an old lady drunk."

Steve leaned forward. "Are you complaining?"

Drake held up his hands. "Not at all. You eliminated my prime suspect before she could poison Howard. Now I can sit back and enjoy the meal. It's not every day I get to live so high on the hog."

"Aren't you afraid someone else might try to take out Howard?"

He shook his head and drank half his glass of pinot sauvignon. "I'm not afraid of these people. I know them too well."

By the third course, Sid had reached the end of his physical endurance. He signaled to Butch, who rose and prepared to wheel the patriarch to his cabin. Sid put his hand on Chad's. "I'm afraid I must lie down now." He looked down the table. "Everyone please stay and finish the celebration."

Before he wheeled Sid toward the exit, Butch said, "As a reminder, the ship docks at nine o'clock in the morning and the wedding will take place on the beach at noon. Vans will be waiting outside the cruise terminal at ten-thirty to take us to the resort on the far end of the island. The full itinerary with instructions is waiting for you in your cabins."

Chad and Anna rose, thanking Sid for all he'd done to make their rehearsal dinner a success.

The vibe in the room changed as soon as Sid's wheelchair rolled out of sight. Carol, who continued to drink her way through each course, cast an accusatory look at her new stepmother. Howard caught her in mid-stare and said, "Daughter, I suggest you look someplace else."

"Or what?" said Carol with a tongue thickened by gin and wine.

"You need to remember that I'm next in line to control your purse strings. Think hard about that."

She wiggled a finger at her father. "You don't scare me. You'll be in prison for killing Mom. Then Tim and Tammy will be in charge. We already figured it out."

"Do you see my arm?" said Howard. "The same person who's responsible for this is the one who killed your mother. If you're looking for her killer, try the other side of the table."

Henry Drake stood. "Let's all relax. This isn't the time or place. Think about what Lucy would have wanted for Chad."

Howard tried to stand, but only made it halfway before he fell back in his chair. "That does it, Drake. I told you never to mention Lucy's name in Shayla's presence. Leave the table."

Carol started a chorus of "Lucy, Lucy, Lucy..."

No one joined her but it had the desired effect on her father. Howard's face turned an unhealthy shade of red.

Shayla rose from her chair. "If everyone will excuse me, I'm not feeling well." She quick-stepped from the room.

Howard did a better job of making it to his feet on the second try. "Shayla, honey. Wait for me."

Carol picked up her bag and stood. She wobbled on her high heels but maintained her footing. "I'm going to find a bar with a better class of people. Tim? Tammy? Are you coming?"

Tim shook his head. "We're not leaving. Chad is our only son and this is his night. Someday he'll be the heir to everything."

Carol's eyes narrowed. "What do you mean 'heir to everything'?"

"Nothing."

"Don't give me that," she shouted. "Grow a backbone and tell me what you know."

Tim's face took on a lighter shade of crimson than his father's, but it was plenty red. "Haven't you noticed? The Green family never passes down the big inheritance to daughters. Do you think Dad is that different from Grandfather? After Dad dies, I'll be in control, then Chad. You'll get whatever we decide."

Carol stood in place as if she were an ice sculpture, then

thawed enough to push in her chair. "If anyone's looking for me, check the bar."

"Which one?" asked Chad.

"Start with the closest and work your way through the ship. I plan on visiting all of them."

Steve leaned into Heather. "That thinned out the herd."

Chad stood. "We understand tensions are running high, but we hope everyone else can stay and enjoy the meal."

Karl stood and raised his water glass. "I'd like to toast the bride and groom. We've set an awful example for you to follow, but some of us are trying to mend our ways. I pray for peace and reconciliation between our families."

"Amen," said Heather as she took Jack's hand.

Steve whispered, "There's a wedding tomorrow. We're not out of the woods yet."

28

Heather gazed upward as she crossed the gangway bridging the gap between the ship and pier. Broken clouds created dappled shadows on the clear waters as cruisers flowed like streams of ants onto the Caribbean island of Cozumel. Sid plowed through the crowd, blasting an air horn mounted to the left arm of his wheelchair. By the time they made it to dry land, Sid had angered most of the passengers he'd passed.

Steve walked on her right side with his cane tapping on the various surfaces of the cruise terminal, past a gauntlet of souvenir shops. Beyond the shops, they encountered waves of vendors hawking wares, selling excursions, and beckoning cruisers with promises of a day at the best beach on the island.

They arrived at a string of vans, waiting to spirit them away to the all-inclusive hotel Chad and Anna had chosen as the place of their seaside ceremony and honeymoon.

While they waited to board a van, Heather noted most of the men had chosen to get in the spirit of the island by wearing Hawaiian shirts and khaki shorts or pants. The shirts were primary colors, mostly bright red, splashed with a variety of scenes including palm trees, sail boats, and marlin leaping from the water.

The women's attire ranged from figure-hugging sarongs falling from a halter neckline for the younger ones to looser, more modest styles for the older women. An azure material scattered with an array of bright tropical flowers was the most popular color palette. The majority of the cruisers chose discretion, while Bella, used to a photographer's camera, chose a two-piece sarong that accentuated her youthful figure and white-blond hair.

Heather watched as the driver helped Ingrid into the van in front of them. Dressed in a somber gray dress, with a black shawl over her shoulders, she looked more like she was attending a funeral than a wedding. From the way she grimaced each time the clouds parted to reveal bright sunshine, the dark sunglasses and massive straw hat weren't doing their job. Her lips looked glued together when Heather, Jack, Steve, Bella, and Adam climbed in and settled in their seats.

The caravan passed resorts on the right side of the road that overlooked white sand beaches and waters in variegated colors ranging from green to deep blue. Once they left behind the congestion and bustle of the city, the space between resorts became greater, and so did the peace of the island. Perhaps this would be a good day after all.

The vans parked on a hairpin-shaped driveway under an awning and dislodged their human cargo. The festively dressed group laughed and talked as they made their way to the entrance, gawking at the beauty of their tropical surroundings. Chad and Anna welcomed them, while a trio of waiters offered tall, slender glasses of something tropical. Carol took one, tossing the paper umbrella on the server's tray. She chugged the drink like water and went for seconds from a passing server.

"The ceremony will start in thirty minutes," Anna announced. She pointed to a large wall of glass. "It will be on the beach straight out those doors, and past the pools. There's a shaded pavilion for those who don't want to stand in the sun. The ceremony will be short and simple, only six minutes, and we'll have a reception line, drinks, and food in the pavilion. After that, you're welcome to swim in the pools or go snorkeling. Someone from the hotel will take care of any equipment you need."

Jack leaned over. "I'm glad you reminded me to bring a bathing suit today."

Chad took over from Anna. "You're all welcome to spend the afternoon with us, but if you prefer, you may go back to the ship after the ceremony or explore the island on your own. A shuttle will leave every thirty minutes after the ceremony, with the last one departing at 4:00 p.m. The ship sails at five, with you or without you."

Anna waved good-bye. "I need to go upstairs with my bridesmaids and change. We'll start on time in..." She looked at her watch. "In twenty-six minutes."

Steve leaned into Heather. "That young lady knows how to organize a wedding."

"They've had their whole lives to plan it."

Jack pulled her close to him. "Are you taking notes?"

She nodded. "Brief service, great location, and give people options. What about you?"

"Make sure the honeymoon suite is nearby."

Steve chuckled. "Maggie and I made that mistake when we got married. Our flight to Florida had mechanical problems so we didn't get to our hotel until two in the morning."

Heather smiled and said, "Duly noted. Don't leave for the honeymoon right after the wedding."

Jack said, "We might as well stroll by the pools and go out to the pavilion."

"Wait a minute," said Heather as she nudged her head to the right and lowered her voice. "Steve, come closer. Jack, look to your right. Check out Howard Green and Ingrid Webber. She's joining him in the alcove, behind those potted plants."

"So?" said Jack.

"My bet is they're up to no good," said Steve. "Can one of you get close enough to hear what they're saying?"

"I might," said Heather. She corralled her long hair into a pony tail at the nape of her neck and donned a wide-brimmed hat. "Hopefully there are enough women in sun hats around here they'll never notice one more." She put on sunglasses and walked with her head down to a seating area mostly hidden by the foliage and slumped into a wicker chair.

"Then we agree," said Howard. "I'll accuse Anna of killing Lucy, and you'll back me up."

"I still think it's more believable if I accuse Chad, but the important thing is to stop this wedding. When will you do it?"

"Right after the wedding begins. We can't trust the preacher to ask if anyone objects. I think they stopped doing that a long time ago."

"Whatever you do," said Ingrid. "Don't wait too long."

Heather slipped from the chair and made her way back to Jack and Steve. "There's trouble brewing. Howard is going to accuse Anna of killing Lucy and Ingrid is going to say she has proof of it."

Steve leaned on his cane. "I was wondering what they would try. Take me to Chad. I have an idea."

"You better make it a good one," said Heather. "There goes Chad and the groomsmen toward the pavilion."

"Jack, there's no time to waste. Heather, grab Bella and Adam. I need a distraction for a backup plan."

By the time Heather made it to the open-air building with the thatched roof, Steve had Chad away from the crowd. The distance and hum of voices made it impossible to hear what they were saying. Chad had a somber look on his face until he draped an arm over Steve's shoulder. The smiles on their faces looked like they were sharing a joke instead of foiling the plan of a potential murder suspect.

A release of tension eased from Heather. She didn't know what Steve said to Chad, or his plan, but he had a way of pulling a rabbit out of a top hat, or, in this case, out of his straw hat. The two men made their way back into the shade where Chad rejoined his groomsmen.

Heather pulled Steve to the side where Jack, Bella, and Adam waited. "What's the plan?"

"Pray that it works," said Steve. "It's the backup plan that I need Adam and Bella's help with."

"Anything you need, just ask," said Adam.

Bella gave an exaggerated nod, which caused her braided ponytail to brush across the top of her sarong. "That goes for me, too."

Steve resettled the hat on his head. "It might involve a bit of a fib, but I want Ingrid to have her mind on more than trying to stop the wedding. Adam, would you be willing to tell your grandmother that your grandfather is considering selling the family home?"

"That wouldn't be a lie; he and I have already talked about it. He's done a lot of thinking since Lucy died. He's a good man; he wants me to help him manage the proceeds from the sale to get him and Grandmother Ingrid set up in separate condos."

Heather asked, "Ingrid doesn't know about Karl's plans to sell?"

Adam shook his head. "He wanted me to tell her after the wedding, but considering how she's acting, I'll be glad to do it now."

Bella cast her gaze toward the hotel. "Here she comes. Do you want me to go with you?"

He shook his head. "She'll strike out at whoever is nearest. There's no need for you to endure her wrath." He gave Bella a wink. "Yet."

Adam met Ingrid and took her as far away as possible, yet remained in the shade. Heather instructed Bella, "Turn away from them. You don't want Ingrid thinking this is your idea."

Heather caught an occasional glimpse of Adam and his grandmother out of the corner of her eye. Then came the explosion. It was mostly in German, but the words, "I'll kill him if he does," came through in English with a heavy accent. Silence reigned under the pavilion for half a minute as all eyes turned to the two in the corner. Adam left his grandmother standing by herself. She went to a table and downed an umbrella-topped drink. The buzz of talk soon took over the silence.

The bridesmaids, each wearing a different color sarong, arrived and waited at the front of the pavilion.

Chad and his groomsmen took their places on the beach. They wore white dress shirts with bow ties and baggy matching bathing trunks in a tropical, Christmas print. Chad topped his outfit with a cummerbund and tuxedo jacket.

The barefoot officiant instructed the people to take off their footwear and move to the white sand just out of reach of the water as small waves kissed the shore. Music began playing softly in the background. The bridesmaids made a slow walk in a single line down the middle of the gathering and took their places.

Next came the bride. Anna's smile and glowing countenance reflected her happiness as she walked toward her groom in a white, ankle-length sarong, that fell in gentle folds to reveal bare feet. Delicate lace cascaded from her dark hair to below her waist.

Holding hands, the bride and groom turned to face the gathering of family and friends.

Heather glanced at Howard who filled his lungs as if preparing to speak. "Chad needs to hurry," she whispered to herself.

"Before we begin," said Chad. "I have a short confession to make." He looked at Anna and smiled. "This ceremony is to satisfy the wishes of our families, who insisted we not elope. We met you halfway. On the morning we sailed, Anna and I were married in Galveston. To honor our families, we'll now renew our vows."

Howard shouted, "No. I won't stand for this. I'll have the marriage annulled."

Chad responded with a laugh. "I'm glad to say there are no grounds for annulment. If we appear tired, it's because we started our honeymoon as soon as I could get to Anna's cabin two days ago."

Karl Webber shouted, "Good boy, Chad."

Those in attendance let their feelings be known with a resounding cheer and applause. Howard Green turned and stormed away, but his new wife Shayla didn't follow him. The six-minute ceremony progressed with no further disruptions. Afterward, neither Howard nor Ingrid were anywhere to be seen.

Shayla came to Heather and Jack. "You two make a lovely couple. Any date set yet?"

"Not yet," said Heather.

Jack smiled and added, "This wedding has given us both ideas. The latest one being, our wedding needs to be sooner rather than later."

A sad smile appeared on Shayla's face. "I understand your eagerness, but take your time and don't make a mistake like I did."

Heather looked at Jack who returned her gaze, both caught in that awkward moment of not knowing what to say.

"It's all right. Please don't feel sorry for me," said Shayla. "I married Howard for all the wrong reasons. Now I'll fix my mistake and move on. There's a lot to be said for marrying for love instead of money. I just wish I didn't have to share a cabin with him on the way home. He hasn't hit me yet, but he's pushed me around. I know what's coming if I stay with him and I don't want any part of it."

"I can help you with that," said Heather. "Chad and Anna are staying here at the resort for five more days. I'll call the ship and arrange it so you can stay in one of their cabins. After all, two cabins are already paid for."

"You can do that?"

Jack laughed. "You might say Heather's got connections."

The celebration began once the photographer finished on

the beach and everyone was in the shade. Sid used the joystick to move his wheelchair to Heather and exclaimed, "Best wedding I ever attended, but it's time for Butch and me to go back to the ship. What's the latest progress on solving Lucy's murder?"

Steve spoke up. "The police will be waiting on the dock in Galveston to take the killer into custody."

"And the person who shot Howard?"

"You'll know who that is before we reach Galveston."

Heather took Steve by the arm as soon as Sid and Butch left. She whispered, "Have you been holding out on me again?"

"I didn't put the pieces together until you were talking with Shayla. All we need is verification of one thing from Leo or Ayana. As soon as we receive it, we'll need to speak with the captain and the head of security. The killer is on the ship and, if I'm right, there will be another attempted murder."

Steve reached into his pocket. "That reminds me, I need to turn my phone back on." As soon as he did, it announced a text from Leo. The mechanical voice announced the brief message.

Call me ASAP.

29

The knock on Heather's door came at 8:02 p.m. Three men, each decked out in a tuxedo, waited in the hallway. Her smile betrayed the pleasure that welled up within her to have her fiancé, father, and Steve show up together on what promised to be a perfect night of food, wine, and solving a murder that had vexed her throughout this Christmas season.

Her father spoke first. "You look lovely."

"I'll second that," said Jack as he tucked her hand under his arm.

"I can vouch for how good you smell," said Steve. He turned toward the elevator. "Let's get where we're going before everyone backs out."

The quartet boarded the elevator and descended. In the main dining room, the maître d' bid them welcome, and they walked the same path to the room where they'd celebrated the rehearsal dinner.

"It's about time," exclaimed Ingrid, who sat near the end of the table on the Webber side.

The ship's head of security came in and shut the door behind him. He gave his name so fast, Heather doubted if anyone caught it. "The captain sends his regrets and requested I take his place. The last night of a sailing is always busy, but he wanted to convey his warmest regards and hopes you'll sail with us again. Also, a special word of thanks goes to Mr. McBlythe for hosting this meal to continue the wedding celebration for the family and friends. He worked with our head chef to choose the perfect wines to accompany our meal, based on the survey each of you filled out."

Heather's father sat at the head of the table with Steve, taking the place of the bride and groom. Heather and Jack sat nearest Steve. Everyone else could sit wherever they desired. She noted the families held ranks with no defectors, except Shayla Daniels-Green. She chose to join the Webbers on the port side of the table while the other Greens sat on the starboard side. Carol Green was conspicuous by her absence.

The missing member of the Green family didn't get past Ingrid's sharp eye. "Are we waiting on Carol to sober up and make a grand appearance, or is she already passed out in her cabin?"

Adam answered his grandmother. "She fell asleep at the resort hotel and missed the boat in Cozumel."

"Drunk again, no doubt."

No one disputed Ingrid's assessment.

Howard spoke next. "The only reason I'm here is for the wine." He looked across the table and glared at his soon-to-be ex-wife. "Otherwise, I'd walk out and leave you losers to pick each other apart."

"Shut up, ingrate," said Sid.

Heather's father stood. "If I may, I'd like to thank everyone for accepting my invitation. This cruise means a lot to me and I hope you find the evening enlightening as well as pleasurable."

Howard added, "We had little choice after the captain said attendance was mandatory."

"I apologize for any offense given, but I know you've all been anxious to hear news regarding your wife's murder." said Mr. McBlythe. "I'll turn this over to Heather."

"Steve and I received word from the Houston Police Department that they'll be dockside to arrest the killer of Lucy Green tomorrow morning."

"Who is it?" asked Tim and Tammy Green at the same time.

"I bet it's someone in this room," said Shayla as she glared at Howard.

"I agree," said Ingrid. "Follow the money and you'll find a wife killer."

Henry Drake narrowed menacing eyebrows as his gaze locked on Ingrid. He looked to be on high alert. Heather wondered how he would react when Steve named the killer.

Howard responded with, "I've said all along that the killer lives next door. Tonight, she's sitting across the table from me."

Steve stood. "I don't mean to interrupt the pleasant conversation, but am I the only person who had to eat salad for lunch because I've gained five pounds in four days? Heather and I will explain all, but not until I've had my last real meal for a week or two."

Grumbling murmurs came from several, expressing their views of who the culprit might be.

"I'll give you a hint if you promise a truce until after the meal." Steve paused. "Is it a deal, Howard?"

"Whatever. As I said, I'm here for the wine. The one wine I'm dying to taste won't come until the meat course. Do whatever it takes to move this farce along."

"What about you, Ingrid?" asked Steve.

"Webbers are known everywhere for our patience."

"That's close enough to a *yes* for me," said Heather. She signaled to the server. "Bring out the first course."

Except for Howard giving Shayla occasional hard glares, the meal progressed in peace, helped along with quality wine. Small conversations broke out toward the end of the salad course and carried through to the cheeses.

Howard played the role of a sommelier, waxing eloquent on the merits of the wine pairings. He took extra time at the meat course to describe his selection. He drank two glasses as he savored the rare prime rib.

By some miracle, the meal ended with dessert and coffee instead of a brawl. Heather then stood. "Thank you for your patience. We can all say the quality of the meal was superb. Our compliments to the chefs, and our thanks to my father."

Applause from all added to the air of bonhomie.

Heather's voice took on a different tone. "Now, however, we must address the tragedy that brought each of us here tonight. I'll sit down while Steve brings our investigation into the death of Lucy Green and the shooting of Howard Green to its conclusion."

Steve pushed his chair back, placed his hands on the edge of the table and stood. He waited several seconds before he said, "These two cases were difficult. In fact, this will go down as the most difficult case Heather and I have faced. It took the combined efforts of Bella Brumley, Heather, me, and the detectives of the Houston Police Department to solve it.

"There were several obstacles that hindered our investigation from the outset. The existence of a longstanding feud meant everyone in the Webber household was a suspect." He pulled on his cummerbund. "Except for Sid, the amount of cooperation from the Green family left much to be desired. It seemed no one was really interested in justice for Lucy."

Steve held up his hands at the first sound of disagreement. "This will go faster if you don't interrupt me.

"Under Ingrid's leadership, the Webbers closed ranks and didn't cooperate either. This left many of you on our list of suspects longer than necessary. We had to do something, and I don't mind telling you, we hope we never have to do it again. Bella volunteered to pose as a maid in the Webber home while feeding us information about the home's occupants."

Ingrid gave a loud snort. "Maid? Don't you mean a spy?"

"And what a beautiful spy she is," said Adam.

Bella dipped her head but followed the temporary embarrassment by taking his hand and mouthing, "Thank you."

"Did she find out anything of value?" asked Sid.

Heather answered as Steve reached for his glass of water. "Not as much as we hoped, but we eliminated some suspects, and we uncovered something we didn't expect. One reason the Greens outmaneuvered the Webbers in the last twenty-plus years is because another spy fed inside information to them."

"Nonsense," said Ingrid with emphasis. "The only person responsible for our loss of fortune is my spineless, incompetent husband."

Steve sighed. "You're not even close, Ingrid. You fed the spy information for years and never had a clue what you were doing. In fact, you two only spoke in German."

Karl was the first to catch on. "It wasn't me, so that only leaves one other person... the cook."

Ingrid shook her head. "Impossible. She's like a sister to me."

Karl pointed. "No wonder Howard outmaneuvered me in every deal. It was your big mouth that cost the family almost everything."

"I don't believe it," said Ingrid.

Steve shrugged. "Let's ask Howard."

Howard's malevolent grin froze Ingrid in her chair. "Be careful throwing around accusations. I've never spoken with their cook in my life."

"That's probably true," said Steve. "But that doesn't mean someone you trust didn't find the informant for you."

Steve asked, "What about it, Mr. Drake? You're happy to do the dirty work for Howard. It only makes sense that you traded his money for information on the Webbers."

"So what if I did? Tell me you've never paid for information. And that goes double for you, Ms. McBlythe. I can't tell you how many lawyers have paid me over the years for information that would give them an edge in a trial."

"You have a valid point," said Steve. "Discovering that the Webbers' cook worked both sides of the fence was a bonus in our investigation, but not what we looked for. We still hadn't found our answer to who killed Lucy Green. To discover the truth, we needed to go next door, to the Greens' home."

30

Eyes shifted from the members of the Webber family to those of the Green clan. Sid moved his wheelchair to the very end of the table so he could get a better view of those who lived under his roof. As usual, Butch stayed as close as a shadow to his employer. Heather noticed all the furtive gazes from both sides of the table as they came to rest on Howard. He squirmed in his chair. "Why is everyone looking at me? Can't you see my arm? I'm a victim as much as Lucy was. It has to be one of the Webbers."

Ingrid spoke up. "I say your injury is a self-inflicted wound meant to turn suspicion from you."

Steve interrupted. "I find it interesting when people who don't have any evidence or first-hand knowledge about a murder believe they can solve it by guessing. Instead of keeping an open mind, they jump to conclusions without the benefit of facts. If Heather and I were to use Ingrid's method, we could manufacture stories for each family member seated at this table."

"Not for me or my family," said Ingrid, who'd regained some of her spunk.

"Especially you," said Steve. "You're the queen bee at your home. You control the purse strings and what's left of the royalties and savings. If I were to use my imagination, I could come up with a dozen theories of how you masterminded Lucy's murder. That doesn't include Howard's close call. I could come up with several scenarios of how you used one or more family members to carry out the crimes."

Heather added, "That sort of speculation could implicate everyone in the Green family as well. Doesn't it seem odd that Carol Green missed the boat in Cozumel? Was she really drunk and passed out, or has she already flown home, packed her bags and absconded to parts unknown?"

At least ten seconds of silence passed as people mulled over the possibility of Carol being her mother's killer before Steve took over again. "Heather and I played a trick on you by planting ideas in your head. We're trying to show you it doesn't take much for our brains to take over and invent ways to make the scenarios possible." He picked up a glass. "Adam's account of Carol's absence is accurate. He and Bella called the hotel before we lost phone service yesterday evening. She overindulged at the wedding reception and fell asleep on a lounge chair. She woke up with a massive hangover and a horrible sunburn."

Steve took a drink of water. "If anyone is interested, she didn't kill her mother or shoot her father."

"Then who did?" asked Sid.

"I'm getting there, but you won't believe the answer without the proper set up. The key to solving a case of this complexity is to throw out all preconceived assumptions. The ongoing feud, and Howard's disagreeable ways, caused most of the Webber family to suspect him, as did some from his own family. From the point of view of the Green family, Ingrid Webber was the likely candidate."

Heather added, "Or a conspiracy of one or more of the family members with Ingrid pulling the strings as the master puppeteer."

Ingrid pointed. "Howard Green thinks like a criminal

because he is one. You can't convince me he had nothing to do with Lucy's death."

Howard rose from his seat. "I don't have to listen to that bitter woman. I'm leaving."

The ship's head of security also rose. "Mr. Green, return to your seat. We're halfway between the Yucatan peninsula and Galveston. There's nowhere to go. Please enjoy another glass of wine."

A waiter appeared with the remains of the bottle Howard counted as the highlight of his meal and poured. Howard nodded his approval. "I have nothing to worry about because there can't be any proof of my involvement."

Steve ignored the comment and placed his fingertips on the edge of the table. "This case boils down to hate and love. I don't want to get too philosophical with you, but there are all kinds of love and many types of hate. Sid fell in love with oil wells and the power that came from them. Howard has the same obsession with power and control. He probably had fond feelings for Lucy at one time, but the lure of winning at all costs eclipsed anything or anyone else."

Howard was swirling wine in the glass and sniffing it. "An amazing bouquet. I love oil wells because they allow me to appreciate wines like this one."

Heather shook her head. She considered how he'd react when Sid's new will left him homeless and having to work if he wanted to maintain his lifestyle with its steady diet of exclusive wines.

Steve cleared his throat and she refocused.

"Next, there's hate," said Steve. "Most of the hate in this case comes from the Webbers, specifically from Ingrid."

Ingrid spoke through clenched teeth. "They ruined our lives. Sid and Howard Green deserve a slow, painful death for what they did to us."

Karl stood and spoke to Ingrid in a soft voice. "Hatred has poisoned your mind. The curses you call down on the Greens are already falling on you. Changes are coming to our lives. Accept what can't change and move forward, then you'll have another chance at joy."

"You old, babbling fool," said Ingrid.

Steve broke in with words that summarized the relationship of Karl and Ingrid. "Love poisoned by hate."

Karl shook his head, while Ingrid remained silent and stewed.

Steve raised his voice and the tempo of his speech. "Let's talk about wine." He waited as the change of topic jarred everyone into listening.

"Good idea," said Howard after several seconds. "What do you want to know?"

"Did you poison your wife?"

"Of course not. Why should I? I had the best of both worlds—a wife who wouldn't leave me, and an open relationship with Shayla. In fact, Lucy's death put a wrench in my plans. I thought no one would care if Shayla took Lucy's place. I still don't know why they objected."

A chorus of voices rose from the table condemning Howard. Steve raised his hands to quell the disturbance, but it took a shrill whistle from Heather to quiet the crowd.

"Thanks, Heather," said Steve. "Let's stay on topic." He paused long enough to take a breath. "Another question for everyone. Did it ever occur to you that Lucy wasn't the intended victim?"

Ingrid was the first to speak. "I'd hoped they intended the poison for Howard and there'd be a second, successful attempt."

"You almost got your wish," said Heather.

Sid had to clear his throat before he said, "Now that you mention it, Steve, Howard would never sacrifice a wine of that quality to kill his wife."

"My thoughts, exactly," said Steve.

Steve took a step back from the table. "Let's assume for a

moment that the intended victim of the poisoned wine was Howard."

"That's easy to imagine," said Shayla. "Everyone hates him."

Steve tilted his head to one side. "I can't argue with that."

"So what?" said Howard. "I don't care if anyone likes me. I added to the family fortune and I didn't hear anyone complaining when I did that."

Steve took a step forward. "The deeper we got into the case, the more we realized that, although everyone in both families had motive to kill Howard, they didn't fit the profile."

"What do you mean?" asked Karl.

Steve nodded to Heather, so she responded. "The poisoning was a sophisticated plan to kill Howard. From the acquisition of a wine that was sure to tempt Howard, to the steps taken to hide the identity of the person who wanted Howard dead, this was a masterpiece in obfuscation. The poison used was tasteless and odorless. While lethal, it was one that didn't act too fast. Lucy simply went to sleep and didn't wake up. The guilty party had to know about poisons, how to get the drug into the wine bottle without detection, and reseal it so it didn't appear tampered with."

Steve took over again. "There's a type of love that can motivate a person to do things that are completely out of character. Since most murders are a crime of passion, this type of love isn't the first thing we look for."

"What kind of love are you talking about?" asked Sid.

"Unrequited love. It can fester in a person, sometimes for years. This is the motive in Lucy's murder and the attempted murder of Howard."

Sid sounded skeptical when he asked, "Are you saying there's someone in Howard's past that loved him enough to try and kill him... twice?"

"Not exactly," said Steve, "but you're on the right track. There was someone in Lucy's past that loved her enough to want to kill Howard when he repeatedly threw Lucy aside for other women and then shamed her memory."

"Who?" demanded Howard.

Steve waited a few torturous seconds and said, "He's sitting next to you."

Howard turned to his left where his daughter-in-law Tammy sat shaking her head.

"You're looking the wrong way," said Heather.

Before Howard could turn his head, Henry Drake stood and pointed. "No way, Smiley. You can't pin this on me."

Steve responded with, "What took us so long was that we didn't go back far enough. While we were sailing to the tropics, the detectives with the Houston Police Department were combing through your school records, looking at photos, and going over your high school yearbooks page by page. It's amazing how many photos show you standing by Lucy. She was your first love, and I'm betting your only true love. What was it like when she went off to a high-dollar university and you were stuck in Houston going to classes at a junior college?"

"High school romances are a dime a dozen," said Drake in a less than convincing tone.

"True," said Steve. "But Lucy was so much more than a high school romance. She was not only a beautiful woman, but the one person who was always nice to you. No one else in school, or later in her home, treated you with the respect she did. Face it, Drake, you admired her."

Drake seemed to have lost his focus for a few seconds. "Lucy was the nicest, most complete woman I ever knew." His tone hardened. "It's a shame someone killed such a fine person, but if you're accusing me—"

Steve cut him off. "You tried to find other women who could live up to the standard you found in Lucy. After three short failed marriages, you knew you'd never find another Lucy. If you couldn't be with her, then being near her would be the next best thing."

"No comment."

"You saw what Howard was becoming and you had the skills to help him with his plots, so you wormed your way in to his confidence. With your help, Howard dismantled the Webber fortune one dirty trick at a time and you got what you wanted, to have Lucy smile and say hello to you every now and then. It satisfied you for a while, didn't it Drake?"

A ten-second pause caused everyone in attendance to shift their gazes to Drake and then back to Steve as he raised his voice slightly. "Each victory over Karl Webber cost Howard Green another piece of his soul. Power affects people in different ways and for Howard, he changed from a faithful husband and father into a man addicted to conquering."

Steve pointed at Drake. "You had a front-row seat as Howard threw Lucy aside for younger women. Did he have you scout out and procure his conquests?"

Heather watched as Drake's jaw muscles flexed.

Steve nodded like a wise professor. "I thought so. You became his accomplice in destroying the happiness of the best woman you'd ever known. Your guilt eventually drove you to do something, to give her back some happiness."

"I've heard enough of this garbage," said Drake.

"Only one more thing for you to think about," said Steve. "Through it all, Lucy remained faithful to Howard and her wedding vows. On the night she was murdered, despite everything Howard had done to her, she taped a sprig of mistletoe to her headboard, hoping he'd come back to her."

Drake shot to his feet. "You're going to have a heck of a time proving anything."

Steve nodded. "Heather and I have to admit that you planned everything to perfection. Lucy didn't like wine that much, but Howard can't live without it. You chose a derelict off the street to purchase the twenty-five-hundred-dollar bottle of wine. You knew he wouldn't be a reliable witness. You paid an informant in the Webbers' kitchen to receive the poisoned wine

Mistletoe, Malice And Murder

and take it next door. You even put a card with it noting the occasion for the celebration—Howard and Lucy's wedding anniversary. The only reason your plan to get rid of Howard didn't succeed was because he spent his anniversary with Shayla."

Steve paused for a breath and another sip of water. He picked up right where he left off as everyone leaned forward, staring at the blind detective as if he were a prophet reading from a scroll. "After you killed the only woman you truly admired, hate filled you. You had to strike out at Howard. It wasn't as neat or as well planned, but you put together a second plan to rid yourself of the man who ruined Lucy's life."

"Proof, Smiley. Where's the proof?" shouted Drake.

Instead of answering, Steve smiled and took his seat.

Heather looked at Howard. "I couldn't help but notice the wine you're drinking is a Musigny Domaine Leroy 2007. Are you enjoying it?"

"Immensely," said Howard.

"I understand the ship allows passengers to bring two bottles of wine with them on board. Did you bring your own wine?"

Howard nodded. "In fact, the burgundy I'm drinking is a bottle I brought."

"No, it's not," said Heather. "The ship's security officer and I went into your cabin while you and Drake were at lunch today. We found the bottle you brought. We steamed the label off and put it on a bottle of wine from the ship's stock. You've been raving over a ninety-dollar bottle of wine while the nine-thousand-dollar bottle you brought is in the ship's security office. It will be handed over to the Houston police along with Mr. Drake..." she paused a split second, "and the bottle of poison we found in his room."

Tammy's gasp was followed by a murmur of comments.

"Once we knew the motive, it was a logical step to what he would do next. Drake knew you would bring wine, so he brought a vial of poison to give it that extra touch of something special."

Howard grabbed Drake by the lapels, raising him to his feet. "After all these years... You were going to kill me? I trusted you."

Drake broke Howard's hold. "You're nothing but a money-grubbing imbecile. You never deserved her. She was always too good for you."

The head of security signaled to a pair of beefy servers, who grabbed Drake by his arms. "Take him to the brig."

Drake struggled against their hold as they led him from the room. His voice faded into the distance as the doors closed. "It should've been you who died. You don't deserve to live."

Karl stood and raised a glass. "Here's to proof. Well done Mr. Smiley and Ms. McBlythe."

The buzz of conversation that ensued was interrupted by a voice through the ship's speakers.

"Attention all passengers and crew. This is the captain. The latest weather forecast indicates we'll soon encounter strong northerly winds and heavy seas. We recommend you return to your cabins within the next half hour. If you need motion sickness pills, stop by guest services. Thank you for your cooperation."

Steve leaned toward Heather and said in a low tone, "There's more change than the weather coming and it's going to be unpleasant for some. I'm glad we won't be around for that storm."

"Yes, me too."

Heather scanned the faces of those gathered at the table. Sid's chin rested on his chest. He was at the end of his endurance, for the night and possibly his life. Butch put a security strap around his benefactor's chest and operated a separate joy stick on the rear of the wheelchair. Heather suspected the church would soon hold another funeral.

Howard threw his napkin on the table and pushed ahead of Sid and Butch, the door rattling shut behind him. Heather could almost feel sorry for the man. After Sid's death, he would have a rude awakening when Jack read the will. His empire wouldn't be what he planned. Her gaze took in Tim and Tammy. They, along with Carol Green, would also have bitter pills to swallow.

With her husband Karl averting his gaze, Ingrid rose and left the room, her head held high in defiance. Sid's death would see Karl's fortunes turn toward a sunnier climate and calm seas. His son, Kurt, and daughter-in-law, Monica, might be disappointed with the sale of the Webber château, but she had no doubt, in his new frame of mind, Karl would be generous to his son.

Heather turned her gaze to rest on Bella and Adam. Would this romance lead to something permanent, or another heartache? Time would tell, but the mental picture that came to her mind was another wedding on a beach, this time in the Eastern Caribbean. She closed her eyes and pictured the beach at the hotel in the Virgin Islands.

A squeeze of her hand from Jack brought Heather back to the present. "We'd better go before the rough seas hit. You sort of spaced-out for a minute. Where did you go?"

"To St. Croix."

"It sounds like paradise. Was I with you?"

She issued what she hoped was a coy smile. "The daydream was sort of fuzzy, but I'm pretty sure you were there."

"What about me?" asked Steve.

"You were there," said Heather without thinking.

Steve unfurled his cane as he stood. "Good. I've never solved a murder on an island."

A Beach To Die For

Escape to the islands with Smiley and McBlythe as they hunt for a killer intent on having a pristine St. Croix beach, no matter who gets in the way.

Warm Caribbean sunshine and the whisper of waves upon the shore beckon blind PI Steve Smiley. He's come for the wedding of his friend, Bella, at her parents' island resort, but the tide turns on the joyous occasion when the man slated to purchase the resort is found dead.

When a guest claims someone is framing her for the murder and pleads for Smiley's help, the vacation is over. His investigation shines the light on a host of people vying for the slice of paradise with the pristine beach and an untouched barrier reef.

With time running out before the bride walks down the aisle, Smiley dives in head first to find the killer before the body count rises and the bride's dreams of a picture-perfect wedding are all washed up.

Scan below to get your copy of the next Smiley and McBlythe Mystery.

From The Author

Thank you for reading *Mistletoe, Malice And Murder*. I hope it kept you turning the pages to find out whodunit! If you loved it, please consider leaving a review at your favorite retailer, Bookbub or Goodreads. Your reviews help other readers discover their next great mystery!

To stay abreast of Smiley and McBlythe's latest adventure, and all my book news, join my Mystery Insiders community. For your convenience you may scan the image below to sign up or go to https://bit.ly/brucehammacknewsletter. As a thank you, I'll send you *Exercise Is Murder,* the case that started it all for Smiley and McBlythe!

You can also follow me on Amazon, Bookbub and Goodreads to receive notification of my latest release.

Happy reading!
Bruce

THE FEN MAGUIRE MYSTERIES

He has no badge and no authority in a county full of corruption, drugs and murder.

Newman County was clean and safe when Fen Maguire left office as sheriff nine months ago. But the dead drug dealer floating down the river says things may be changing.

When he discovers a stash of drugs and a coded notebook, Fen launches his own investigation into the murder. Can he uncover the layers of corruption in his beloved county? Or will this be one time justice doesn't prevail?

Keep reading for a preview of book one,
Murder On The Brazos.

Murder On The Brazos
Excerpt

All was as it should be... until the body floated by.

A sigh escaped as Fen Maguire put his 4B sketching pencil away and mumbled, "At least this one isn't my responsibility."

The lifeless form eased to a stop in a tangle of flotsam, anchored by a fallen hackberry in the muddy water of the Brazos River. A third of the tree's roots clung to rusty earth, thirty yards from Fen's interrupted workplace.

Instead of punching 911, he called the non-emergency number to the Newman County Sheriff's Department and waited for a familiar voice to answer.

"Sheriff's department. How can I help ya'?"

The mental image of a woman with big hair and an encyclopedic knowledge of everything going on in the county flashed in front of him.

"Brenda, it's Fen. Grab a pen."

"Sheriff Maguire? Is that really you?"

"It used to be. The last election took care of the title you used. If you want to keep your job, you'd best not let Sheriff Newman hear you call me sheriff."

"Ain't much chance of Miss Lori sticking her head in here on a Sunday morning—or any other morning, for that matter."

His gaze shifted back to the river when the body moved, turning it right-side up. Fen knew if he didn't get Brenda on task, she might talk for twenty minutes. "I'm on my property, about a mile down from the bridge. There's a body hung up on a tree. Call Billy Ray. Tell him to get his team together and put in at the boat ramp by the bridge. There's a clear spot on the bank where I'm standing. The ambulance crew can help them get the body out of here."

"Do you want everyone to come to your place?"

"You know I don't want them here, but I have little choice.

I'll call Sam and have him open the front gate. He'll direct everyone to where I am."

"Any chance the victim's still alive?"

"No sign of life and I don't swim in the Brazos. Call the justice of the peace on duty and tell him to come and make it official."

"Expect a crowd. You know how everyone loves to run lights and sirens."

The last comment didn't earn a response, so Fen pushed the red icon on his phone and shoved it back in his pocket. He spun around at the sound of a voice speaking over his shoulder, and instantly regretted the sudden movement as a bolt of pain shot from his right knee.

From the ground, he looked up and shook his head and spoke through clenched teeth. "It's a good thing I don't carry a gun anymore."

Sam smiled and squatted beside him. "It's like the old days when we used to play cowboys and Indians. I'm getting you back for all those times you pretended to win and I let you."

Fen moved his bum leg, making sure it still worked. "How long have you been listening?"

"Long enough. I spotted the body downstream from the bridge and followed it here as you set up your easel." Sam pointed. "It's bad karma that the body got hung up on that hackberry instead of floating downstream. It could have been someone else's problem."

"It's still not my problem, or yours. You're making your morning rounds, checking on cattle, and I found the body. There's no use in both of us having to write a report." Fen looked around. "Where's your horse?"

Sam stuck two fingers in his mouth and blew a piercing whistle. A saddled roan mare came running from behind a thicket of brush. Sam turned his attention back to him. "I'll open the gate for your visitors. Do you need your cane?"

"And an ice pack, if you have one in your saddlebag."

Murder On The Brazos Excerpt

Sam went to Fen's four-wheeler and brought back a walking cane. "You need to get that knee fixed."

It was another statement that didn't earn a response.

Sam reached under Fen's arms and helped him to his feet. It took only three steps for Sam to reach his horse and effortlessly pull himself into the saddle. The sound of hooves pounding earth gave way to a distant siren. The ranch foreman would make the first officers wait long enough to aggravate them. A small payback.

Fen hobbled to his four-wheeler and took the load off his leg by sitting in the passenger's seat. It wasn't long before a black-and-white highway patrol SUV pulled alongside and the tall, lean figure of Sergeant Tom Stevens slid out, leaving his door open. He settled a buff Stetson on graying hair and spoke a single word greeting. "Sheriff."

"Not anymore," said Fen. "I'm glad you're the first on scene."

"Where's the body?"

Fen pointed. "Follow your nose. You can't miss him."

Sergeant Stevens moved to the river, pulled out his phone and took photos of the body and the bank leading down to the water's edge. He raised his voice enough to cover the distance to where Fen waited. "Did you get pictures of him before he got tangled?"

"Sort of. I took a short movie. I also got still shots after the hackberry grabbed him. He was face-down until a little while ago."

"What about photos of the bank?"

"Yeah. No footprints prior to mine and yours."

A pickup truck from the sheriff's department dropped into the river valley, several hundred yards away. Emergency lights flashed and blinked, but the deputy had at least turned off the siren.

The highway patrolman climbed the incline, turned when he made it to Fen's side and looked at the river. "What do you think?"

"I'd start by looking around the boat launch by the bridge." Fen dipped his head toward the body. "By the looks of him, he's been on the bottom for a while. It takes time for the gasses to form that brought him to the surface. I think he'd have hung up on something along the bank if he'd gone in farther upstream."

"Are you going to tell Sheriff Newman your theory?"

Fen held up his palms. "Leave me out of this. You know Lori and her father would like nothing more than to see me face-down in the river instead of whoever your victim is."

Tom placed a hand on Fen's shoulder and gave it a squeeze. "You honored Sally's wishes. I would have done the same thing."

A lump once again formed in Fen's throat, making it hard to swallow. Tom removed his hand and announced, "I need to make a few phone calls. I'll get a state trooper to the boat ramp and tape it off before Lori..." His voice trailed off. "You know what I mean."

Tom gave a nod.

"Do me a favor," said Fen. "Put out a call over your radio that you need the justice of the peace to respond. I don't want it known that I already told Brenda to call him."

Tom issued another quick nod. The door to Tom's SUV closed with a thunk. Muffled, unintelligible words of the radio transmission were all he heard.

A pimply faced young man exited the county patrol car and looked over the top to Fen and gave a nod. He was the last deputy Fen hired before his late wife's sister took the oath of office as the new sheriff.

Instead of speaking, Fen pointed to a spot on the river. The deputy nodded he understood, walked down the sloping river bank, putting his hand over his nose and mouth. When he returned to Fen, he asked, "What should I do?"

"Remember your training. Take things one step at a time and do what your supervisor tells you."

"How do you secure a crime scene when it's in the middle of a river?"

Murder On The Brazos Excerpt

Fen lifted his shoulders and let them drop. The answer to the deputy's question arrived as his radio came to life with the voice of Sheriff Lori Newman. She asked if any officers were on the scene yet. The deputy swallowed, gave his call sign, and told her he and a state trooper were there.

In an excited voice, Sheriff Lori said, "Tape off the crime scene."

"10-4. But, how? It's in deep water."

Fen let out a groan. "Tell her to disregard your last transmission. You'll handle it." What Fen didn't see was that the deputy had already depressed the transmission button on his radio.

"Who said that?" demanded Lori.

The deputy responded in a meek voice. "That's Sheriff Maguire."

The next radio broadcast came from Sgt. Tom Stevens. He began by stating his badge number, followed by, "I'll take over securing the area until a supervisor from the sheriff's office arrives."

"My ETA is twenty minutes. Make sure no one contaminates my crime scene."

Fen rolled his eyes, then directed his attention to the distant rise where two more vehicles from the sheriff's department came with lights flashing. One still had his siren activated. Tom gave instruction to the first deputy to string yellow tape along the wooded river bank for about a hundred yards upstream and downstream.

A sheriff's department lieutenant, new to the department since Fen left, approached and looked down on him. "What's your name?"

"Fen Maguire."

"Your full name," he demanded.

Instead of answering, Fen pulled out his wallet, retrieved his driver's license, and gave it to the lieutenant.

After a thorough examination, the lawman quirked a smile, and said, "So you're James Fenimore Maguire." He clipped the license under a pen in his shirt-pocket and walked back to his truck.

Fen had learned not to judge a book by its cover, but had a feeling he and the lieutenant might not see eye-to-eye.

More emergency vehicles arrived, including volunteer firemen, an ambulance, and three additional deputies. A Toyota Camry also came down the slope into the river valley. It pulled into a field away from the official vehicles. Fen watched the woman exit the car and come toward him.

It had been nine months since he'd last seen her. He'd been in the midst of trying to solve his last murder case before his tenure as sheriff was up and he'd not paid much attention to her looks. He guessed Lou Cooper to be in her early forties. She wore a navy jacket over a light-colored blouse, gray slacks and shoes that could pass for casual. She also had pretty eyes. A little too intense, but pretty all the same.

She scanned the crowd and honed in on the four-wheeler. "Mr. Maguire, it's been a while."

He nodded an affirmative answer. "You still look like a big-city reporter."

"That's because I am, at heart. Since this is your land, do you mind if I take notes?"

"It's fine with me, but this is an active crime scene. Sheriff Newman will be in charge as soon as she arrives."

Fen motioned for her to come closer. She leaned in and he caught a whiff of her perfume. "Stand back and don't ask questions for a while. Some of these deputies are new and don't know to keep their mouths shut. You should get most of what you need by listening."

She whispered back, "Why don't you tell me?"

He grinned through the pain of his knee. "I know better."

About twenty-five minutes after Lori's last transmission, her

Murder On The Brazos Excerpt

voice came over the multitude of radios. She directed the transmission to her lieutenant. "Where is everyone?"

The lieutenant responded, "Didn't the ranch worker tell you where to go?"

"No one's at the gate, only a map. I'm following the directions."

Fen closed his eyes and wondered what Sam had done.

It didn't take long before Lori's sharp voice came over the radio again. "Lieutenant Creech, I'm stuck. Come get me."

"Where are you?"

"How should I know?"

Fen looked at the hapless lieutenant. "Tell her to describe the terrain."

Lori spoke of what sounded like a seldom used path that led to a bog. Fen knew right where she had gone, and it wasn't anywhere near the river. "Tell her to stay in the car. It'll take a tractor to pull her out."

The lieutenant relayed the message.

"I don't have time to wait on a tractor. Come get me now!"

Fen looked up at the lieutenant. "I'll need to show you how to get there. It's a rough, narrow trail. The four-wheeler is better suited for where we need to go."

The lieutenant shook his head. "From what Sheriff Newman's told me about you, I can't trust anything you tell me."

Fen shrugged. "Suit yourself. Good luck finding her."

The lieutenant stroked his thick, black mustache. "How 'bout I arrest you for obstructing an investigation?"

Sergeant Tom Stevens took the number of steps necessary to invade the lieutenant's personal space and issued an icy stare. "Back off before your mouth overloads your badge." Without looking away, Tom spoke to Fen. "Where's Sheriff Lori?"

"Blackman's slew. Not over fifty yards from where you killed that feral hog last winter."

Tom gave the next command. "Your truck, Lieutenant. You'll need a new paint job after today."

Fen watched the two men drive away, then tested his leg and took a few tentative steps while leaning on his hickory cane. Not too bad, but he dreaded the swelling that was sure to follow. He watched from a distance as the officers milled about, not knowing what to do until the rescue boat arrived. It was a disorganized mess, but they pulled the lifeless body out of the water and brought it to shore. Most everyone viewed the victim, and because of the condition of the body, backed away with haste.

Judge Stone arrived, put on blue gloves, and motioned for Fen to join him. "Do you know him?"

"Hard to tell. Something about him is familiar."

The justice of the peace asked the paramedics to roll the body over. A gloved hand lifted a soggy shirt as Fen and the judge examined the victim's back. Nothing but a few abrasions. Next, the judge lifted a thatch of mud-stained hair from around the left temple. He continued to pull back the hair at the base of the skull. "Uh-oh. This is a homicide."

Fen closed the distance and stared at a small hole, no larger than the diameter of the pencil he'd been sketching with. "That's not just a homicide; it's an execution."

"No exit wound," said Judge Stone.

Fen looked at the ambulance attendant. "Could you get a towel and clean off the mud from the back of his belt?"

With a few swipes, the belt revealed a hand-tooled name—Clete. Fen blurted out, "Cletus Brumbaugh. I thought he looked familiar."

The announcement brought renewed interest in the body, and people formed a tight circle around him. "Turn him over," came a voice from someone. "Yep. It's Clete, all right."

Fen took out his cell phone, called Tom, and gave him an update.

It wasn't long before Lieutenant Creech's truck barreled across the river valley. After sliding to a stop, a shrill voice overpowered all the others. "Everyone get back."

Like Moses parting the Red Sea, Lori Newman's command

caused the first responders to make a path. She took a cursory glance at the body and then fixed her gaze on Fen.

He gave her a quick head-to-foot look. From the knees down, she was nothing but drying mud. She had another brown smudge that went all the way across her forehead and into a lock of sandy-brown hair. Other than a tear on the hip revealing pink panties, her designer dress looked unscathed.

Lori's forehead wrinkled. "Who made this map?" She waved a piece of paper in Fen's face.

He shrugged. "Sam, I guess."

"Then that ex-con's going back to jail where he belongs."

Fen jerked the paper from Lori's hand and gave it a quick glance before she could take it back. Through gritted teeth, she said, "I'm glad you did that. Now you're going to jail, too."

Fen set his feet shoulder length apart. "Look again, Lori. There's nothing wrong with that map other than you had it upside down."

Snickers and more than a few laughs came from those assembled.

Tom had taken his time getting to the scene. "Sheriff Newman, I need to talk to you."

"What is it?" she snapped.

"You'll need to go to the boat ramp by the bridge. A state trooper has the area taped off. She believes there's evidence suggesting the boat ramp may be the original crime scene. I told her to call Danni Worth to do the crime scene investigation."

"That wasn't your place."

Tom gave her a fatherly smile and scanned her mud caked legs. "You were busy, and I only did what you would have done."

Fen wondered if Lori would have remembered to call Danni, or was she so pig-headed that she'd mess up another crime scene? Either way, it wasn't his problem.

While Lori occupied herself by telling her officers what to do, Tom motioned for Fen to step away from the crowd. They moved to the shade of a massive pecan tree, where the sergeant faced the ambulance. "Danni's coming here after she's finished at the boat ramp."

Fen nodded. "There won't be anything to look at but tire tracks and footprints from the first responders."

The corner of Tom's mouth quirked upward. "My guess is, Danni will ask you for a glass of iced tea and a long conversation later."

A groan was Fen's only response.

Tom chuckled. "Look. Lori's sending her officers farther downstream. There goes Danni's search area."

Fen shrugged and tried to look disinterested. He would have limited the searchers to one man, Sam. The half-Choctaw Indian knew the difference between trash and something usable in court.

Fen's thoughts then went to Danni Worth. He hadn't seen her since the last homicide he investigated. That was a few months after Sally died and his world stopped spinning. Danni had been too willing to help him grieve.

The ambulance loaded Clete and took off at a slow pace. Fen turned to Tom. "Would you mind asking Lori's lapdog lieutenant for my driver's license? I'm not sure he has any intention of giving it back to me."

Tom nodded. "Things sure ran better when you were sheriff. I hope you're planning on running again."

Fen pointed to the September sun. "I might consider it when that freezes over." He scratched two days' growth of whiskers on his chin. "You're close to retirement. Why don't you throw your hat in the ring?"

Tom didn't reply, which told Fen the highway patrol sergeant had already considered it but the election wouldn't be for three more years.

While Fen contemplated how he could help Tom get elected, Lori strode toward them. "Mr. Maguire, you'll need to come to the sheriff's office and make a formal statement today."

"I'll be there tomorrow morning."

Murder On The Brazos Excerpt

Lori shook her head with vigor. "You're coming with me today."

"Can't."

"Why not?"

"My attorney doesn't work on Sundays, and I'm not answering questions without him."

While Lori's face reddened, Fen shifted his gaze to her ruined sandals. "I hope you put on bug spray before you came. The chiggers in this Johnson grass are thick this year."

Lori looked down at her bare legs and stomped her foot. Tom must have taken pity on her. "Come with me, Lori. There's nothing else to do here and we should both be at the boat ramp. I'll fill you in on what Fen told me and show you the photos I took."

Lori agreed and took off at a quick pace. Tom hung back and spoke in a soft voice. "Good luck with Danni when she comes calling."

Fen extended a hand and received a firm handshake. "Good luck with Lori. Try to keep her from messing up this case. Few people liked Clete, but he didn't deserve to die the way he did."

Get your copy of Murder On The Brazos today!

About The Author

Drawing from his extensive background in criminal justice, Bruce Hammack writes contemporary, clean read detective and crime mysteries. He is the author of the Smiley and McBlythe Mysteries, the Fen Maguire Mysteries, the Star of Justice series and the Detective Steve Smiley Mysteries. Having lived in eighteen cities around the world, he now lives in the Texas hill country with his wife of thirty-plus years.

Follow Bruce on Bookbub and Goodreads
for the latest new release info and recommendations.
Learn more at brucehammack.com.

Printed in Great Britain
by Amazon